LORI-ANNE COHEN

BOOK 1 IN THE *VAMPIRE'S KISS SERIES*

VAMPIRE'S KISS

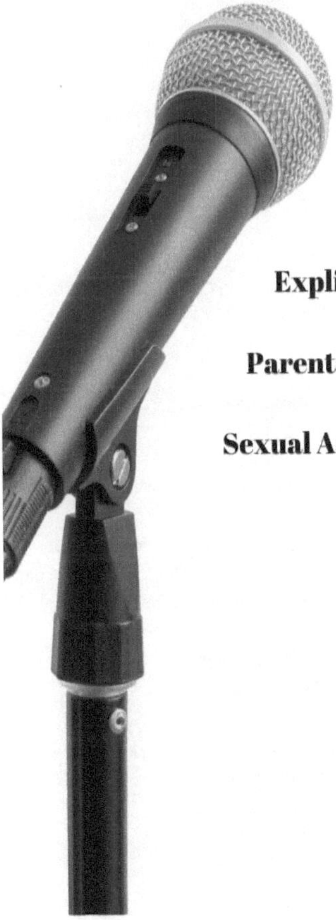

Content Warnings

Drug Use

Violence

Language

Explicit Adult Content

Parental Death (off page)

Sexual Assault (Discussion of)

CHAPTER 1

Adelaide Gold hadn't sung in front of a crowd for years. The last time had been Enshe was in college; she'd sung at a cousin's *quinceañera*. Tonight, she was going to sing in front of people again—vampires and humans actually—and she was very nervous but also excited. For the first time, she would be singing rock music, not the standards she had grown up listening to and singing in her father's band.

Oh, standards were fine, and the smoky tones of her voice lent themselves well to singing them, but that was not where her musical heart lay. She'd always wanted to sing rock and pop. Her father wouldn't hear of it, though. He had hated rock music, though, her mother had loved it and cultivated that love in her only child.

For years after her mother died, Addie had sung with his band. And it was all standards, all the time. It was not what she had wanted to do as a young woman. Hell, she'd been a teenager when he had drafted into the group. Spending all of her free time with her father and a bunch of middle-aged men was like having several fathers when all she wanted was one mother: hers. When he had passed away, she'd stopped singing and went to college to get her degree.

Addie had taught high school English for years and had enjoyed it. She'd married and had enjoyed that for a while as well. But she'd grown unhappy and had a feeling he was too, so she asked for a divorce. It's too bad he'd turned into a raging asshole during that time. Maybe he always had been, and she never saw it. What was true is that they never really knew each other, and neither of them cared enough to fix that.

But she was ready to move on to the next chapter of her, and that chapter included finally singing with a rock band—even if it was in a vampire club.

She sat at the table in her smallish kitchen and stared at the plate of food: chicken and a plain baked potato. She had to be careful what she ate before performing tonight. She wasn't that hungry but she'd need the energy, so she forced herself to eat.

She really wanted this to work out. It was her dream, and she wanted it to be a success. She didn't want fame. She just wanted to have a regular place to perform. She had lucked out with this place, and she knew it. Few places wanted singers in their 40s. Not only had she been offered the job on the spot, but the pay was also excellent. Vampire clubs paid notoriously well, from what she'd been told. She thought it was to keep people quiet about their existence, but she was happy not to have to take anything part-time. The money was enough to pay all of her bills, and buy some new things for her place. Right now, that was more than enough.

Elias Schrader strode into the club and looked around. *Where the fuck is he?* "Darian!" he yelled.

A tall, very pale, very skinny man with a mane of black hair and a lot of eyeliner came out of the back of the club. "What?" he yelled back.

"Do I have this right? Did you hire a fucking warmblood to be your new singer?"

"Yes, Elias, I did." Darian was calm, as he always was when Elias blew up at him. Elias went to yell some more, but Darian put his hand up. "Hear me out, okay?"

"Fine. But this had better be good."

"It is," Darian promised. "The new singer knows about vampires already."

Elias was incredulous. "How?"

"Her friend Miranda is dating Stellan. Miranda sent her here when she found out we needed a new singer. And she's fucking great."

"So, she knows Stellan. But she's not part of this world," Elias huffed.

"We have humans who work here."

"The blood groupies don't count."

"Maybe they should," said Darian. "But no, she's not part of our world. But it didn't put her off. We agreed if she couldn't handle it, she'll leave. Adelaide seems like someone who knows what she can and can't handle."

"Her name is ... Adelaide? Is she ninety?"

"Coming from a vampire, several centuries old, I find that comment hilarious."

"The liability of this is a problem. If something happens to her here, we could be in real trouble."

"Thought of that. Peter worked up a contract for her to sign, absolving us. But I am not going to let anything happen to her. None of the guys are."

"You fucking her?" Elias asked.

Darian frowned at his friend. "No, I'm not. If you recall, I prefer men. And no, I am not biting her either. Not everyone is as depraved as you are, Elias." Darian shook his head. "I just like her. Sometimes warmbloods and vampires can be friends."

Elias laughed, but there was no humor behind it. "Not really. But I apologize. You're right. Not everyone is like me."

"Man, I'm sorry. I didn't mean that." Darian ran his hand through his hair.

"Yes, you did," Elias said. "And you aren't wrong." But he didn't need the reminder from someone he considered a friend.

Darian sighed. "She's a bit older, so the chances her head will get turned is lower than if she was in her twenties or even thirties. She's starting over, and she's got a fucking phenomenal voice."

"They all get their heads turned. Just keep her the fuck away from me."

"You don't want to meet the singer for the club you own?" Darian was incredulous.

"No. Not if she's human. Trust me, it's better that way." And with that, Elias stalked off to his office.

"Well, that went better than expected," Darian muttered.

CHAPTER 2

The club was packed, as was typical for a Saturday night. It was loud and hot, bodies crushed together as they danced and drank. Vampires and humans alike melted into the shadows if they were looking to partake in more decadent activities.

Elias saw it all. Nothing escaped his eagle eye or his preternatural hearing. His club, Vampire's Kiss, was a place where both vampires and humans could mix. The name was a sly nod to the fact that vampires could find warmbloods here willing to let a vampire drink from them. Not just willing but excited to do so. Vamps had groupies, and Elias provided a safe place for humans and vampires to indulge. He referred to them as blood groupies. The only rule he had was the exchange of blood or sex, was entirely consensual on the part of the human. If a vampire failed to follow that rule, he was banned from the club.

He was curious enough about the new singer to make his way to his regular booth, picking up Elise, one of his regular blood groupies on the way. He didn't stay away from all humans, just most of them. This one knew what he expected from her: blood and sex. And nothing else.

She sat on his leg while he idly played with one of her nipples through her dress.

"Elias," she breathed. "I was hoping you would find me tonight." She tried to touch him.

"No touching!" he told her sternly. "You know the rules. You sit, be silent, and do not touch me unless I tell you to." He never told her to.

She pouted but removed her hand. "One day, you'll want me to touch you."

"Quiet," he said. "Or I won't drink from you tonight." She instantly shut up. He was going to have to re-think this one. She was getting entirely too attached.

On stage, Darian was introducing their new singer. "Please give a warm welcome to our new singer, Addie Gold!"

Addie walked out on stage to healthy but not overly enthusiastic applause. Elias's eyes widened. Addie was about five-foot-five with exceptionally long dark wavy brown hair that almost reached her ass. And what an ass it was. Round and lush. Her skin spoke of Hispanic or Spanish heritage, and it set off the white, V-necked t-shirt she was wearing, along with tight black jeans. She had good-sized breasts and a small waist. The word "voluptuous" came to his mind, and he was instantly hard from the sight of her.

Addie opened her mouth and started belting out *Piece of My Heart* by Janis Joplin, and Elias almost moaned. Darian was right. Her voice was amazing. It was deep and smoky, and it went right into your soul. Well, it would have if he had one. His eyes traveled to the audience, and they were right there with her, putty in her hands as she sang about heartache. He now understood why Darian had to hire her.

Elise reminded him she was there by wriggling over his erection. She probably thought it was due to her. It wasn't, but she was going to reap the benefits. Because one thing he knew was he really needed to stay away from Addie Gold.

Addie didn't meet Elias for the first two months she was there. He was in the audience every night, though, watching from the back. He was very tall, with short, black hair, a beard, and dark eyes. He looked dangerous.

When she said as much to Darian, he had laughed but said Elias was indeed dangerous.

That should have been the end of it, but Addie was fascinated by him. His eyes followed her as she moved across the stage. She didn't hate the feeling. She relished it, honestly. He watched her like he was hungry for her, making her feel powerful. She'd begun asking about him casually to other staff members. Some people wouldn't tell her anything, but she did get a couple of people to talk. But everything they told her about his supposed depravity was heard thirdhand. No one had seen anything. It all centered around his sexual exploits and appetites. But even though he always seemed to have a woman with him, he barely paid attention to them.

She sighed. Maybe one night, she'd meet him. She was walking back to her dressing room after the first set when she heard a ping. Her hand went to her ear. One of her diamond stud earrings from her second hole was gone. The earrings had belonged to her mother, and losing one would break her heart.

"Shit!" She started searching the floor, but it was a bit dark, and she didn't have her phone for the flashlight. She bent over further, backing up until she hit something solid. It was a man with a raging hard-on. She couldn't say how, but she knew exactly who it was.

"Lose something?" A deep, gravelly voice asked her.

Addie closed her eyes briefly. *Why me?* She stood and turned around to meet her boss finally. He was holding her diamond stud in his hand. "I did, actually. I see you found it." *Ay dios mío*, he was even better looking up close.

He was well over six feet, with dark eyes that looked black in this light. Dark, close-cropped hair and a beard accentuated a hard, but handsome face. He had full lips, which were currently smirking at her. He was broad shouldered and she knew that he was all muscle. She felt dwarfed by him. But it wasn't frightening, it was exciting.

He rolled the earring between two fingers. The stud looked so small in his huge hand. "Hmmm," he said. "What will you give me for its safe return?"

Anything he fucking wanted. He smelled amazing—like sin, like chocolate, like everything she'd ever wanted, wrapped up in one very dangerous vampire. "A thank you," she replied tartly.

His eyes widened at her tone. "Is that any way to speak to your boss?"

"Oh? Are you my boss? I wasn't sure since I've been here two months and haven't met you yet." She put her hands on her hips and looked at him.

"I should put you over my knee," he growled at her. "Teach you a lesson." That had just popped out, but something about her hands on her hips slayed him. She'd probably quit now, and Darian would be furious at him.

He started to apologize when he saw it. She was turned on. He looked hard at her. Her pupils were dilated, and her nipples had turned into hard pebbles. She had liked what he had said. *Shit*.

Addie felt as if she was melting. She wanted to throw herself at him. He was likely trying to scare her, but he'd only made her horny. Brown eyes flashed at him. "I am pretty sure that's an OSHA violation. So how about you give me my earring back, so I can take my break before I have to sing again. In your club. For your patrons."

He stared at her. He stepped closer to her. She stepped back. *Smart girl*. He reached out and picked up her hand. Her palm opened, and he dropped the earring into it, closing her fingers over it. "There you are," he said. "Go take your break, little bird."

She swallowed hard. "Thank you." She turned to go but made the mistake of looking over her shoulder. He was still standing there, and before she thought about it, she opened her mouth again. "Mind your manners from now on, vampire."

He stared at her and then bared his fangs. "Not fucking likely. Now I suggest you go before I really do put you over my knee."

Addie didn't need to be told twice.

He showed up for her second set, which was unusual. He had a woman, one of the groupies, on his lap. His hand splayed on her waist while one finger rubbed the woman's breast. Addie swore she could feel that hand. But once again, he was paying no attention to the woman. He was staring at her, his eyes dark. He was smirking.

She turned to Darian and suggested a change of song. Darian eyed Elias and grinned. "Sure, I'll let the band know."

A minute later, the band broke into the beginning chords of *You're No Good* by Linda Ronstadt.

Elias caught Addie's eye and smiled. *Game on.*

Darian slipped into Elias's office after closing. Elias was sitting at his desk, drinking whiskey, and looking out into the night. Or what was left of it. The club closed later than any other club in the city. Elias greased the palm of many a city official to make sure they could keep their 4 a.m. closing time. The live music, though, was over by 2 a.m., so Addie was long gone.

"Is someone brooding?" asked Darian, sitting and pouring himself some whiskey.

"I could fuck kill for you hiring that woman." Elias flipped around and stared at his oldest friend.

Darian grinned into his glass. "Oh, did you two meet?" he asked innocently.

"You know we did. She was bent over, looking for an earring. If I weren't already dead, it would have killed me. Her ass should be illegal."

"I hear that it is in California," Darian joked.

"You aren't funny." He sighed. "I need to stay away from her. I know that."

"Why?" asked his friend.

"What do you mean, 'why?' You know me. You know the kind of sex I like, what I'm like with women."

"You don't care about those women," Darian pointed out. "And those women know exactly what they're getting into. You aren't forcing anyone. It's consensual."

"I still treat those women like shit, and I don't care. I have no soul. It's true. I know my past; dark, violent, fucked up." Elias took a sip of whiskey. "I give those women pleasure, or pain, for a certain amount of time. Then they go on their way. No more, no less. This is what I am."

"Oh, what fucking nonsense," said Darian. "You aren't that. It's what you do, but I don't think for one minute that it's who you are."

"Because you always want to think the best of me."

"No, Elias. I see you. I see you for who you are. Everyone else sees the person you want them to see, but I *know* you."

"I told Adelaide I'd put her over my knee if she didn't watch her tone."

Darian looked at him. "Of course you did. What did she do?"

"She told me to mind my manners."

Darian laughed. "That is great. Man, I love her. Perfect answer. She's obviously not scared of you."

"She should be," Elias said morosely.

Darian stood. "You're an idiot. Look, you're a vampire. And you are a dangerous one, that is all true. But you are not a soulless hell beast either. Just maybe get to know her."

"Get to know her?"

"Yeah, like a regular person. Since the club is closed tomorrow, Stellan is having a small party. Addie will be there, and you should come."

"Absolutely not!"

"Don't be a coward. You might have something like fun. And don't bring another woman."

"I'm not coming!"

Darian opened the office door and turned to look at Elias. "Yes, you are." And with that, he left the room.

CHAPTER 3

When Elias walked into Stellan's apartment the next night, he immediately looked for Addie. He caught Darian's eye, and the other vampire smirked at him. Elias gave him the finger, and Darian laughed but gestured to Addie's location.

She was standing against the wall in the back corner, talking to another vampire, who was trying very hard to make inroads with her. He was sweet, well, as sweet as a vampire could be, but she wasn't interested. She didn't want sweet. She wanted dangerous.

She looked around. Would Elias come tonight?

Then, Stellan's booming voice called out. "Elias! I didn't think you'd come! How are you, old man?" Addie smiled. Stellan was a lot. A big, loud personality who worked hard but played harder. Her friend Miranda adored him. And he adored her. She tried to pay attention to the sweet vamp, but her thoughts strayed to Elias. She couldn't believe he had shown up. Would he speak to her?

A few minutes later, as she tried to stifle a yawn, he approached them. "Jack, I think you've been hogging Adelaide's attention for long enough," said Elias, clapping the other vampire on the shoulder.

Jack blanched and scuttled off quickly, making his apologies. Addie looked at Elias. "Was that necessary?" she asked him.

"Yes, it was. I wanted to talk to you alone. So, it was time for him to move along." She was wearing a long black column of a dress, with of all things combat boots. She looked adorable. Her hair was in one long braid down her back. He could picture his fist wrapped around that braid while she was on her knees, his cock in that mouth of hers.

Christ, he needed to get a handle on this attraction to her.

"Are you used to getting what you want?" Addie was playing with fire, and she knew it. But she couldn't help herself. She was sure he was messing with her. She was a woman in her forties, with great hair and a little too much flesh. He could not seriously be attracted to her. Could he?

"I am," he said in a low voice. He leaned towards her and sniffed. "You smell like summer rain and cut grass," he said.

She blinked several times. "Do I? Do you like those scents?"

"I do. Very much." He moved a little closer to her. "You can smell me if you feel like it."

"Is this how vampires flirt?" she asked.

"No, just me. Go on, smell me," he replied.

"I already know what you smell like. Sin and chocolate." She wanted to touch him. He was so close that she could reach out and put her hand on his chest.

He smiled at her, baring his fangs. "Do I really? I like that. Do you like those things?"

"I like chocolate," Addie said. "Not sure about sin. It depends on the sin, I suppose."

"I bet I could make you like sin," he said.

"I bet you could make an angel like sin," she replied.

"As I said," came his reply.

"I am no angel," she said. "Don't make me out to be one. I don't bite the same way you do, but I can bite."

He leaned down and whispered in her ear. "Promise?"

She put her hands on his chest, feeling the heat coming from him. "I think I may be in over my head now. I am just a singer in your club."

"A singer with the best ass I've ever seen. I want to sink my teeth into it." She removed her hands from his chest. "No, little bird. Keep touching me. I like you touching me." And he did—something else he needed to get a handle on.

Addie was saved from saying anything else by the arrival of her friend, Miranda. "Addie! There you are. I've been looking for you. Elias, I need to steal my friend."

Elias smiled at the redhead. "Of course, Miranda. I'll see you later, Adelaide."

Miranda dragged her off. "Okay, hold on. We're going to the bedroom. I want details."

Thirty minutes later, Addie had filled her friend in. "Wow," said Miranda. "Elias is never like that with any female. Not that I am aware of anyway. Stellan knows him pretty well."

"I heard he's had a bit of a tough past. Do you know anything about it?" asked Addie.

"Nope," said Miranda. "He doesn't talk about it. Would Darian know?"

"Yes, but they're tight. I would never ask him to spill secrets about Elias."

"So, you sneak around and ask other people?"

"Naturally," Addie laughed.

Miranda gave her friend a serious look. "Addie, I've heard things about him, though. I know you can handle yourself, but just be careful, okay?"

"Okay," she squeezed her friend's hand. "How are things with you and Stellan?" Addie desperately wanted to change the subject.

"It's so weird the best boyfriend I've ever had is a vampire. He's not as scary as your vampire, though. I think I'd pass out."

"You're happy, though?"

"I am so happy, Addie. He's so good to me and for me."

"You've always been a daytime person."

"True, but it's been fine rearranging my schedule somewhat. It works out. There's only one thing, though."

"What is it?"

"He hasn't fed from me. And I am not sure why."

"Is that a big deal?" Addie asked. "Don't vampires feed on humans all the time?"

"Yes, they do. You've seen it at the club, right?"

"Yes, mostly the wrist." It was very weird when Addie first saw it, but now she was used to it.

"Wrist is the most common for those kinds of transactions. Vampires don't mate often, but when they do, they feed on either the neck or heart vein. That's what Stellan told me. He hasn't even fed from my wrist. I thought we'd be mates, but maybe not?"

"I am sorry, babe. But he'd be crazy not to want to be your mate." Addie thought. "You haven't been together all that long. It's a big step for him and you."

"True. And he is one of the top vamps in the city. Along with Elias."

"Is he? I didn't know that."

"He is. But you're right. I will just give it time."

"Good, just be patient." Miranda always wanted things quickly, but sometimes, it wasn't possible.

"Now, go over everything Elias said to you again."

Chapter 4

By the time Miranda and Addie were done talking, Elias had disappeared. Addie sighed; she'd see him at the club soon enough. Addie left soon after that. Jack had come around again, trying to warn her off Elias, and the whole exchange had irritated her.

Once home, she changed into PJs and pulled out the song Darian wanted to her learn. It would hopefully take her mind off Elias. But it wasn't working. She could not stop thinking about him. His hands, his chest, his voice, even his fangs. She hadn't had sex in a long time and hadn't missed it all that much—until Elias.

She sighed, stretched, and got back to the song.

Elias had disappeared quickly from the party. He'd needed to think. He should stay away from Addie, and he knew now he wouldn't be able to. He didn't want to. Which was why he found himself on the small terrace outside of her living room window like a creepy stalker.

She was wearing shortie pajamas that didn't fully cover the smooth, pale curve of her ass. He sighed and tried to rearrange himself.

There was a noise below, and he looked. Probably just a cat. The terrace door opened, and he turned back to see her staring at him. "If you're going to be creepy, come in and do it."

He had the decency to look chagrined as he went into the apartment. "I'm sorry. What I was doing was awful, and I won't do it again. I know better, and I know how frightening it would be to a woman, especially one who lives alone."

She blinked at him. "Well, I can't even yell at you now. But you're right. Please don't do that again. It was ten seconds of pure fright before I realized it was you. And no, you really don't understand how frightening it would be to a woman because you are a large man. But I appreciate the thought."

"I really am sorry," he said.

"Forgiven. This time. Are you hungry? I'm hungry."

"Um, sure?" While vampires needed blood, they did not need food. But most kept up the pretense of eating and drinking simply because they enjoyed it. Elias was one of those vampires.

"Good, come with me." She walked into the kitchen, and he followed her. It was tiny but warm and inviting. "Is there anything you don't like?"

He sat and watched her as she got out eggs, cheese, mushrooms, and spinach. "No," he replied. She took out a wrapped package, sighed, shrugged, and opened it. It was a petit filet mignon. She started the heat under a cast iron skillet and seasoned the steak.

He suspected she'd been saving it. Darian had let it slip she had to start over with little to no money. He felt humbled by the small act. He was going to open his mouth to stop her, but he heard the sizzle and smelled the meat. He'd make it up to her somehow.

He watched in silence as she cooked the steak and made one large omelet which she split in half. She put the omelet and steak in front of him, with just the other half of omelet on her plate.

"What would you like to drink?" she asked. "Water? Wine?"

"Water is fine," he said. She poured them water, then sat to eat.

He cut a chunk of steak and put it on her plate. She shook her head. "Oh no," she said. "That's for you. I wasn't sure the omelet would be enough."

"Adelaide," he said in a silky voice. "Take the steak."

"But ..."

"If you don't, I will tie you to the chair and feed it to you."

"You wouldn't!" she exclaimed.

"I would. And the whole time, I'd be thinking what I really wanted to be feeding you was my cock." She opened her mouth and closed it again. He could feel her desire right then. He smiled a little and ate a piece of steak.

She also cut a bite of steak and put it in her mouth, chewing. They ate in silence, but it wasn't awkward. For her part, Addie was too busy picturing being tied to a chair while she sucked him off. She was pretty sure he knew that's what she was thinking about. He kept smiling wickedly at her.

He had one bite of steak left and held the fork out to her. She shook her head. "Let me feed you," he said softly. She licked her lips, took the proffered meat, chewed, and swallowed.

"Are you satisfied?" she asked. "I can make you something else."

"I am full where it concerns food. But I am not at all satisfied. Not yet." Her eyes widened. He stood and stared down at her. "You need to tell me to leave now if you don't want anything to happen between us. I am not a patient man, but if you need more time or don't want me at all, tell me now." Elias would never force himself on her.

Not want this? All she thought about was this. She looked at his erection and then into his eyes. "Do your worst, vampire."

He moved the table out of the way with one hand, picked her up, and set her on the counter. "We really need to do something about that mouth of yours, little bird. It's going to get you into trouble one day."

Before she could reply, his lips were on hers. She gasped, and his tongue swept into her mouth. Her tongue hesitantly met his, and he groaned. His hands dug into her hips, and she gasped. He stilled for a moment until she pulled back and sucked on his bottom lip, letting it be known that she didn't want him to stop. He growled and kissed her again. He was demanding with his kiss, wanting everything she had to offer. Her hands were balled into fists on the counter. He pulled away.

"Adelaide, touch me."

She was helpless to do anything but obey the command. Her hands went to his shoulders, and her legs wrapped around his waist. He ground against her core, and she writhed, trying to find release.

He pulled back and laughed. He opened her pajama top and flicked one nipple, then the other. She hissed. He could smell how aroused she was, and it made him burn hotter for her. He licked one nipple while putting his hand inside her pajama shorts. He palmed her sex, pressing none too gently, and she bit back a curse.

Her sex was slick. "God, Adelaide, you're so wet. I admit that I like that I did this to you." He slid two fingers inside of her and began to pump. She rode his fingers while his mouth toyed with her breasts.

She was gripping his hair. "Elias, God ... please!"

"Not God," he said. "The devil, maybe." He took her mouth in another searing kiss. "I need to taste you, baby." He removed his fingers, and she whimpered. "Don't worry. You'll come soon enough." He lifted her ass and removed her shorts. Then he spread her legs, getting on his knees. He just looked at her, looked at her glistening wetness. It made him so hard. He would need to fuck her soon.

She gripped his hair and moved his head closer to her sex. He blew on it, and she nearly came undone. With one long, slow lick, she moaned. He laughed and started licking and sucking her in earnest. Her hand was in his hair again, grinding against his face, trying to find her release. His hands were gripping her ass, and he pulled her forward so she came off the counter as he held her in place. Her legs sat on his shoulders.

He squeezed her ass, and then his finger found the tight rosebud. He stroked while he bit her nub, and she came all around him.

He looked up. She was breathing heavily, and her eyes glazed with her orgasm. He stood and pulled her off the counter, turning her around, so she faced away from him.

"Do you know what I have wanted to do this ass?" he asked her. She didn't say anything. He gave it a light smack. "I asked you a question, little bird."

She took a shaky breath, still coming down from that orgasm. "No, I don't know. Will you tell me?"

"Say please," he said throatily.

"Please," she said, desire evident in her voice.

"First, I will take you from behind, so I can watch it as I fuck you. But I want to lick it, suck it, and I sure as hell want to bite it." He slid his finger into the crack again, whirling it around her rosebud, and she inhaled sharply. "Does that feel good?"

"Yes, Elias."

"Say my name again."

"Elias," she breathed.

He unzipped his pants and pulled his cock out. He rubbed it against her ass, and she moaned. "Adelaide, my sweet Adelaide." He re-positioned himself. "You are going to feel so good." With that, he rammed himself into her, making her scream his name.

"God, yes, Adelaide. You feel amazing." He pulled out almost all the way, then rammed into her again. "Put your hands on the counter, Adelaide. Palms down. Don't move them."

She did what he told her to. He put one hand on her hip and the other on the back of her neck, holding her head in place while he fucked her. Hard and fast and rough.

She should hate this, but she didn't. She loved every moment of it. She felt safe with him, this dangerous vampire. If she said to stop, he would. But she wasn't going to tell him to stop, not at all.

"Elias. More, please. More."

"More what? Harder? Faster?"

"Yes. All of that. Rougher," she said.

He stilled for a moment, not quite believing what he'd heard. "Did you say 'rougher'?"

"Yes, I did."

He kicked her legs even farther apart and gently pushed her head down further. She laid it on the counter while he groaned. The hand on her neck fell on her other hip. He pulled back, squeezed both hips, and thrust into her, hard. He kept thrusting harder, manhandling her until he could feel she was close to another orgasm. He leaned down, and while he didn't bite her, he ran his fangs down her back, and she screamed, coming a second time. He leaned over her, thrusting into her while he talked dirty to her, and she came a third time, with him coming right after her on a yell.

They stayed like that for a long time until they caught their breath. When he stood, she missed his weight on top of her. He carefully lifted her, massaging her hands, neck, and shoulders before picking her up. She wrapped herself around him and put her head on his shoulder. "Where is your bathroom, Adelaide?"

"Through the bedroom," she said a little drowsily.

He carried her into the bathroom, setting her carefully on the side of the tub. He wet a washcloth with warm water and carefully washed her. She stroked his cheek. "No one has ever washed me before."

"I used you quite forcefully," he said. "It is the least I can do."

"You did not use me. Okay, maybe you did. But in the most delicious way. I feel great."

"You don't feel ... bad about what we did?"

She looked at him. "No, why would I? You like rough sex. You're kinky." She shrugged. "I seem to be as well. It's news to me but not unwelcome."

He looked at her, then kissed her soundly. "If you're sure then?"

"I am." Her eyes widened. "Oh! We didn't use protection."

"Ah, that. I can't get you pregnant and I can't give you or get anything from you."

She nodded. "Safe, then. Good." She yawned.

He looked at her, then kissed her soundly. "We both have to get to bed. And sadly, I cannot stay here."

"Ah, okay. That makes sense, of course. You're a vampire."

"I'm old enough that I don't necessarily always sleep or need to sleep during the day. But your room won't get dark enough."

"If it did, would you stay?"

He thought for a moment. "Yes, Adelaide. I would." That answer surprised him, but it was true.

She nodded. "That's good enough for me." She yawned. "I am very tired."

He picked her up again and carried her into the bedroom. He pulled back the blanket and set her on the bed. She grabbed the blanket and pulled it back up. "I should let you out," she said. "So, I can lock the door."

"I'll go the way I came in, and I can lock the door."

"Really?"

"Yes, don't worry about it." He leaned down and gave her a soft kiss.

She rubbed his cheek. "Good night, Elias." And with that, she was sound asleep.

He stared at her for a few minutes, knowing he needed to leave soon. He had, in one evening, broken all his rules when it came to human women. And instead of feeling regret, he was elated. And afraid. She would be his weakness; one his enemies could exploit. He would have to tread carefully.

He gave her one last look and departed; certain everything would change now.

CHAPTER 5

Addie woke at noon the next day. It was the best night's sleep she'd had in ages. She stretched and realized she was a bit sore. Deliciously sore. She had no regrets about last night, but doubts were creeping in.

She didn't know where she stood with Elias. Had this been a one-time-only thing? Did he expect to slot her into his regular rotation of groupies? Because that was not acceptable. She wouldn't watch him fondle other women while she was on stage singing. She sighed, threw the covers off, and sat up, wincing a little. She was glad she had another night off since the club was closed on Mondays. She could have a long, hot soak in the tub and not worry about the time.

She grabbed her phone, and there was a message there from Elias.

Little bird, I enjoyed last night. I'd like to see you again tonight, but I won't be available until after midnight. Let me know if you're free.

Addie's nipples tightened, thinking about seeing him again. She quickly texted back and was surprised his reply came through almost immediately.

I will be by tonight then. Adelaide, no touching yourself today when you think of me. No making yourself come.

Addie took a shaky breath. That should not be hot, but it was. She texted two words back: *Yes, Elias.* Then, Addie got up to make coffee and start her day.

In his bedroom, Elias smiled at her last reply. He hadn't slept, but he was trying to rest some. He thought of Addie and grew hard immediately. He could toss himself off thinking about her and that lush body of hers, but he'd rather wait until he had the real thing.

It had been a long time since he was excited about something. He was annoyed he couldn't see her until after midnight, but he had a standing monthly meeting with the other vampires. It was his meeting, but he couldn't cancel. He was hearing rumblings about rival vampires wanting to come into his territory. Because, no matter how Stellan felt about it, Elias was currently the one in charge.

He also wasn't convinced that Stellan wasn't the one sowing the seeds of dissension currently. He'd been acting cagey lately, and Elias didn't like it one bit. He didn't know if this had to do with Miranda or the fact Stellan wanted more territory and more power. He liked the other vamp—as much as he liked any vamp that wasn't Darian—but Stellan was mercurial and bored of things and people easily. He didn't have the edge needed to run a wider territory.

Elias sighed and rubbed his eyes. That could all wait for this evening. For now, he was going to try and think of more pleasant things—namely Addie. Then maybe he'd be able to sleep for a bit.

Stellan pounded his fist on the table and glared at Elias. "What fuck, Elias! Why not?"

Elias looked bored at the outburst. "Stellan, I admire your ambition, I do. But you bore easily, and the shipping routes need constant vigilance. Tamir is better suited to the area than you are." Tamir bared his teeth at Stellan, who gave him a sour look back. "Why are you suggesting that Tamir give up his territory?"

"Because Tamir is getting lazy. He spends all of his time and money on whores and partying with his friends."

Tamir growled. "That is a lie," he said. "And I would think carefully about you say next my friend."

Elias sighed. "Stellan, if any area of the city is losing money, it's yours. Tamir is delivering on time and on budget. If he chooses to whore in his free time, that's his business."

"I can't control the financial industry!" Stellan shouted.

"Actually Stellan, that is actually what you're supposed to be doing. You're the money man. You're good at it. And if affords you the lifestyle you like."

"I want more!"

And there it was. Stellan didn't really want the trade routes. He wanted Elias's position. He'd take Tamir's, then work his way to Elias's if given a chance.

He stood in front of Stellan. "You want my job then," he said quietly. "You want to run the whole thing." Stellan shook his head. "Don't lie. I can practically smell it on you. You've been trying to cozy up to me for weeks now. You want me to step down."

Two other vampires were in the room aside from Elias, Stellan, and Tamir. Genevieve and Elizabeth stepped up to stand behind Elias. Tamir followed suit. "Yes, Stellan," said Elizabeth silkily. "We all sense this to be true." Elizabeth and Stellan had been lovers at one point; the break-up had been acrimonious, and Elizabeth was still angry. Vampires had long lives and longer memories. Grudges could be held for centuries.

Stellan stared at Elias. "Yes. Yes, I want to run the city. I don't deny it. You spend all your time at that fucking club of yours, Elias. You have no idea—"

"I have no idea what, Stellan? What do you feel you need to tell me about my city?" Elias's voice was dangerously low. "You think you can take me, Stellan? I will rip your throat out and leave you to the sun if you try."

Stellan's eyes widened. "That's not what I meant, Elias." He put his hands up in supplication.

"You want the butcher back, Stellan? Is that it? You want to see how I mete out justice firsthand? If you think you can take me, come on. Let's see what you've got, old man."

There was a tense silence as the two men stared at each other. Stellan lowered his eyes first, ceding to the alpha vampire.

"Truce," Stellan said. "I had to try. But fine, we leave things as they are."

Elias nodded and moved back to his seat. The other vampires relaxed. "Is there anything else this evening?" Everyone shook their heads. "Good. We're done here then."

Sometime after midnight, there was a loud knock at the door. Addie looked through the peephole. Elias looked pissed. *Shit.* She opened it, and he strode in.

He turned to look at her. She was wearing a black sheath dress that came to just above her knees and no bra. He said nothing but backed her against the door, placing an arm on either side of her head. He leaned down and nipped her bottom lip. She groaned, and that's all he needed. He pulled her to him roughly and ravaged her mouth with his own. His hands squeezed her ass, and she rubbed herself against him while she gripped his shoulders. The kiss asked for everything she had to give, and she gave it willingly.

He pulled back and smiled wolfishly. Her lips were swollen, and desire filled her eyes. "Little bird, you are a sight right now." He picked her up and carried her over to the couch, setting her down gently. He chose a large chair across from her.

She licked her lips. "Tough day at the vampire office?" she asked.

"It was," he answered.

"Do you want a drink then?" He shook his head no. "Anything to eat?" Again, a negative response. "Me?"

"Yes, Adelaide. I most definitely want you. And I mean to have you tonight. But you have something to say."

"It can wait," she said.

"No, it cannot. What is it? I don't want this in the way of what I plan to do to you tonight."

She looked at him. "What is this exactly?"

"Excuse me?"

"Is this just sex? Is this sex and you feeding on me? Is it more? Because, Elias, I won't watch you feed from another woman. I won't watch you fondle another woman while I'm on stage."

"Is feeding from you on the table then?"

"It is." She'd thought about it all day, and it excited her.

This was a pleasant surprise. "You want to date then?"

She laughed. "I don't think you date. If you're with a woman, you're with them. But I will not put up with you being with vamp groupies if we're having sex."

"Is that a dealbreaker then?"

"Yes, it is." She crossed her arms in front of her.

"No more vamp groupies. If I need to feed, I will feed from the wrist of a male." Elias didn't need to feed as often at this point, which was handy right now. "No more fondling other women. I don't want to fondle anyone else anyway."

She relaxed. "So, you won't be feeding on me then?"

"Come here," he commanded, his tone full of dark promise.

She moved over to the chair, and he pulled her onto his lap. He leaned her back and ran his fangs over the side of her neck. She gasped. "Adelaide," his voice was soft, "I will feed from you. Not tonight, but soon." He licked her neck. "Right here, where your pulse is, while I'm fucking you." He moved his hand over her nipple, then pinched it. "But once I feed from you, there is no going back. You'll belong to me. For always. I will never let you go."

His hand moved under her dress to her sex, parting the slick folds. "You're so wet," he breathed in her ear. "Did you touch yourself today, little bird?" She hesitated for a second, then shook her head. "Adelaide!" He pinched her clit, and she bucked under him. "Tell me the truth."

"I started to," she said quietly. "When I was in the tub, but I didn't come."

"Is that the truth?"

"Yes, it is." She nipped his earlobe as her arm came around his neck. "I wanted to wait for you."

"Good, little bird," he said, kissing her. "Undo my pants and take my cock out."

She slid off him so she could. She unbuckled his belt and unzipped his jeans. Then she slid her hand in and grasped him. He groaned. She pulled him out and gave him two strokes. "Elias, please?"

"Please, what?"

"Please, fuck me."

"No, Adelaide. Tonight, you fuck me. Straddle me, take inside you."

She got back into his lap, straddling him. She guided him to her entrance and impaled herself on him. "Oh, God," she said, moving on him.

Elias reached up with both hands and ripped her dress in two. "Ride me, Adelaide." He latched onto her breast, sucking and licking, moving from one breast to the other while she rode him. Her hands gripped his biceps.

She started to come when Elias put his hands on her hips and stilled her. Her eyes widened. "Elias! What the fuck?"

He took one hand and smacked her ass. "Excuse me, Adelaide?"

"You heard me. Why did you stop me?"

She looked so aggrieved that he wanted to laugh and had to work to keep a straight face. He smacked her ass again. "Adelaide," he said, gripping her hips tightly. "I am stopping because you touched yourself today when I told you not to. So, I am making you wait a little."

"You absolute fucker," she exclaimed

"You want your ass smacked again then?" She shook her head, though she really did. "Liar," he breathed. "But this is what will happen if you do it again. Do you understand?" She nodded. "No, answer me."

"Yes, Elias. I understand." His cock inside of her was almost too much to bear. She'd probably agree to never sing again if he asked her to right now. And he knew it. But this whole thing was so unbearably hot.

"Good girl." He kissed her roughly. "You may continue." He leaned back in the chair, his hands still on her hips. She rode him again, faster and harder this time. Almost as if she were afraid he'd stop her again. She was getting close. "Come, little bird. Come for me." She clenched on him, and he groaned, his hands digging even harder into her hips. "Oh, baby, that feels so good."

She paused for a moment, clenched one more time, and came. She rode her orgasm as he pulled her to him, his hands on her ass, helping her pump him to his own orgasm. A moment later, he came on a yell. She collapsed against him.

He stood, taking her with him, and walked into the bedroom with her. Addie reached out and turned on the light. He looked around, the windows catching his eye. "Are those black-out curtains?"

"They are," she cuddled closer. "I heard some women talking about them one night at the club. I weighted them with magnets so they should be more secure against letting light in." She looked at him. "The bedroom doesn't get a ton of light anyway.

He just continued to look at the curtains. "Elias, say something. You're freaking me out. Should I have waited or not have done it?"

He hugged her to him, knowing he was in real trouble here. Something about the gesture had broken down some of that carefully built wall around his emotions. "No, little bird, I am glad you didn't wait. This gives us much longer to play. What a treat."

She beamed at him. "Whatever you want, Elias."

The problem was, Elias might want it all now.

CHAPTER 6

Later, in bed, Addie looked at Elias. "You ripped my dress," she accused.

Addie was on her stomach, head resting on crossed arms, while Elias lay on his side, stroking her back and ass. He smiled at her. "I did. I'm sorry."

"No, you aren't. You're very proud of yourself. Some of us are not wealthy, club-owning vampires, you know."

"How do you I'm wealthy?" he asked, nipping her shoulder. Christ, he wanted to feed from her. But what he'd told her was true. Once he did, there was no going back. He wanted them both to be sure.

Addie snorted. "Your clothes. I've seen your car, and Darian told me where you live. You're not a poor little bird like me."

He looked at her thoughtfully. "Why are you poor? I mean, I know you're divorced, but did you not get alimony or a settlement?"

Addie shook her head. "No. I declined alimony."

"Why?"

"Because fuck him, that's why! He offered it to me like it was some magnanimous gesture, you know?" Elias nodded. "He had the kind of lawyers I would never be able to afford. He owned the house we lived in. I moved in after we got married. I didn't go into the marriage with a lot, and the few things I did have, he stole and sold right out from under me."

Elias sat up. His dark eyes had taken on a murderous gleam. "Excuse me? Are you telling me that he made significant money but sold your things?" She nodded at him. "What did he sell?"

Addie propped herself up on one arm and looked at him. "You won't like it."

"No, I fucking won't. Tell me anyway."

"He sold my mother's piano and my first edition books. The first editions were either from my father or ones I had saved to buy. There weren't many, but I was proud of them."

Elias rolled his shoulders and cracked his neck. He was going to find out who this fucking asshole was, and he was going to bleed him very slowly. "What was his reasoning?"

"Elias, calm down. It's done now. I am not the first woman to marry a man who wasn't what he seemed."

"This is true, but none of those women are lying naked next to me."

"I hope the hell not!" She sat and ran a hand through his hair, rubbing his head. "I went to the house one day to pick up more of my things, the books included, and arrange pick up for the piano. They were gone. He said I couldn't prove they were mine, and they were in his house, so he sold them." She sighed. "The thing is, I could prove it, and I did. But it didn't matter. They were already gone."

"You refused to take a settlement for them?" he asked.

"My mom's piano, Elias? She taught me to play on it. No amount of money could replace it. Why bother? The books sucked, but they're books. If I got them once, I could get them again." She leaned up and kissed his jaw. "My boss pays very well."

"You realize I am going to kill him."

"You can't kill Dan," Addie said. "Society frowns on murder."

"I will not get caught, Addie. I've killed before, you know."

She stared at him. "Humans?"

He nodded, ashamed suddenly at his confession. "Yes. I suppose you're horrified. I'll just get dressed and—"

"Oh, for God's sakes, don't be an idiot. I know you have a past. But don't kill Dan. He's honestly not worth it."

"I don't suppose Gold is your married name?"

She smiled. "No, Elias, I don't suppose it is. Come now, lay down." She laid back and patted the bed next to her. "I don't want you to leave."

He laid down and stroked her cheek. "I've done terrible things in my life," he said.

"I know. I can see it on you." She kissed him on the mouth, taking his bottom lip in her teeth and biting gently.

"You can bite me harder, little bird," he said. She did, and he growled his approval, instantly hard. He rolled over, hovering above her.

Her legs wrapped around his waist, her back arching. His hands found her sex and stroked. "Yes, Elias. Please."

"Again, little bird?" he asked.

"Again," she breathed.

"Hands above your head. Hold your headboard." She did so. "Keep them there, Adelaide, until I tell you differently. Do you understand?"

"Yes, Elias."

"Good." He kissed her hard and rough. "Let me clarify something from earlier. I won't have any other women, but you won't have any other men. Yes?" She nodded, and he gave her a wicked grin.

He guided himself to her sex, rubbing a moment and enjoying her little moans before he drove into her. It was quite a while before they spoke again.

Elias slept, but in his dreams, he was sure he could hear Addie singing at some point. It was a beautiful song. Sad and sweet, but full of hope. When he dreamt, it was usually phantoms from his past come back to haunt him. He didn't know if it was her or the song, but he didn't dream. No one haunted him during his slumber. It was the most peaceful rest he'd had in ages.

When he stepped out of the darkened bedroom, Addie sat crossed-legged on the couch, reading. She looked up and smiled. "Hello! Did you have a good rest?"

"I did, actually." He sat next to her and pulled her onto his lap. "Were you singing earlier?"

She laughed. "I was. I'm trying to learn Darian's new song." She gestured at an old, beat-up electronic keyboard sitting on the table. "Did I keep you up?"

"Not at all. I liked hearing it." He frowned. "Darian's new song? Darian wrote a new song?"

"Yes, it's really lovely."

"Are you sure *he* wrote it?"

"I am. He said he did. Why?"

"Darian hasn't written a song in ... I can't even tell you how many years." He kissed the top of her head. "You must be his muse."

She shoved at his shoulder. "Hardly."

"You went out too, I think?"

"I did. I had an early lunch with Miranda. Then I ran some errands, boring stuff."

"Necessary things," he said.

"Yes, but I bet you don't pick up your own dry cleaning." He looked mystified at this. "That look is exactly my point."

"I am a very busy and important vampire. I can't do my own laundry."

Addie laughed. "What bullshit. But fine. I wouldn't do it if I didn't have to either." She pulled his hair a little. "Hey, you never said why you were so angry when you got here."

"I don't want you to feel like you're in the middle of something."

"Ah. It's about Stellan then, yes?"

He nodded. "Yes. He wants more power. More control of the city. He wants my job, basically."

Addie pulled away, an incredulous look on her face. "Um, what? I thought you all were well, sort of equal. That's what Miranda seems to think."

"Likely because that's what Stellan told her. There is a vampire Assembly of the top five vampires in the city. But there must be a leader, and that, little bird, is me."

"Ah, okay. I definitely don't think it was explained that way to Miranda."

"That doesn't surprise me. Stellan can be a great guy. But he is ambitious, in quite a grasping way. He's been making trouble for the other vamps of the Assembly, Tamir especially. But he full out has admitted he wants my job."

"But you think that's not the extent of it?"

"Very observant. No, I don't. I think he wants to unseat all of us and run it himself."

"Putting his own people in your places." He nodded. "What a shit."

"Yes, he is. Adelaide, about Miranda ..."

"I won't say anything, Elias. I have not ever been a person who talks about her relationships a lot. It's possibly because I've not really had close friends through the years. I've known Miranda since college, and I am very fond of her, but I don't kiss and tell."

"Does she?"

"Oh, does she! I've always known everything about anyone she was dating."

He wanted to ask her to tell him if Miranda said anything important, but he didn't think it was fair to do that. And it seemed like Stellan wasn't telling Miranda the truth anyway.

His phone pinged, and he picked it up off the table. He read the message and groaned.

"What is it?" asked Addie.

"A delegation of elders from the main Assembly is coming to the city."

"When?"

"Tonight. Fuck! This means I will be scarce for the next week or so. I wonder if Stellan contacted them. He's really beginning to piss me off."

Addie frowned. "Bummer, but I understand." She was just a human, after all.

"Adelaide, I am not ashamed of being with you. Nor is this me trying to move on. These are old vampires. Cruel, somewhat depraved, and far too curious. I don't love that you're going to be at the club to sing, but I am hopeful they all hate rock music enough to stay out. I have other clubs they may like more. I don't want them to know about you because I am trying to keep you safe." He was stunned by his own words.

"Your face, Elias. Did you surprise yourself?"

"I did. I am not protective of anyone. But here we are."

"That's bullshit. You are protective of Darian but thank you. I am pleased to know that I rate you being careful of me."

"You won't say that when I am cold and professional to you if they're with me."

"Are you going to be fondling or feeding from a female during this time?"

"Absolutely not. I promised you."

"Then we're fine. I must get ready for work, speaking of which. So, I need to shower."

"What a wonderful coincidence, so do I!" He stood, picked her up, and slung her over his shoulder.

"Elias! Put me down!"

"I will," he said, stalking towards the bathroom. "In the shower. We should have just about enough time."

"For what?" The blood was rushing to her head, but she couldn't help being delighted.

"For me to fuck your brains out. It's going to have to last both of us."

"I can't be late!"

"Sure, you can. You're fucking the boss after all."

"Good point. Onwards to the shower then!"

Elias and Addie walked into the club together. She waved at Darian and went off to her dressing room, and Elias headed for Darian.

"You're sleeping with my singer," said Darian.

"You wrote a song," came Elias's reply.

Darian seemed startled. He didn't think Elias paid close attention to that. "I did. You're still sleeping with my singer."

"You haven't written in years. The song is beautiful, Dar. I heard Addie singing it while I was in bed."

Darian looked excited suddenly. "It's perfect for her, right?"

"Absolutely perfect." Elias paused. "I'm elated to see you're composing again."

"How the fuck can I be pissed you at for sleeping with her if you say things like that?" Secretly though, he was elated they had found each other. He just had to give his friend a hard time.

"You can't. And I am not going to stop. She doesn't want to, and neither do I."

"You don't do anything by halves, do you?"

Elias shook his head. "I do not. I don't think she does either." Addie and Elias both knew, without discussing it, that things were moving quickly.

"The elders, though." Darian was worried.

"I know. I agree. I am going to try and keep them out of here. Help me keep an eye on her this week?"

"Absolutely."

"I am also concerned about Stellan. The good thing is Addie doesn't gossip about her own love life with Miranda. So, Stellan doesn't have much to go on."

"I'll keep an eye out for him, too," Darian said.

"Thanks, Dar. I let her know that if we come in, I will act indifferent or cold to her."

"Which bothers you. You like her, don't you? A lot!" Darian hooted.

"Shut up, you asshole!"

Darian laughed. "You old softie!"

"I take back what I said about your song, dickhead." Elias shook his head. "Okay, I need to go get ready for the onslaught. I will try and come by around this time each evening to check in."

"And to see Addie!"

Elias started for the front door. "You are such a fucking pain in the ass. I don't know why I'm friends with you."

"I'm the only one who can stand you!" Darian shouted after him. Elias made a rude gesture and was gone. "Well," he said quietly. "I *was* the only one who could stand you." Darian smiled. It was about time his friend had something nice in his life.

CHAPTER 7

Elias spent the next week squiring three ancient, ugly, depraved vampires around town. They, unfortunately, did want to visit Vampire's Kiss, but a water pipe put the kibosh on that. Elias broke that water pipe with his bare hands, hardly believing what he was doing. All to protect a human woman. It had taken work to mask her smell on him, but he wanted to do nothing to alert them to her presence in his life.

Thankfully, Tamir stepped in and was able to offer a night of entertainment that catered directly to their depraved desires. Tamir was a bit of a degenerate, and it worked to their advantage in this case. There were plenty of humans for the ancients to feed from. And plenty of drugs for the humans to do before being fed on.

"Do I even want to know where you got these people and the drugs?"

"No, you do not."

Elias sighed. "Tamir, I assume you're running a side shipping enterprise. I will ignore it as long as it doesn't affect this city. But if shit starts to go bad, it stops. This is not negotiable."

Tamir nodded. "Yes, Elias. I am not running drugs again. Purely recreational."

Elias hated drugs. But he'd never be able to stop them coming in with Tamir in charge of shipping. All he could do was regulate it and keep one eye on Tamir. "The people?" he asked.

"Elizabeth," replied Tamir, gesturing to the other vampire in the corner.

"Are they all sex workers then?" asked Elias. Elizabeth ran that trade in the city and she took the job seriously. Her people were very well taken care of, but she had strict guidelines if you wanted to work for her. Elias knew he could learn a few things from her.

"That, and the usual groupies. One of your regulars is here if you're interested."

Elise was in the corner, on the lap of an Elder. The vampire had his hand up Elise's dress, and his mouth latched onto a breast as he fed from her. The most troubling thing was Elise's eyes were on Elias. Even if Addie had not been in the picture, this would be it for Elise. He'd never touch her again.

He shuddered, and Tamir laughed. "Agreed, my friend. But I can find you another plaything."

Elias shook his head. "No, thank you. I am fine."

Tamir seemed surprised. "Really? Are you sure?"

"I am." The only person Elias was interested in was Addie. Everyone else paled in comparison. "Is Stellan here?"

"Yes. Gen has eyes on him." Genevieve had spies all over the city working for her and Elias. Here, it was to keep an eye on Stellan and his people.

"Has he been talking to any of the elders?"

"Yes. And yes. He has mentioned you in not so glowing terms. But the elders don't seem to give a shit. The city is running fine, you're making money, so they're making money. Beyond that, they don't care."

"Well, that's something then."

"Have they said why they're here?"

"Just a general visit to see how it's going. This party should help them feel even warmer toward us."

"I know how to throw a party, my friend. Are you sure you don't want to have a little fun?" Tamir asked.

"Positive, but thanks." Elias sighed. This week could not be over soon enough.

Addie poured Miranda some more wine. "I feel awful about that water pipe breaking, but I am delighted it means we get to have a ladies' night."

"Agreed!" replied Miranda.

"Where is Stellan this evening?"

"Oh, business meeting with the old vampires. He's wining and dining them."

No, he's not. But Elias was. He kept in touch with her via text, so she knew exactly what was going on. She was just curious if Miranda knew. It bothered her that Stellan had obviously lied to her. She also didn't love that Elias was there. God knows what kind of temptation there was. But she was pretty sure he had engineered the water pipe issue to keep the Elders out and away from her. A guy that would do that would surely be able to keep his dick in his pants and his fangs in his mouth, right?

But all she said to Miranda was, "Oh, that's nice."

"Where is Elias?"

"I'd think with Stellan and the Elders," she replied mildly.

"Oh, of course. That would make sense. They're partners, after all." Addie managed not to roll her eyes. "How are things going with you two?"

"I haven't seen much of him this week," she replied. She hadn't seen him at all, really. But the texts! Earlier this evening, he had sent one that made her hot, just thinking about it.

Little bird, tonight I want you to touch yourself. I want you to think about me fucking you from behind while I play with your ass.

And if I don't?

Again, that mouth of yours. I will have to fill it with something so you stop talking back. Are you going to do what I ask?

Do you want me to use my fingers, vibrator, or dildo?

He had taken a little while to respond to that. *Little bird, you never cease to surprise me. Use your fingers, but I plan to watch you use the others the next time I see you.*

"Addie!" This was from Miranda.

"Oh! Sorry. My mind wandered. What did you ask?"

"I asked you what he was like in bed?"

Addie did roll her eyes then. "You know I'm not going to answer that," she replied.

Miranda shrugged. "I figured maybe you'd changed. Friends share that stuff."

"I know, but I don't feel comfortable doing that."

"Come on! I tell you stuff!"

And I wish you wouldn't. "You do. I don't mind that you tell me, but I am not comfortable sharing. It doesn't make me any less your friend."

"Is he bad in bed? Is that why? Stellan says he has ... issues."

Miranda took a sip of wine as Addie considered pouring the rest of the bottle over her friend's head. Without a doubt, Stellan had indeed told Miranda this. But she also knew Miranda was baiting her. "Miranda, this is a shitty thing to do to a friend just because you're not getting your way. I am not going to give you details. I am happy, and that should be enough."

Miranda had the grace to look embarrassed. "You're right. I'm sorry. Forgive me?"

"Of course." She picked up a take-out menu. "Now, what kind of pizza do you want?" she asked, effectively changing the subject.

A few days later, the Elders were gone, the club was open, and both Addie and Elias were cranky. For Addie's part, while she enjoyed their texts, she wanted Elias in person. Miranda kept texting her, going on and on about how important Stellan was, and it was beginning to grate. A lot. Was Miranda trying to convince Addie or herself?

Elias missed Addie. He missed her voice, face, laugh, and of course, that ass of hers. He was horny and pissed off at continually being on call with the Elders. Stellan had behaved, as far as anyone knew. But it was what they might not know that was the problem. He was looking forward to seeing Addie, and that alone gave him pause.

Addie stepped into her dressing room, and something was different. She poked her head out the door and stopped the club's general manager. "Miles, do you know where this chair came from?"

Miles glanced into the room, and there was a large armchair in there. Much bigger than the one that had been there before. "Oh, that? Yeah, Elias said he was replacing your chair."

"Ah, okay. Thanks." She closed the door and looked at the chair. It was Elias sized. She smiled. Her phone pinged, and she looked at the incoming message.

I am running a bit late tonight, little bird. I'll be there for your second set. Do you like the chair?

She ignored the fact that her heart did a flip flop. *I do. But it's so big. Whatever shall I do with a chair that big?*

Whatever I tell you to, Adelaide. Heat pooled in her belly. It was going to be a long first set.

The minute Addie stepped off stage, the energy was different. Elias was in the club. But where the fuck was he hiding? She stomped back to her dressing room and slammed the door.

"Be careful, little bird, you don't want to take the door off its hinges."

"Elias!" Addie ran across the room and launched herself at him. He caught her easily, settling her across his lap. "About fucking time!" She grabbed him and kissed him. "God, you feel good. You feel even better than I remember."

"Mmm, you feel good, too," said Elias. He palmed her breast while he leaned down to kiss her. "That short skirt is going to kill me."

"I wore it for you," she said.

"Yeah?"

"Yeah," she replied. "I have an hour."

"A whole hour, huh? Let's see what trouble we can get into."

Her heart sped up. "Whatever you say. I need you."

God, he needed her, too. He wound his hand around her hair and pulled her head back, scraping her neck with his teeth. "I know what you need, Adelaide." He pinched a nipple. "Go lock the door."

Addie got up, locked the door, and turned back to him. She stood before him, waiting. His eyes darkened, and his mouth watered.

"Good, little bird. Now, take your clothes off. Slowly."

She licked her lips, and he almost groaned. She slowly pulled her silver and black top off. She was wearing a black lace demi bra. She went to take it off, but Elias held up his hand. "Wait. Play with your nipples, and then cup your breasts for me."

Addie rolled both of her nipples between her fingers. Then she cupped both breasts and squeezed, never breaking eye contact with him. "How does it feel?" he asked.

"Good. But I'd rather it be your hands."

He laughed. "I'm sure. Take your bra off." She did. He gestured for her to continue. She removed her skirt and panties until she was naked. He looked at her for a moment. "You are so damned beautiful."

She waved him off. "Oh, stop, I'm okay." Addie had gained some weight in the last few years, and her curves were considerably softer than they used to be.

"Do not talk about yourself like that, Adelaide. You are beautiful to me." He looked her up and down in a way that made her blush, as much as it made her hot. "Fuck, I do love those curves of yours."

"Well, *gracias*." She'd never stood naked like this before with someone staring at her.

"Spread your legs," he commanded. She complied. "Now, touch yourself."

She'd never done that in front of another person before either. She'd wanted to, but her ex had made a face at her and said no. Him doing it was entirely different, though.

"Now, Adelaide!" His voice was like a velvet whip. She moved her hand down her body, to her sex. "Good, little bird." He watched her, his eyes turning darker. "Take two fingers and put them inside of yourself. Fuck yourself for me, Adelaide."

She groaned but did as he asked. She circled her nipple with her other hand. She concentrated on what she was doing, barely hearing the growl. She was immediately swept up by Elias and slammed against the wall. Her eyes widened. "Did you not like that?" *Why did he stop her?*

"I liked it too much. It was the hottest fucking thing I have ever seen." His voice was gravelly, and his eyes were black. He reached between them to pull his cock out. With one swift move, he was inside her, and she screamed. He pounded into her, and the photos on the wall crashed to the floor. They ignored them.

"Elias, yes! God, yes!" Addie was digging her nails into his back.

"Yes, mark me, Adelaide! Fucking hell, yes!" He pounded into her with a fury he didn't think he had ever felt for any woman, human or vampire. He was more beast than man at this point as he slammed into her repeatedly, their orgasms building.

Addie came on a yell, and Elias followed a moment later.

"Fuck," he said. "I have never lost control like that."

Addie wrapped her arms around his shoulders. "Well, one thing is for sure, everyone knows we're having sex now."

He laughed as he carried them back to the chair. "Very true. It's fine. I've been getting a lot of odd looks and hearing whispers about me not feeding from someone. This should stop that."

She pulled back, looking aggrieved. "Are you not feeding at all? Elias!"

"Relax, little bird, I am. Bagged blood. I don't need as much anymore, so bagged blood will do me until I feed from that gorgeous vein of yours."

"Okay, then." She looked at him. "This is insane."

"What's insane?"

"Us. This. How do two people who haven't known each other that long have this kind of connection? Even if it's just sexual..."

"It's not just sexual," Elias bit out. Pretending it was otherwise was at an end now. He'd claimed her in a way so the whole club would know it.

"Don't sound so annoyed about it." She laughed at the look on his face. "Plenty of people like me."

"No one likes me," he said darkly.

"Oh, what nonsense. I like you."

"I can't imagine why."

"Stop fishing for compliments, buddy. I married someone I didn't this strongly about."

"Why did you marry him?"

"I thought I loved him. No, that's not fair. I did love him, but both of us changed, and the marriage couldn't sustain that change. Also, he's an asshole."

He sighed. "Fair. So, do we slow down?"

"If that means less sex, no. Absolutely fucking not."

He laughed. "Thank goodness."

"Let's play it by ear. Everyone knows now. Let's see what fallout there is."

"I'm the boss, Adelaide. There will be no fallout."

Addie stood and bent to pick up her clothes. "Not for you maybe, but I don't want people to think I am getting special treatment."

"Technically, Darian is your dotted line. But you will get some shit, especially from the vamp groupies."

Addie pulled on her panties and skirt. "Some of them do that now." Next came the bra and shirt. She sat to fix her makeup. "I can handle your groupies. They're human."

Elias started to say something when there was a knock at the door. He flicked his hand, and the lock clicked.

"You asshole! Why did I lock it if you could do that?"

"Because I told you to, Adelaide." He gave her a look, and she shivered. "Come in!" he barked.

Miles came in, looking a bit nervous. "Elias, we have a little problem."

"Naturally. What is it?"

"Stellan is out front," said Miles, his eyes flicking to Addie quickly. Addie quietly continued fixing her makeup.

"And?" Elias sounded bored.

"He's got a human with him?"

Addie turned. "Miranda?"

Miles shook his head. "It's a man. The man wants to see Addie."

Elias reared up. "Excuse me?"

Miles backed up. "He wants to see Addie. He says he knows her."

Addie stood beside Elias, her hand on his arm to calm him. Miles' eyebrows raised at this. The boss rarely allowed a woman to touch him. Addie must be special.

"Miles, did he give his name?"

Miles swallowed. "He did. He said his name was Dan Tremont. He says he's your ex-husband."

Addie was trying to catch up with Elias as he marched out front. "Elias! Hold on a minute! Wait!"

Elias stopped. "I am going to fucking kill your ex-husband—as soon as I find out who he sold your piano to."

Addie's eyes softened at this. "Oh, Elias." She touched his cheek and heard gasps behind her. "Does no one ever touch you?"

"No. It is not an intimacy that I generally invite."

Addie smiled. "Really? Interesting. Listen, I know you want to go out there guns blazing. Or fangs blazing in your case, but can we play this cool? What is Stellan doing with my ex? We need to get to the bottom of that."

Elias stared at her. "I hate that you're right. But you are."

"It's just very odd. Dan is like Stellan. Grasping was your word. But I think Stellan had to go out of his way to bring Dan into his circle. And the worst thing you can do is act like this is more than a small annoyance."

"True. Okay."

"You can still be scary if you want. And you can feel free to make it clear we're together."

"That is very petty of you," Elias smiled.

"Yes. Do you blame me?"

"I don't. Let's go."

They walked out to the front of the club, side by side. Stellan and Dan were standing near the stage. "God, his face is so stupid," Addie said under her breath to Elias, who had to hide a laugh. He liked when his little bird was fired up.

Dan's jaw dropped when he saw Addie. He'd never seen her dressed like this, all glammed up for the stage. "Addie! Is that you?"

"Daniel, you know it's me. Hello."

"You look so different." Addie said nothing. "How are you?"

Addie dipped her head, then lifted her eyes to Elias and then back to Dan. "I'm good. You?"

Elias grinned. He couldn't help it. She was so adorable right now.

Dan looked at Elias, then away quickly. "I'm fine. I am here with Stellan. You know him, right?"

"I do. Hello, Stellan. Where's Miranda?"

"Home tonight. Hello, Elias," he said.

"Stellan," came the reply. Elias moved closer to Addie, putting his hand on her ass. He was gratified when Dan's eyes narrowed. "How do you know Stellan, Daniel?"

"That's a funny story," Dan was nervous.

"I bet it is," said Elias.

Stellan broke in. "I've been looking for new talent. Someone whose ambitions match my own. I'd heard good things about Dan."

"Really?" said Addie. "How odd."

"Come on, Addie, water under the bridge now. You're doing fine." He looked at Elias again. "It seems."

"No thanks to you," she pointed out.

"Anyway," interjected Stellan. "I'm bringing him on board to help me with some special projects I have in mind. He's great at making money."

"Is this true, Addie?" asked Elias.

She shrugged. "Couldn't tell by me."

Dan turned red at this. "I treated you fairly, Addie."

"Hey, Dan, you sell any pianos lately?" Elias's voice was deadly quiet.

Stellan's brows furrowed. "Pianos? What is this about pianos?"

"Danny Boy here knows, don't you?" Dan nodded jerkily. "Stellan, are you staying for the second set?"

"We are indeed. Would you like to join us?"

"Ah, I'm afraid not. I like to sit alone, so I can watch Addie sing. As you know, she's amazing. Dan, I don't know how you let her get away, but I'm very glad you did."

"Totally understand, old man." Stellan was all forced cheerfulness.

"But I'll come by afterward to talk for a bit while Addie changes." He turned to her. "Does this work for you?"

"It does. But now, I really must go. Darian is giving me the sign." She turned to the other man. "Stellan, Daniel." She turned back to Elias, stood on her tiptoes, and kissed him. His arm wound around her waist, and he deepened the kiss before letting him go. "Everyone in here for sure saw that," she whispered.

"Good. Go sing, little bird."

The second set was the best Addie had done to date. Between Elias watching her and proving a point to her douchebag ex, Addie felt very powerful and beautiful and sexy. Dan's often sour look spurred her on.

Elias may not be a good man or vampire, but he was hers. And she was damned if she was ever going to let him go, even if he didn't know it just yet.

CHAPTER 8

Darian headed over to Elias's table after the second set. He wasn't sure who the warmblood with Stellan was, but he didn't like it.

"Great set," said Elias. "When are you debuting your new song?"

"Soon. Addie had some ideas about it, so we're going to work on it together." Darian sat. "Who's the human with Stellan?"

"Addie's ex-husband, Dan."

Darian gaped. "Are you fucking kidding me?"

"I wish I was. Do you know he sold Addie's mother's piano out from under her during the divorce?"

Darian's eyes darkened. "What the fuck? What an asshole! Why is he with Stellan, though?"

"That is the question, isn't it? I told you Stellan is looking to take over from me, yes?" Darian nodded. "I believe that is what this has to do with. I am not sure if he's trying to provoke me to make it look like I am too volatile to be in charge or just needling me. Addie hasn't gossiped about us, but Miranda is aware there is a relationship."

"And she either told Stellan of her own volition, or he asked her, and she answered. She's an awful gossip, to be honest."

"I am beginning to sense that." Elias ran his hands through his hair. "I'll have to discuss that with Addie. See how she feels about it." He caught Darian's grin. "What is it, Darian?"

"You really like her, don't you?"

"It's not like that," Elias insisted.

"You broke a water pipe in your own club to keep her safe from the Elders. You let her touch you in front of people. Do not tell me it isn't like that. You can bullshit anyone else, not me, brother."

"Oh, 'brother' now, is it?"

"We do share a sire, Elias."

Elias sighed. "We do, and I am glad of it, Darian."

"Me too. Now, tell me the truth."

"I'm ... fascinated by her. Everything about her ... She is not at all what I expected. So yes, I do like her. But it's all happening so quickly."

"Nope. You're a vampire. She isn't. You may have time, but she doesn't have the same kind of time." Neither of them mentioned she could become a vampire. That was not something to discuss now. "Besides, you two look like you belong together."

Elias scoffed. "Oh, that is ridiculous."

"It is not. When you came out from the back, I saw it. It's not surprising you're a couple. You two fit."

"I'm worried I am going to hurt her. And that is not something I've worried about in the past with women. And that is making me ashamed of myself."

"Good. Do better," said Darian. "No one is saying you have to make friends with Elise, but maybe the club keeps an eye on her and other the ladies. I know what they can be like, well, some of them. But maybe they wouldn't be if the club did better by them."

Elias nodded. "You're right. I'll talk to Miles about it. See what we can do to keep a better eye on things, and see how we can do right by them for the service they provide."

"That's a good plan. I think you should keep your distance from Elise though."

"Agreed. Okay, I need to talk to Stellan and the asshole right now. Then, I'll take Adelaide home."

"Cool. She's a keeper, Elias."

"Yes. I am just not sure I am. I am not sure I can change."

"Has she asked that of you?" Darian saw it though; Elias was already changing.

"Not yet, but she might."

Darian stood and debated whether to ask the question that popped into his head. "Does she know?"

"About my past? No, she doesn't. I will tell her, just not yet."

Darian nodded. "Okay, but it's better she knows. Sooner rather than later." With that, Darian walked off. Elias went over to talk to Stellan, though his preference would be to rip the other vampire's throat out.

When he got there, Dan wasn't at the table. "Where's your new pet?" asked Elias.

"I could ask you the same thing," Stellan smirked.

"Do I refer to Miranda as your pet, Stellan?"

"No, you do not."

"Then never refer to Adelaide that way again." Elias's voice was silky, but there was steel underneath it. Stellan's eyes widened, and he nodded. For all his bluster, Stellan was the weaker of them. He'd not been bred for battle in the same way Elias had been. And he didn't have Elias's bloody and violent history. To win, Stellan would have to be sneaky. He could never beat Elias in a fight.

Stellan cleared his throat. "Dan left immediately following Addie's set. I think he might be regretting divorcing her."

Elias bit back a grin. That would not work with Elias, and he was shocked Stellan was trying it. "I doubt it. He's an insecure man. It's why he could never make Adelaide happy." *Take that, you piece of shit.*

"Perhaps," Stellan answered as he roughly grabbed a passing redhead. He pulled her onto his lap and went to put her wrist to his mouth.

"Stellan, did you ask the young lady if she was willing to let you feed on her?" The woman's head came up, and she smiled at him gratefully.

"Does she have a choice?" Stellan's snarled.

"In this place, she does. You know the rules. She may be with someone. She may be on her way out for the night. Ask her and see if she's willing."

"Woman ..." Stellan began.

"She has a name. It's Clara." Clara, for her part, seemed surprised Elias knew her name. To be honest, he only knew it because she was the sister of his bar manager.

"Clara, may I feed from you?" Stellan was pissed and there'd be payback, but damned if Elias wasn't enjoying himself right now.

"Absolutely, it would be my pleasure to let you feed on me." Clara seemed amused by this turn of events, but there was something in her voice that made him think that she was not okay with it.

"Are you sure, Clara?"

She nodded quickly at him. "It's fine, Elias. Really."

Elias nodded at her and stood. "Stellan, I am not sure what game you're playing with Addie's ex, but if you or he hurt her, you're both going to be very sorry." With that, Elias went to find his lady.

"Miranda, I know he's your boyfriend. But why did you tell him Elias and I are together? I told you that in confidence." Addie was curled in the armchair in her dressing room, talking to Miranda on speakerphone.

"Addie, I'm sorry. I didn't think it was a big deal," Miranda answered, confused.

There was a knock at the door, and Elias poked his head in. Addie gestured for him to come in. He picked Addie up and deposited her on his lap as he sat. She smiled, putting her finger to her lips, so he didn't say anything.

"He hired my ex-husband to work for him. That is a big deal, and he's doing it to poke at Elias."

"And how do you know he hired Dan?"

"Randi, where do you think Stellan was tonight?"

"He said he had business, and he was working late."

Addie closed her eyes briefly. She opened them, and Elias nodded at her. "He was here tonight, honey. At the club. With Dan."

"At the ... club?" Miranda sounded even more confused now.

"Yes. He brought Dan here on purpose. Maybe they talked business, I can't say. But it was obviously done to upset Elias and me."

"Addie, come on. Why would he want to do that?"

Addie was shocked. "Miranda, does Stellan not talk to you about what's going on with him?" Elias rubbed his face. Stellan was supposed to be a good boyfriend, better than Elias. But at least Elias told Addie what was going on.

Miranda sniffed. "Of course he does!"

"Then you know he's looking to unseat Elias from the Assembly."

"No. They're partners. Why would he do that?"

"They aren't partners. Elias oversees the city, and Stellan works under him."

"Oh, I suppose Elias told you that! Well, he would, wouldn't he?"

"He did, yes. But I've also heard it from others."

"Addie, of course, *he* would say that." Miranda ignored the second part of Addie's comment. "And I've been with Stellan for a lot longer than you've been with Elias. What's it been? A week? Two?"

"Okay, Randi," Addie replied quietly. "You've made your point."

Miranda sighed. "I'm sorry, that wasn't very nice of me. And I didn't mean it. I'm just ... he's still not ... he hasn't fed from me yet."

Elias's eyes widened. "I know, I'm sorry. Let's not discuss it anymore, huh? But whatever I tell you about Elias is between us, yeah?"

"Okay, Addie, sure. Stellan should be here soon, so I will talk to you later."

"Sure, night, hon."

"Stellan is sure as shit not going to be there soon. At the moment, he's feeding from a redhead named Clara. And he's a glutton."

Addie looked upset. "Will he fuck her?"

Elias shrugged. "No. Clara doesn't fuck the vampires who feed on her." That much, he did know. "Why is she so upset that he hasn't fed from her?"

"She is hoping to be mated to him. At least that's what she said."

"So, she thinks they'll be mated if he feeds from her?"

"She said he told her if he fed from her neck or breast, where her heart was, yes. I can see by your face this is not true."

"Oh, God, Addie. No, it's not. There are a few things to unpack here. Firstly, it is rare for a vampire to have a human mate. The reason it's rare is that for them to be fully mated, the human would have to take blood from the vampire. Not a lot, and the human would have to keep doing it every so often. but It's not about where you feed from."

"Oh! Well, that makes a lot more sense, to be honest. What does the human get out of it?"

"Extended life span, no real aging to speak of. The problem is if the vampire dies, the mate dies."

"Why not become a vampire?"

"You can do that. I have heard of humans deciding to become a vampire after mating with one. Becoming a vamp and then mating is usually what happens."

"Interesting. So, Stellan is lying to her because he doesn't want a mate?"

"It's worse. You can only have one mate. We can love more than once, but we only mate once. Stellan already had a mate. She died."

Addie was shocked. "Oh, Elias! I am dead sure Stellan hasn't told her that. I am not sure what to do. I'd tell her, but I don't think she'd believe me."

"I don't think she would either, little bird."

"How did his mate die?"

"Some humans caught her and pushed her out into the sun."

"Oh, that's horrible!"

"It was awful."

"What happened to the humans?"

"You don't want to know, so please don't make me tell you. Stellan didn't do it himself though. He hired muscle to take care of it."

She kissed him on the cheek. "That's fair. What happened to your mate?"

He looked at her and smiled. "Why do you think I had a mate?"

"I just assumed. You've been alive a long time."

"I've never had a mate," he replied. "I never felt I deserved one."

She laid her head on his chest. "Everyone deserves to be loved, Elias."

"I don't. Didn't." *Don't—I don't deserve it.* But sitting here with her like this, he recognized that not deserving it and wanting it were two different things.

CHAPTER 9

A week later, Addie was getting back from running errands, and as she walked to her building, she saw a familiar face. She sighed. "Dan, how did you know where I lived?"

"Well, hello to you, too. I asked my divorce lawyer for the address."

Ah fuck. All the paperwork for the divorce had come to her here. She'd forgotten. "Ah, yes. Though, if I had wanted you to have the address, I would have let you know. What do you want?"

"Can we go inside?" he asked, throwing her what he thought was a charming smile. At one time, that would have worked on her. Now, not so much. She'd rather have Elias glower at her. At least that was an honest expression.

"No," she answered shortly. "We cannot. What do you want?"

"Addie, come on!" Dan held his hands in a beseeching gesture. "I care about what happens to you, and I am perturbed about you being with this ... vampire."

Addie just stared at him. "Oh, where do I even begin with you? You do not care about me. You proved that when you were such an asshole during the divorce. It is none of your business, and need I remind you? You were with a vampire last night."

"I am not fucking Stellan!"

"Really? Because you seemed to have your head very far up his ass last night."

"Addie, this isn't you. This is that vampire talking."

Addie made a show of looking around as if she was searching for something. "Well, I don't see him here. So, it must be me speaking."

Dan's face darkened. "His influence is what I meant."

"I know what you meant. It was an idiotic statement. I am a grown-ass woman, and no one puts words in my mouth. Tell me what you want and go away. I need a nap before work tonight."

"I didn't know you had such an amazing voice."

"I know you didn't. You weren't interested in that. Get to the point. You're pissing me off."

Dan dropped his eyes, sighed, and looked up. He was doing his very best to give her the sad puppy look. She was unmoved. "I just—well—I want you back. I want us back!" He sounded so earnest when he said this.

Addie looked at him for a moment and then burst out laughing. She couldn't help it. It was the stupidest thing he could have said. And she knew it to be a complete lie. Stellan wanted her away from Elias, and this was his very ham-handed way of doing it. Addie would no sooner stop laughing, then she'd look at Dan's face and be off again.

"I don't see what's so funny about this!" Dan sounded offended. "I am a damned good catch."

"No," Addie said, trying to get herself under control. "You are not. You neglected me during our marriage. You didn't care about anything good that happened to me if it had nothing to do with you. You were awful during our divorce proceedings. You sold my things out of spite. You were pissed that I wanted out of the marriage. I was not in love with you anymore. You made me miserable. Why would I want to get back together with you?"

Dan's mouth was hanging open. "I didn't sell your things out of spite!" Addie just looked at him. "Okay, I did. You're right. It was wrong. I was just so upset that you wanted to break up our family."

"Our family? Are you high? It was just you and me. We didn't even have a pet."

"I've changed! Really, I have!" Dan seemed desperate.

Addie sighed and picked up her bags. She stepped closer to Dan. "I will say this slowly so you understand each word. You go back and tell Stellan to stop fucking with me and Elias, especially Elias. Whatever this is, it's not going to work. And frankly, I am shocked he thought sending you was a good idea. You must have loaded him with outrageous lies about how easy it would be to get me back. Do not ever come to my place again. If you do, I will have you arrested for harassment."

"You wouldn't do that!" Dan was practically shouting.

"Yes, I would. Then, I will let Elias have you. I bet he'd enjoy that." Addie walked up the front stairs. "Now, go away. Shoo." She pulled out her key, opened the front door, and went in without saying another word.

Addie dropped her bags and rubbed her face, groaning. She had to tell Elias, and he would not be pleased.

She made tea, climbed into bed, and stared at her phone. She tapped out a message, hoping he was asleep. He had an early evening meeting, so he'd stayed at his own place.

Just to let you know, Dan was waiting for me here when I got back home today.

She waited and groaned again when the three dots signifying he was replying appeared.

What the fuck, Adelaide. Are you okay? What did he want?

He said he wanted to get back together. But I don't believe that.

Her phone rang. "Hi, Elias," she said.

"Adelaide," His voice was low and gravelly, and it did something to her insides, even though he was pissed off. "What the fuck is going on? Are you alone now?" The thought of her going back to her dickhead ex was messing with his head right now.

"Yes, I am alone. In my apartment, in bed, talking to you."

"I am going to have to fucking kill him," he replied.

"Babe, don't be silly. You don't need to kill him. I laughed in his face and threatened him with both jail and you."

"Wait? What? You did what?"

She explained the whole thing to him ending with her threat to call the police, then to turn him over to Elias. "Then I walked into the building and left him standing there like the total idiot he is."

"I thought the divorce was maybe because he was dumb enough to cheat on you."

"Maybe he did. I just knew I wasn't happy. And when I looked at why, it was a bit of teacher burnout, but mostly, it was him. Are you still in bed?"

"I am. Naked and missing you," he replied.

"I miss you too. I haven't even seen your place yet."

"We can come here tonight if you want." Well, that was a first. He'd never brought a woman to his place.

"Sure, I'd like that. Don't kill Dan before I see you."

"Hmmm. Maybe. I am going to have to call Stellan, though. I agree with you. This was definitely his idea."

She laughed. "Babe, really, you have nothing to worry about. I am going to have a short nap and then head to the club early. Darian and I are going to work on his song for a bit."

"Fine. I won't kill him. Today. I will see you later tonight then." His voice dropped. "Be good, little bird."

She shivered. "Of course, Elias."

After they hung up, Elias smiled to himself. She called him 'babe,' and he didn't mind it. She said it in this really sassy way that turned him on. He was going to kill her ex one day, though. Eventually, that little twerp would cross a real line, and Elias would be waiting on the other side.

He dialed Stellan's number, knowing the prick would be asleep. He hadn't been around as long as Elias and Darian and, as such, needed more rest. "Stellan, if you send Dan over to talk to Addie again, you will be very sorry." Stellan would be waiting for a threat. Something he could take to the Elders. "If you continue to try and usurp my authority in this way, I will have no choice but to inform the Elders and petition to have you replaced." *Take that, asshole.* "If you truly feel you are more qualified than I am to oversee the running of this city, then I suggest you handle it more professionally. You are more than welcome to go to the Elders and petition them yourself. Keep Dan out of Vampire's Kiss. Adelaide finds his presence offensive." He ended the call.

He rolled over to try and get a little more sleep but it would be impossible. He sighed and decided to work before he showered. He wished Adelaide was there with him. He liked having her close. Sometimes she stayed in bed and read. He'd watch her twirl her hair around her finger as she reacted to the words on the page. He hadn't lied to Darian; she absolutely fascinated him.

But over the last week or so, he'd come to realize that the one thing he really wanted was to feed from her. He was trying to wait—trying to give it time. But he didn't want to. Bagged blood was fine, but warm blood from a person was better. Blood from someone you were close to could not be beaten. He wanted that closeness between them. And it scared the hell out of him.

When Elias walked into the club that night, Darian and Addie were on stage. They were sitting on stools with guitars, and Darian was making notes. He walked over to sit at the bar and watch them.

"Scotch, boss?"

"Yes, the Lagavulin 16. Double." A moment later, the drink was in front of him.

"Let's go through it once more, Addie," said Darian. "If we're going to put it in tonight, I want to make sure it's perfect."

"Sounds good. I think doing it acoustically is the way to go. You, me, two guitars."

"Agreed."

Darian played the opening chords, and Addie started to sing, with Darian coming in on harmony. It was a beautiful song, and as he listened, it was a very specific love song. Darian had finally written a song for Samuel. They weren't mates, but Darian had been very much in love with the mercurial vampire.

Samuel, for his part, had loved Darian the best he could. But something in Samuel had been broken long before he and Darian met. It had all become too much for him one day, and Samuel had walked out into the sun. Darian's heart had broken, and he hadn't composed anything since.

Elias's heart swelled listening to it. He was a bastard, but Darian wasn't. He was tough, but he was artistic and sentimental. He had been loyal to Elias for so many years, even when Elias hadn't deserved it.

When the song was over, Elias applauded, along with the employees. Addie saw Elias at the bar and her face broke into a bright smile, and something inside Elias shifted. "That was amazing!" he said, making his way over to the stage.

Addie leaped up and bent over to kiss him. "It's so good, right? It almost makes me cry every time I sing it."

"It is," said Elias. He looked over at Darian. "You have outdone yourself, Darian. Samuel would have been proud."

Darian's eyes turned sad for a moment, but then, he smiled softly. "I'd like to think so."

Addie turned to him. "Oh, I should have figured that out. It's a love song for someone you lost."

Darian stood and grabbed Addie's guitar. "It is. I lost him a long time ago. But I am finally starting to make peace with it."

Addie hugged him. "I'm glad. Art helps, I know." She walked back over to the end of the stage where Elias was. "But now I must get ready to debut this little beauty. Thank you for letting me work on it with you."

"Thank you, Addie. You made the song better." He turned to put the guitars away, and if he had a tear in his eye, no one needed to know that.

Elias wrapped his arms around Addie's legs and lifted her off the stage. She was squealing with delight as he carried her to her dressing room. Neither of them noticed the smiles and looks everyone gave each other.

Elias deposited her on the floor as soon as they reached the dressing room. She batted at his shoulder. "You did not need to carry me," she said, still laughing.

"No," he leaned down to kiss the tip of her nose. "I just wanted to."

She wrapped her arms around him. "You doing okay? You look like you've been thinking big vampire thoughts."

"I have been." He wrapped his arms around her, cupping her buttocks with his hands. "I will never get enough of your ass, Adelaide Gold. I dream about it."

"Lucky for you, here it is, in the flesh."

"Oh, and what flesh." He leaned down to kiss her. Addie expected him to be hard or rough, but it was gentle, almost tender. But with no less of an explosion in her body. He pulled back. "But I have been thinking about something."

"Oh? Enlighten me," she replied.

He took one finger and ran it down the side of her neck. His tongue followed the trajectory of her finger. Addie shivered. His mouth hovered over her pulse point, and he sucked the skin there. Her grip on him tightened.

"Tonight, Adelaide," his voice, more sinful than usual, "I want to feed from you. I want to feel your pleasure when you come while I'm feeding from you. The decision is yours, baby, but I hope you say yes."

His hands were kneading her ass, and she could barely think straight. But she knew her answer. "Yes, Elias. God, please, yes."

"Good! Whew!" Relief flooded through him.

"Now, though," she said, pulling back, "You have to go, or I will never be ready in time."

He laughed. "Fine, but tonight ... we're out of here quickly after your second set."

"Absolutely!" She pushed him out the door. And once she was alone, she did a bit of a dance. This was a good step. Elias was one step closer to being hers.

Chapter 10

Addie changed quickly after the second set, wanting to get on with the next part of the evening. She was nervous but also excited. If you told her a year ago she'd be excited about a vampire biting her, she'd have said you were crazy. Hell, a year ago, Addie didn't think vampires were real. It was a little unnerving, if she thought about it for a minute, how comfortable she was in this world. The club was a microcosm of the vampire world, and she hadn't seen its very dark underbelly yet.

She walked out to the front of the club to meet Elias when Elise stepped into her path. *Ah shit.* The vamp groupie had been shooting her daggers since it became obvious she and Elias were together. There was something unhinged about Elise, and Addie always tried to be pleasant to her. She wasn't worried for herself; she was worried Elise would do something to hurt herself.

"Hello Elise, you look lovely tonight." Addie kept her voice calm and even.

Elise's eyes narrowed. "You think he will be interested in you in a month's time? A year? You're fooling yourself. You're just the next slut in line. A pussy for him to …"

"Oh, hey now, what's this?" Clara, the pretty redhead, came up to them. With her was Mei, looking worried.

"Hey Clara, Mei," said Addie calmly. So maybe she did need to be a little worried for herself, but she didn't want Elias over here. He'd make it worse.

She had to be able to fight her own battles. "Elise and I were just chatting. I think she might be a little tense, though. Maybe she needs a drink?"

Clara looked at her and smiled softly. "I think so. Mei, can you take Elise to the bar?"

"No problem," said Mei. She put her arm through Elise's. "Come on, honey. Let's get a drink and have a good chat."

"Mei, put it on my tab, huh?"

"I don't need you to buy me a fucking drink, you whore!" Elise hissed.

"No, but I owe Mei one, so you both should get one." Addie shrugged like it meant nothing. Mei gave her a thumbs-up that Elise couldn't see.

"You do! Come on, babe, let's get a little lit, huh?" Mei guided Elise away.

"You are kinder to her than she deserves," said Clara. "But thank you."

"Of course. I know she hates me, but I worry for her."

Clara nodded. "I don't think any of us realized she was this obsessed with Elias until you came along. But I can't regret that."

Addie's eyebrows lifted. "Really? Why is that?"

"Because since he's known you, he's made sure all of us ladies are looked after. The club has always been good about making sure any feedings were consensual, but he's much more involved with enforcing it now. It makes a difference that he's personally involved."

"Oh," said Addie softly. "I hadn't realized that." She opened her mouth to speak but closed it again.

"I can see you want to ask me something. Go ahead," said Clara.

"No," said Addie. "I am not one to poke my nose into people's business. I am not free with my own, and I don't want to be a hypocrite."

Clara laughed. "I'm actually the same way. So, I am going to do you a solid. I suspect you were going to remark that I don't seem to be your normal groupie, yes?" Addie nodded. "You're not wrong. I have different reasons for being here. But, at this point, I like to keep an eye on the gals."

"Thank you," said Addie. "You didn't have to say anything, I appreciate it."

"You are welcome. May I ask *you* something?"

"Of course, it's only fair."

"Are you sure you know what you're doing?"

Addie looked at her for a second, then burst into laughter. "Only about fifty percent of the time. The other fifty percent, I am totally winging it." Addie took Clara's hand and squeezed it. "But I know I want to be with him, and I'll figure the rest out as I go along."

Clara squeezed back. "Okay, then. I will be keeping an eye on you, too, though."

"Who's going to keep an eye on you, though?"

"No one. No one ever has."

Elias walked up to them. "I'm sorry to interrupt. Is everything okay?"

"Everything is fine, Elias." Addie let Clara's hand go after a final squeeze. "We were just chatting."

He nodded. "Clara, is Elise feeling well?"

Clara looked at Addie, who nodded. She'd talk to Elias about it later. "She's a bit off tonight. We're keeping an eye on her, though."

"Good, let Miles know if you all need anything. I have a proposal I'd like to discuss with you soon if that's alright?"

"Oh! Sure, no problem. Have a good night, kids." Clara walked away.

No one had ever kept an eye on her, she'd said. That must be the darkness she saw there. Well, Addie would be keeping an eye on her from now on. She looked at Elias. "Ready?"

"I am. Are you, though?"

"I am indeed. Let's go!"

Elias lived on the top floor of an apartment building in a decidedly fancier part of town than Addie lived in.

She whistled low when they walked into the apartment. The room had floor-to-ceiling windows on two sides. The view of the city was amazing. "Dan really wanted to sell his house and live in this building. He never managed to make it work. But we'd walk by a lot, and I always wondered who lived here and why they felt they needed one-way windows."

"I think you'll be glad of it tonight," he said to her in a low voice. "Oh?"

"Hmmm," he said, leaning down and dropping a kiss on the back of her neck. "Oh, yes. I've been thinking about this all night." He stood and put her bag down. "What's in this thing?"

"Just stuff I need," she replied. "I planned on staying tonight if that's okay."

"I insist upon it," Elias replied. "Christ, you look sexy," he said.

"You may be biased."

"Possibly, but you do." She was wearing another long black sheath dress. This one was slit up both sides, showcasing knee-high, stiletto black boots. Her hair was slicked back into a high braid, something she knew he liked.

"Thank you, then." She walked over and gave him a soft kiss. His arms came around her, and he deepened the kiss. She sighed into his mouth, and the heart that had long ago stopped beating flipped over. She pulled back. "Did your heart just beat?"

"It did. Every once in a blue moon, it will."

"Oh, that's very cool."

"Would you like a drink?"

"Does that affect, well, anything?"

"One or two drinks wouldn't, no."

"Good to know. But no, not right now. Maybe later." She walked over to the windows and looked out. "This view is amazing. And it's so quiet here!"

He walked up behind her, putting his hands on her shoulders, massaging them a little. She leaned back into him.

"It was a selling point for the place," he said. He started dropping kisses on her neck and shoulders.

"What about the sun?" she asked.

"I have blackout shades that come down, either by a voice-activated panel or an app on my phone."

"Smart," she replied.

"Thank you," he said. "My bedroom, bathroom, and office have no windows, and every room has a reinforced steel door. I've done a lot of work to the place. Between the view and the quiet, it was worth it to me to put money into the place."

"This room is smaller than it should be, isn't it?"

"Observant. It is. I wanted my bedroom suite and office to be bigger."

"So ..." she started to say.

He turned her around. "Adelaide, we can discuss the apartment later."

She took a breath. "Nerves." *I think.* "I am both excited and nervous. It's not like anyone has fed from me before."

"I fucking hope not," he growled at her. "We don't have to do this now, little bird."

She gave his chin a light nip. "I want to," she replied. "Will it hurt, though?"

"At first, it might. But then you will only feel pleasure. Mine, mingled with yours. I will have you so on fire at that point that any pain should be minimal."

"Oh, how you talk," she said.

"Just the truth. But as I've told you, once I do this—we do this—there's no going back. You will belong to me, and I will not let you go."

She looked at him. "What makes you think I'd ever let *you* leave."

He pulled her to him and kissed her savagely. His tongue plunged into her mouth, and she met it with her own. She grabbed his biceps and wiggled closer to him.

He pulled back. "Don't think that little nip you gave me went unnoticed."

Her eyes widened, all innocence. "Who, me?"

"Yes, you. What am I going to do with you, little bird?" He walked around her. "Always with that mouth of yours getting you into trouble." He pulled her dress up. "You aren't wearing underwear, Adelaide."

"No, Elias. I'm not."

"I do not recall instructing you in this regard."

He sounded so formal; she loved it. "I took matters into my own hands."

He yanked and pulled the dress over her head. She was naked except for her boots now. "You also did not wear a bra. Was this also a decision you made?"

"I did, yes."

His eyes glittered darkly. He pulled her to him, bent her over his arm, and gave her ass one hard smack. She groaned. He laughed low. He gave her a second whack, and she wiggled over his arm. "Stay still, Adelaide. Or I will have to smack your gorgeous ass again." He gently rubbed where he'd smacked. "Do you like when I do this, Adelaide?" She nodded. "Answer me," he commanded.

"Yes, Elias."

"I know you do," he said.

"Then why did you ask me?"

Whack! "Are you talking back now, little bird?"

Adelaide had done that on purpose, and he had to smile. She was so turned on, and she wanted him to do it again. "No, Elias."

"Didn't think so." He stood her up. "Keep your boots on."

She nodded at him. "Of course," she replied. He took his shirt off and her mouth watered. The muscles, the tattoos; he was simply perfect.

He grabbed a cushion off the couch and put it on the floor. Then he palmed himself and gave her a wicked smile. "On your knees, Adelaide."

She fell to her knees on the cushion, hands at her side, and looked up at his face.

"Good. Very good," he said. "Now, take my cock out and take it in that mouth of yours." She did so with shaking hands. Not nerves, desire. She ran her hand down his length and was gratified by his shudder. She smiled and took him in her mouth, sucking gently.

"Told you we would need to do something about that mouth of yours." He wrapped her braid around his hand and tugged. "All of me, Adelaide, take all of me in that pretty mouth of yours." He pushed her forward to take more of him in her mouth.

She moaned around his cock, and he paused. She looked at him, letting him know all was good as she relaxed her throat and took him to the root. She gagged for a moment but quickly acclimated, working him with her mouth. He groaned this time. "God, Adelaide. That feels amazing! I love how you look with my cock in your mouth."

Her eyes watered some, but she smiled around him and took his balls in her hand, squeezing them a little. "Harder," he moaned. She did it harder, and his hold on her hair tightened. She sucked harder, and he rocked his hips towards her, fucking her mouth.

All too soon, though, he stopped her. "I don't want to come like this. Well, I do. But not right now." He lifted her. "That was amazing, Adelaide." He kissed her deeply. She wound her arms around his neck. He backed her against the window, setting her on her feet again. The cold glass felt wonderful on her overheated body.

While he would feed from her tonight, he wanted to ensure that she received her own pleasure. "Spread your legs for me, Adelaide." She did, and he got on his knees. He kissed her breasts, belly, and the tops of her thighs before his tongue lapped at her sex. She bucked off the window, and his hand held her in place.

"Your pussy is so wet, Adelaide," he said. His hands went to her ass, and he stroked a finger down the slit and circled the tight rosebud. She whimpered as she grabbed his hair and pulled it hard. He laughed. "That's right, little bird. Pull harder." He took her clit in his mouth and bit. Addie screamed his name, and he used his fingers to bring her to orgasm, letting her ride his hand.

He stood. "Christ, you are a sight." She was breathing hard, flushed, eyes glittering. With the city lights spread out behind her, he'd never seen anything so lovely.

She reached for him. "Elias, please, I need you inside me."

He toed off his shoes and socks and then took off his jeans. He moved into the circle of her arms, and she wound them around his neck, burying her face there. "Are you doing okay?" he asked quietly. She nodded and tightened her arms around him.

"It's a lot. I am feeling a lot. But none of it bad," she said.

He was feeling similarly if he was honest. He took a breath and then lifted her. She wrapped her legs around him, and he carefully backed her against the window again. "Are you ready?" he asked quietly. She nodded. "Addie, honey, it's important to me that I have your verbal consent."

"Oh, of course! Yes, Elias, I am ready." She paused. "I trust you."

Three little words, and he was undone. He hadn't realized how much he had needed to hear that until she said it. He entered her gently and thrusted slowly at first, then faster. Her legs tightened around him as he continued to hold her up. She pulled her head up and kissed him. She was getting close again. She leaned her head back and to the side for him, knowing instinctively what to do.

He groaned and whispered her name. He licked her neck, and as he pumped faster, he leaned down and put his fangs on her, going slowly until her blood filled his mouth. She tasted sweet. He had known she would.

Addie felt a moment of panic, a moment of pain, and then it was gone. Pleasure like she'd never felt filled her. Not just sexual, though that was pretty intense. But she felt good all over. She now understood the vamp groupies a little better, though she was sure it only felt this good because it was Elias.

Her hand cupped the back of his head. She stroked his hair and tightened even more around him. She closed her eyes and gave herself over to the feelings.

Elias couldn't believe it. She was holding his head while he fed from her. No woman had done that. It had been hundreds of years, but she was the first to offer him affection during feeding. He pumped harder and faster until she was gripping him so tightly, moaning and bucking against him while he fed from her.

She came on a scream, and a moment later, he came as well, calling her name. He licked her neck and then healed the bite marks. He licked his lips and sighed.

Her eyes were huge when they met his own. "You are mine," he whispered into her hair.

"Yes," she answered. "And you are mine. I will hunt you down if you ever try to leave me."

He laughed. "I wouldn't dare, Addie. I wouldn't dare."

They weren't mates, and that was just fine. This was enough of a commitment, and she was absolutely content.

Elias kissed the top of her head and walked to the back of the apartment.

"Where are we going?" she asked.

"Bedroom. I have a huge bed and hours until dawn. I have plans for you, Adelaide. Such plans."

CHAPTER 11

Addie rolled over and looked at Elias. "This bed," she said, "Is enormous."

He laughed. "It is. I had it specially made. I like room when I sleep." He was a big man, even in life, when he had been stuck in small cells or rooms, he had sworn one day, the room where he rested would be enormous. As would be the bed he slept in.

Addie looked at him as if she knew what he was thinking and stroked his cheek. "It is very comfortable."

Something had been niggling at Elias since he had fed from her earlier. "Addie," he started, knowing he would probably fuck this up somehow. "When I fed from you, I got some glimpses into you. Things you may not even be aware of."

She frowned at him. "Does that happen often?"

"It never has before. I have only ever fed from the neck of one other person, and it didn't happen with her." Addie's eyes narrowed. "Settle down, little bird. That was centuries ago."

"Is she why you haven't done it in so long?"

"Yes, it was. And stop deflecting. I got glimpses of your life with your father and Dan. And some good-looking kid that I admit I wanted to thrash."

She smiled. "Ah, that must have been Nigel. He was a trumpet player we had to hire last minute on a European tour because ours took sick. He was the only other young person in the band. And my first lover." She sat. "But I am curious what you saw. Or thought you saw."

"How old were you when your mother died?"

"Fourteen. It was sudden. She wasn't sick or anything. One day, she turned to me to say something, and the next, she was gone. Aneurysm."

"Christ, Addie, that's awful."

"It was pretty terrible. Dad barely took any time to mourn and, well, if I'm honest, I am still mad about that. I know he loved her, but the band always felt more important. When I asked him about it, he told me the band was still there and we had to move on. Then, he told me I had to sing in his band. Weekends, summers, any random evening gig they had."

"Told you? Fucking hell, Adelaide! You were fourteen! And you had just lost your mother! You needed time to grieve."

"I know," she said in a small voice, "But I couldn't say no."

"How long did you stay with the band?"

"Until he passed away when I was 22. We did a tour of Europe. I am still not sure how he managed it. But there was a lot of nostalgia for big band and music standards at the time. I celebrated my 21st birthday in Amsterdam. When the tour was over, I stayed with Nigel for a while. I was slowly starting to assert my independence—thanks to Nigel, actually—and I insisted on time off. I stayed a month, and it would have been longer, but dad called me to come home. He was sick, and I needed to take care of him."

"He demanded that you take care of him?"

"He did, but I would have anyway. Nigel and I parted because I would not have time for him. He offered to come out, but it was more than I could handle."

"That's reasonable, little bird. But I have to ask why you stayed with the band so long."

She looked at him, sorrow in her eyes. "Elias, he had never really paid attention to me before. I thought he was showing me he loved me. So, I was a good and dutiful daughter. I did what he told me."

"Until you didn't and stayed in Europe. But then he got sick, it must have felt like that was payback for starting to live your own life."

"It wasn't my fault!" Addie burst out. "How was I to know? I was an adult, and I wanted something else for myself."

"Of course, it wasn't. But you still blame yourself. I felt it."

"You still blame yourself for things!"

"Yes, I do, as I should. But we will get to my mistakes another time. It's why you are so calm with people like Dan and Elise. You're used to tamping down all those feelings. You keep the peace. Have you ever yelled at Dan? When he sold your mom's piano, did you yell at him?"

Addie jumped out of bed. "No! I didn't yell at him, you asshole! I stared at him and then walked out of the room. What could I possibly say? I don't like confrontation!"

"Why not?" She was yelling at him, and that pleased him.

"Because what if they stop loving you? Or caring about you? My father said I had to be …"

Elias got out of bed and stood in front of her. He put his hands on her shoulders and rubbed gently. "What did he say, Addie? What did he tell you?"

"He said I had to be good, quiet. Because no one likes you when you yell and scream. My mom had a temper. She used to yell at him in Spanish when they fought and he hated it. Good girls do what their fathers say, he'd always tell me." She looked at him, shock plain on her face. "So, even though I didn't love Dan anymore, the habit of not causing a fuss was so ingrained that I let the piano sale go." Her face crumpled.

Elias scooped her up and brought her over to his large, oversized chair. He sat her on his lap and rubbed her back. "Okay, Adelaide, cry now. Cry for your mother, cry for your childhood that was over too soon. Cry for all of it. You are safe with me."

"I can't," she whispered.

"You can. Addie, you just yelled at me, and I'm still here. I am not going anywhere. I am a complete fucking asshole, but even I recognize that how your dad treated you wasn't right. Just fucking cry."

She looked at him and opened her mouth to speak, but she started to cry. He tightened his arms around her and let her sob, though it broke his heart.

He had no idea why he'd gotten those glimpses into her life. Into the unhappiness and loneliness that he saw there. But once he saw it, he couldn't ignore it.

She cried for a long while, and he just held her. Finally, she sniffled and looked at him. "I'm really sexy now, huh?" she said.

"Absolutely. I love a red nose and waterlogged eyes." He grabbed her some tissues. "Better?"

"Yes." She wiped her eyes and blew her nose. "My mom sang with the band before I did. And now I remember her telling me that at least she got to spend time with him. But when she was home, all her attention was on me. That was the difference. His wasn't."

"She was your mother first, a singer second."

Addie nodded. "I think you're right. She never missed anything at school or a recital." She sighed. "I see it so clearly now. Dan had that same kind of cavalier attitude. I think he did love me for a time, to the best of his ability."

"That isn't saying much," Elias retorted.

"No, it's not. But I started to chafe against it because I wanted to start singing again. He didn't like that."

"Why didn't you become a music teacher?"

"When my father died, I wanted out of a career centered around music. I played and sang a bit for myself. And I taught piano while I was in college. Eventually, I began to miss it."

"Makes sense," he replied.

She gave him a shocked look. "Oh my god, Elias! Is this why I like you telling me what to do during sex so much?" She didn't just like it, she loved it.

"I can't say that what happened to you with your dad didn't play into it, but there is absolutely nothing wrong with what we do. But if you want me to stop doing it, I will."

She shook her head. "No, I don't want you to stop. I love what we have, it's ours, and I love how you make me feel. I don't feel less or minimized. I feel powerful and very sexy."

"Why do you think that is?" he asked.

"Because you respect me, and I trust you." This was the answer he had wanted. "I know you'll stop if I say no, and I know you'd stop if I didn't like it. I am not sure why, but I've trusted you from the beginning."

He hugged her to him. "I trust you too, and no, I can't explain that either. That being said, if you want to continue with this, you will need a safe word."

She nodded. "I do want to continue. I have things to learn, and I will come up with a safe word."

"Good girl." He grinned at her. "But you know, if you ever want to, you can tell me what to do."

Addie's eyes lit up. "Yeah? You'd like that, would you?"

He grinned at her. "I would. I am more than happy to let you lead me." He kissed the top of her head. "Addie, I probably shouldn't have dumped all of that on you, but I thought it was important."

"No, it's good that you did. I've spent many years ignoring it, not understanding why I was so quietly angry all the time. I felt better when I moved into my own place." She grinned at him. "Hey, you're my rebound guy!"

He growled at her. "No, I am not your 'rebound guy,'" he replied. "I'm keeping you. It's too late. You had your chance to get away."

She kissed him softly. "I'm teasing. Stop growling at me, Elias."

"Is this you telling me what to do?" he asked silkily.

She laughed outright at this. "Well," she said airily, "It's certainly a start."

CHAPTER 12

When Addie walked into the club the next night, Darian took one look at her and knew Elias had fed from her. He could scent it on her.

"Elias fed from you," he stated.

Her eyebrows shot up. "How could you possibly know that?"

"I can smell his scent on you in a different way." He tapped his nose.

"What? Will everyone be able to tell?"

"Yes, Addie. It is a clear signal to any vampire interested in you to back the fuck off." She gave him a sour look. "But your scent will be on him as well."

"Is that also a back the fuck off signal?" she asked, crossing her arms.

"It is, though less of one since you are human," he replied. "I take it he did not share that bit of information with you?"

"He did not." She sat across from him. "What can I expect?"

"From him or other vampires?"

"Both, I think."

"Most vamps will respect the bond you're forming. Some may try and test it. Just for fun."

"And if Elias catches wind of that?"

"He will kill the other vampire. And not even you will be able to stop him from doing it. He fed from your neck or breast; I assume?" She nodded, reticent to give up that information, but she sensed he needed to know. "Feeding from the wrist— as you know already—is commonplace.

Most of the time, vampires do not feed from the neck or breast unless there is an intimate relationship. I suspect yours is more intimate than most and you are bonding differently. Because of this, he may be less reasonable as it relates to you."

"He knows I would never betray him," Addie replied.

"Yes, he does know that. You are not the issue. The other vampires are." Darian believed Elias and Addie were mating. He wasn't about to share that with either of them, but he was pretty sure about it. Vampire and human matings were rare. They may be in for a bit of a ride.

Addie nodded. "I see. Okay, I will be mindful of that then. Is he going to get pissy about anyone who works here talking to me?"

Darian shook his head. "I don't think so. I hope not. But we will have to see. I'm safe enough, as is Miles. The other band members are also fine."

"Good. I have two problems that I can see right off the bat: Elise and Miranda. Elise, because someone will mention it in her presence, and she won't be happy. Miranda, because Stellan hasn't fed from her, and they've been together longer."

"Who would tell her, though? I am assuming you won't."

"I am not planning on it at the moment. But Stellan might."

"Oh, that's very true. And you can't very well tell him not to say anything."

"I can't, no."

"It's a different relationship, Addie."

"Yes, but it's moving much faster than hers. She's going to hate that. It's already tense between us."

"How come?"

Addie sighed. "I don't know how to friend, it seems."

"What does that mean?"

"I don't share confidences with her. She doesn't get a lot of details about my life, especially how things are with Elias. And it pisses her off."

"Why don't you?" Darian didn't care, but he was curious. He didn't think much of Miranda, so her pettiness didn't surprise him.

"I had female friends when I was young. But after my mom died, I spent a lot of time with older men. God, that sounds awful. But it was just the musicians in my father's band. At a time when girls were getting together and gossiping and meeting boys, I was singing in a band, in places I was often too young to be in otherwise. I never developed that skill. I always thought it was better to keep my business to myself."

"I don't think that's necessarily bad," Darian replied.

"Me neither. Or I didn't until Miranda pointed out something was wrong with me."

Darian's eyes darkened. "May I be honest?" She nodded. "Is there a reason you have people in your life who think this? There is nothing wrong with you."

"I mean, there's probably a lot wrong with me. I've started unpacking my childhood. Well, as of last night." She had started looking for a therapist to help her unpack her issues around her father and Dan.

"We all have shit in our pasts. Miranda thinks something is wrong with you because you don't friend like she does. But you listen to her spill all her stuff. You support her. That's a good friend. Maybe she's a bit envious or jealous of you."

"Why would she be?"

"You are smart, funny, and talented. You are also very self-possessed. The vamps here really like you, whereas they merely tolerate her."

"Darian, I don't know about all that."

"It's true."

"I don't like confrontation. So, I keep my feelings to myself." And she was doing it again, but she recognized it at least.

"I get that. But you don't back down with me or the band. And you don't back down with Elias, I bet."

"Elise ..."

"You are careful with her because she has some issues. That just makes you kind."

She smiled at him. "Thank you. Why don't the vamps like Miranda?"

"They think she's desperate and needy," Darian replied, which was the truth. "She is always hanging off Stellan and trying to pull focus back to her, as if she's the first warmblood to date one of us."

Addie wanted to argue, but she couldn't. She'd seen Miranda in action. "She's insecure about the relationship because he hasn't fed from her."

"And it shows," came the retort. "Even if he feed from her, it doesn't mean he's going to stay with her. Does she know that he feeds from the ladies here?"

Addie shook her head. "No. I've seen him do it, just the wrist. But Clara has implied she won't let him feed on her again."

"She won't. She says he's greedy and makes it hurt on purpose. Clara is different, though. She can pick and choose. She's like you—people like and respect her."

"Stellan won't like that," Addie said.

"No, he won't. But either Elias or Miles will set him straight. And I think Elias has something in mind when it comes to the Clara and the other ladies."

"I feel comfortable talking to Clara."

"I am not surprised. She's no bullshit. She has been through some shit in her life, and she's very comfortable with herself."

"Hard-won, I think."

"Agreed. But you're both alike there."

"Truth," said Addie. She looked at him. "Darian, thank you. You're a good friend. You're like a brother to me. I am grateful for Elias, but also for you."

"Oh, Addie. That's very sweet. I feel very much the same. I am so glad I hired you."

Addie stood and leaned over to kiss him on the cheek. "I'm going to start getting ready now. Thanks for the talk. It helped."

"Anytime, sis, anytime."

Addie was finishing her makeup when there was a knock at the door. "Come in!" she called.

The door opened, and Clara stepped into the room. "Hello," she said.

"Clara! Come in, have a seat."

"Thanks," she smiled at Addie. She sat. "This chair is huge. Did Elias put it here?"

"He did. It is Elias-sized. How are you this evening? You're not usually in on Wednesdays."

"I'm good. No, not usually. Elias wanted to talk to me. He got caught up with Miles, but he said he'd come grab me if I wanted to stop in and see you."

"I'm glad you did." Addie took off the light robe she usually wore to protect her clothes. "You look like you have something on your mind, girl."

"Yeah," Clara bit her lip. "I want to ask you something, but it's also not my business."

Addie sat back. "Go ahead, shoot!"

"Did Elias feed from you last night?"

"He did. Is that going around the club already?"

"It is. I know it's not my concern ..."

"You keep an eye on Elise. I get it. Is there any way we can minimize this for her?"

"I hope that most people won't mention it in front of her. But it's bound to come up at some point. She's not here tonight either. Tamir invited her to a private party that he's hosting. Thankfully."

Addie nodded. "Maybe people will calm down about it in a couple of days."

"So, another personal question, how did it feel?" Addie looked at her. "It's different for me."

"It hurt for a second, then it was wonderful. I think it was because Elias made sure of that."

Clara nodded. "I've heard it can be like that. Nice to know it's true. Okay, tit for tat. You can ask me something. Or two somethings."

"I don't need to do that."

"I know. That's why I'm okay with it." Clara smiled at her.

Addie thought for a moment. She had a question she wanted to ask, but she felt it was too personal. "What's up with Stellan being greedy when it comes to you?"

Clara laughed. "That's not what I thought you were going to ask. You've talked to Darian."

"Yes, sorry. It's the Miranda connection."

"I understand. He makes it hurt, and it doesn't have to. He also takes more than he needs to, more than he should. And he's crude. He called me a whore and a slut the last time, and I don't like that. He's got a real ugly side."

"This makes me worry for Miranda," said Addie. "But I don't know that I can tell her any of that."

"She won't believe you," said Clara. "Keep an eye on her if you can."

"I will," said Addie. "Is that your natural hair color?"

Clara burst out laughing. "That's what you want to know?"

"It is!"

"I am a natural redhead, but this is kicked up. I do hair for a living. I own a salon. You need a trim, by the way."

"I'll call for an appointment. Where is your place?"

"Corner of Fourth and Riverside."

"I live on Riverside," Addie said.

"And I live on Fourth! Who knew we were neighbors! I have time tomorrow, come in around two o'clock. You don't go to anyone else. Just me."

"Yes, ma'am!" Addie saluted. There was another knock, and Miles and Elias poked their heads in. "Hello, gentlemen!"

"Hello, ladies!" smiled Miles. "Addie, you have twenty minutes."

"Thanks, Miles!" Miles clapped Elias on the shoulder and went off to give the rest of the band the time check.

Elias came over and kissed Addie. "Hey, gorgeous!"

"Hey, yourself!"

Clara fanned herself. "You two generate way too much heat for me."

Elias laughed. "Sorry about that."

"Please don't be. I'm a hopeless romantic after all."

"I am sorry I kept you waiting," said Elias. "Do you still have time to talk?"

"I do," said Clara. "I will meander over to your office, give you a little time to kiss your lady some more. See you tomorrow, Addie."

"2 p.m. on the dot. I will be there." Clara let herself out.

"What's tomorrow?

"Clara owns a hair salon, and she's giving me a trim. Shoulder length?"

"Don't you dare!" He glared at her. She laughed and kissed him. "Stellan returned my call finally."

"And?" she asked.

"We're all having drinks after your second set tonight."

"Where?"

"A private room here."

"You have private rooms here?"

"I do. He's bringing Miranda. So, I hope that means he'll behave."

"Shit. I hope he doesn't say anything about you feeding on me."

"Oh, that would get messy. Let's hope for the best." He pulled her to him. "I may miss part of your set. But I will be out there as soon as possible."

"No problem. You're there every night. You know you don't have to be."

"I want to be,"

She snuggled into him. "You going to tell me what you're talking to Clara about?"

"Afterwards. I am not sure she'll agree to my proposal. Have a good set, little bird."

"Mmm, thank you. Go, don't keep my new friend waiting any longer."

"Yes, ma'am!"

Once they were settled in his office, Clara leaned forward. "Before we start, I wanted to thank you."

"For what?"

"Keeping an eye on us as of late. It's appreciated, and it's made a difference in our treatment."

Elias frowned. "You're thanking me for something I should have been doing all along."

"True, but you're doing it now. So, I wanted to thank you for starting? I guess?

"You're letting me off easy, which I thank you for. To that end, I wanted to talk to you about something. Well, a couple of things. The ladies listen to you. They respect and like you. True?"

"True," Clara replied.

"I'd like to offer you a job. A part-time job, as I understand you own a hair salon."

"I'm listening." Clara would not mind doing a little less hair. She enjoyed it, but she needed to work a lot to make ends meet.

"So, I'd like to try and monetize what you ladies offer to my patrons here."

"I'm sorry?" Clara was not sure where this was going.

"I knew I was going to fuck this up. Not for me—for you. I'd like to either pay you all for the service you offer as hostesses, let's say. If that doesn't feel right to you, the serving staff would like to give you a cut of their tips."

Clara looked at him in shock. "What would be my role?"

"I'd like to formally hire you to manage the ladies. Ensure they have what they need, handle any issues that may come up, and make sure they feel safe. I think they would feel more comfortable going to you than to Miles or me. But we'd step in whenever we needed to. I assume most of the ladies have outside jobs and may not need or want the money, but I'd like to offer it. You all keep my customers happy the same way the bartenders do or the live music does. You provide an important service, especially for younger vamps." Elias paused. "Have I completely insulted you?"

Clara shook her head. "No, you haven't. Now that I know you don't mean to make money from us. But I am confused about the tipping thing? The staff suggested this? Was it my brother?"

"No, it was the wait staff's idea. And they discussed it with the bartending staff since they pool tips. Your brother is my bar manager, and he takes a smaller cut of the tips, by choice. That's what gave me the idea to see if you'd be interested in a job. Miles even suggested giving you the title of assistant manager, and I agree."

"I'm ... well, speechless. Almost. What are we talking about salary-wise?"

Elias wrote something on a piece of paper and pushed it toward her. Clara goggled.

"Elias, this is ridiculous. That's too much money. I am only in here four nights a week and not even the whole night most of the time."

"That's fine. You can still make your schedule. Though, I'd want you available via phone for emergencies. I ask that of Miles, your brother, and myself."

"Of course," She thought about it for a moment. She could cut back at the salon, just keep her regulars. She could also start putting away a little money. Maybe even buy a place one day. "Okay, I accept your job offer. I will come in five nights a week, but not the entire night since I own a business. But I would be available by phone. As for the other, I would like a chance to speak to the ladies about this. It'll take a few days to get everyone's opinion. Most ladies do not need the money as they come from wealthy families, but they may enjoy making their own money. I'd hate to break into the server's tips, though."

"They believe they make what they do for tips because of you all. Clara," *Should he say this?* "You are the best person for this job. Not only because of how much you are liked and respected, but you don't let vamps feed from you as often as you used to. You spend most of your time making sure the ladies are okay and you are impartial. That's important."

"You've been watching me," Clara laughed. "In between watching Addie."

"I'm always watching Addie. But I also see what goes on in my club. I've chosen to stop ignoring it."

"Can we thank Addie for that?" It was ballsy of her to ask, but she wanted to know.

"Yes, we can." He stood. "Speaking of, I'd like to go watch her set. Talk to Miles. He'll take care of all the paperwork. Let me know what the ladies decide."

"Will do. And thanks, Elias."

"Thank you," he replied. "Also, Stellan is coming in tonight with Miranda, sometime during the second set. You may want to make yourself scarce."

"Will Addie need me? You know what Miranda can be like."

And with that, Clara won Elias's loyalty and protection. "I don't think so. Maybe mention it to Mei if you get a chance. Then go enjoy your night off."

She was going home to leftovers and *The Real Housewives*. But she'd enjoy the downtime. "Okay, I will talk to Mei. But if Addie needs or wants me, feel free to call."

They walked to the front together. Elias went to his booth, while Clara went to find Mei. Things, she thought, were looking up.

CHAPTER 13

Someone knocked on the door to Addie's dressing room. "Come in!" she called.

The door opened, and Elias came in, shutting the door behind him. He leaned against it, taking her in. Addie was still wearing the tight leather pants she'd worn on stage. But she'd changed into another black t-shirt that said "Rock Goddess" in red crystals on it. She'd also changed into low-heeled boots.

"See something you like?" she asked Elias in the mirror as she re-applied her lipstick.

"Yes. All of it. But right now? That ass in those pants."

She turned and smiled at him. "Do we have time?"

"Sadly, no. Stellan and Miranda are waiting for us."

"Boo!"

He grinned at her. "You are insatiable."

"Yes." She rubbed her stomach. "Also, hungry."

"Lucky for you, I ordered in some food for this."

"You're my favorite," she replied.

"You look a little worried. Is it Miranda?"

"Yes. I am just concerned Stellan is going to open his mouth about you feeding from me. It would upset her."

"I am not sure she deserves your consideration."

"Be nice. She's insecure, sure, but she's a good person."

"Who makes you feel bad about the kind of friend you are."

"You've been talking to Darian!"

"No. Well, yes. But I didn't need to talk to him about this. It's obvious. Can't you be friends with Clara instead?"

Addie rolled her eyes. "I can be friends with both."

"I don't suppose I could tell you not to be friends with Miranda?"

"Elias, telling me what to do in the bedroom is one thing. Telling me in my life is quite another. I will not put up with you forbidding me to do things."

His eyes darkened. "I don't like anyone making you feel bad about yourself. You've had enough of that."

"Elias, I understand what you're saying. But she's my friend, and I will not abandon her." She stroked his cheek. "Don't start growling about it. I appreciate the concern, but my independence is too hard-won."

He sighed. "Okay, fine. But I don't have to like it."

"No, you don't. You need to accept it."

He nodded. "I will not let you be disrespected, though. Please bear that in mind. If you do not quash it, I will."

"Yes, Elias," she replied mildly. "Let's go. I don't want to keep them waiting any longer."

He opened the door to her dressing room, and she scooted out in front of him. "Elias, what would happen if you got caught here with the sunrise?"

"What is your dressing room missing?" He took her hand while they walked along.

Addie thought for a moment. "Oh! Windows! It doesn't have windows."

"Correct. None of the dressing rooms do. Neither does my office. If I get caught here, I can bunk down in my office. Anyone else can bunk down in the dressing rooms." Addie had a pained look on her face. "What is it?"

"I've been locking my dressing room door. Just out of habit, I guess. I won't do that anymore."

He squeezed her hand. "Yours is off-limits."

"No, Elias. That's not right. I don't keep anything too personal or valuable here. If my dressing room can provide a safe place for a vamp, I'd like that."

"If that's what you want, that's fine. But if you should lock it, Miles, Darian, and I have master keys, so don't worry too much."

They reached the back rooms, and Elias opened the door, ushering Addie in. Miranda and Stellan stood. "Addie!" Miranda ran over and hugged her friend. "You look amazing!"

"Thanks," replied Addie warmly. "But you're the one who looks amazing!" Miranda was wearing a short red dress that clung to her body and red strappy sandals. Her hair was in a tight bun, and she was perfectly made up.

"Aw, this old thing!" she joked.

"Miranda," said Stellan. A command in the one word. Miranda went back to his side, causing Addie's eyes to narrow.

Stellan's eyes lit on Addie in a way Elias didn't like. "Adelaide," he said smoothly. "You look well." He turned to Elias. "Good evening, Elias."

Miranda looked confused. "Stellan, you're being very formal. We're all friends."

"Are we?" Stellan asked Elias.

"I'm not sure we are," replied Elias. "Are you going to send your new puppy over to Addie's again?"

Miranda looked at Addie. "What are they talking about?"

"Stellan sent Dan over to my apartment," replied Addie.

"What? Why?" Miranda looked at Stellan. "You didn't do that, right?"

"Of course, I didn't, Miranda." Stellan looked at Elias. "I didn't send Dan to Addie's house. The poor guy must still be in love with her."

Addie snorted. "He was barely in love with me when we were married."

Elias's eyes hardened. "Stellan, you sent him over to Addie's with the sole purpose of trying to get her away from me and to enrage me. You know it, I know it, and Addie knows it."

Miranda shook her head. "No, no. Stellan wouldn't do that." She looked at Addie. "You have to believe that."

Addie shook her head at Miranda. "I saw Dan here with Stellan, and then a couple of days later, he shows up at my house. It seems very odd timing." She put her arm around Miranda. "But why don't we sit? Have some snacks. I'm starving." This is not how she had wanted this meeting to start.

Miranda stared at Stellan, ignoring Addie. "So, you were here that night? You told me Adelaide was lying."

Addie mentally kicked herself. "Randi, sit. Please." Addie poured her friend a glass of champagne. "Here, have some champagne. Take a breath, honey."

Miranda took the champagne, and Addie rubbed her back while her friend drank. She looked at Elias, willing him to do or say something. He nodded briefly.

"Stellan, let's sit and discuss things." Elias pulled out a chair and sat. He looked at Stellan, who sighed and sat. Addie pulled out Miranda's seat, pushing her into it. Then went around the table and sat next to Elias. He pulled her chair closer to him and draped his arm around her shoulder. She pinched his leg, and he grinned.

Addie leaned forward, made a small plate of food for Miranda, slid it across the table, and then one for herself. "Now, Stellan," Addie began, "Please tell Miranda what you were doing here with Dan."

Elias tried not to grin. Addie wasn't letting Stellan off the hook. She just wanted her friend to have a drink and some food.

Stellan gave her a sour look. "I'm sorry, babe," he said to Miranda. "I had a client that wanted to come here—insisted, really. I didn't want to upset you, so I told a white lie. I didn't want you to think I was here because I wanted to be." He looked at Elias. "No offense."

"Oh, offense taken, but continue," Elias replied mildly.

"I meant that I didn't choose to be here. My client wanted to be here. And yes, I hired Dan. I had no idea he was Adelaide's ex-husband. But he's good with money. I have every right to hire him." He leaned over and stroked Miranda's arm. "Baby, you gotta believe me. I would never do anything to upset your friend. I love you." He nuzzled her neck, and Elias had to keep from rolling his eyes.

"You told me my friend lied to me, though," she pouted at him.

"I know, baby. I froze. I didn't know what to say. I'm sorry I did that. Honest. I'll make it up to you." *That was rich. It was me he lied about. I'm the one who should be pissed off.*

Miranda smiled at him with watery eyes. "I knew there must be a good reason. I forgive you for lying to me about being here." She looked at Addie. "It's just business, Addie. You can see that, right?"

Elias looked at Addie. She looked so disappointed in her friend and a little sad. "Stellan," he said before Addie could answer. "Dan is not allowed in here. Adelaide does not want him in here, so that's final."

"Fine," said Stellan shortly.

"Now, have you given any more thought to what I said?"

"About?" Stellan took a sip of scotch.

"About what you're doing. If you don't stop playing these games, I will report you to the Elders. And if you think you can do better, you can petition them yourself."

Miranda's brow furrowed in confusion again, but she kept silent.

"If you would just see reason, we wouldn't have to go through this," Stellan huffed.

"Reason? You want what's mine. I run this city; you report to me."

"Stellan, you told me that you and Elias ran the city together. What is going on?" Miranda asked. All Stellan's lies were coming to roost, it seemed.

"I'm sure I never said that. Or you misunderstood."

"I know what you told me!"

"Well, I should be running the fucking city. But your friend's boyfriend doesn't want to step aside."

Miranda looked at Addie. "Addie? Did you know this?"

"I did," said Addie quietly. "I told you, remember? You didn't believe me."

"Well, what makes you think Elias isn't lying?" Miranda sounded resentful now.

"Because I see him here. In the club. I talk to people, and they talk to me. I know it's the truth because I've seen it with my own eyes."

"Elias, why don't you and Stellan run it together then?"

Elias turned to Miranda, wanting to be gentle for Addie's sake but also wanting to shake this delusional woman. "That's not how it works. The lion is the king of the jungle, right?" She nodded. "In this jungle, I'm the lion. It's not about who has the best business acumen. It's about who is capable of holding the city. Stellan is not."

"How fucking dare you!" Stellan stood and tossed the table aside. Addie jumped and pulled Miranda to the side.

"Don't do this, Stellan. If you want to try and run the city, do it the right way. Petition the Elders. If you win the petition, I will step aside."

"Just like that?" the other man scoffed.

"Just like that. No retaliation. I will work for you with no issues." Until the day Elias or another Assembly member killed him. Because if Stellan took over, he was sure they'd have to murder him at some point.

"You're a fucking liar! You're a monster, and everyone except your little girlfriend knows it."

Elias didn't flinch, but just barely. "Stellan, I am warning you."

"I am going to take this city, and I will kill you. Adelaide will work for me. Maybe she'll see reason and re-marry her ex."

It happened too fast for Addie to see. One moment Elias and Stellan were staring at each other, and the next, Elias had Stellan against the wall. Miranda gasped and went to move towards Stellan. Addie held her.

"Addie!"

"They're vampires Miranda. Do not get in between them."

"Oh, the vampire expert now, are we?"

"Don't take my head off. You know I'm right."

Elias was growling and holding Stellan against the wall with one hand. "I know what you're trying to do. Stop it." He let Stellan go. "Get the fuck out!" He looked at Miranda. "If you'd like to stay and visit Addie, you will be under my protection."

Miranda looked so conflicted. "Stellan?"

"You are not allowed to stay, Miranda. I don't care who you are friends with!"

"Addie, I don't know what to do." She whispered to her friend.

"Miranda, go with Stellan now. It's fine." God, her friend was well and truly hooked.

Stellan snarled at Elias. "You think you've changed, don't you? You haven't. You've fed from her, and now she's tamed you."

Addie closed her eyes and groaned. *Shit.*

"No one has tamed me. Just because I choose not to kill you here and now doesn't mean I'm tame. And don't you worry about us. You're going to have enough to deal with Miranda now."

"What do you mean?"

But that question was answered when Miranda rounded on Addie. "He fed on you? When? Were you going to tell me?"

"He did. Last night and I don't know," Addie answered honestly.

"You don't know? Are you mates now?"

Addie shook her head. "No, that's not how it works. At least not for us. I didn't want to hurt you. I knew it would."

"Hurt me?"

"Because Stellan hasn't fed from you, and you've been together longer." Addie could not help thinking about how really juvenile this whole thing was. What a stupid thing to be upset over. Why was she protecting Miranda over this?

"But you aren't mates?" She whirled to Stellan. "Is this something else you've lied about?"

"Randi, baby …"

"Don't you fucking dare!" Miranda screeched. Back to Addie again. "Do you have to fucking get everything?"

"I don't, Randi. I really don't."

"Everyone likes you, your vampire fed from you, you're talented and smart and gorgeous. Why do you have to have it all?"

Addie was shaking her head. "You're just upset. You're all those things too."

"Why are you making me hate you?" She pulled her hand back as if to slap Addie when it was grabbed from behind. Gently but firmly.

"Miranda, I know you are Adelaide's friend. But I absolutely cannot allow you to hit her or harm her in any way. You are angry at Stellan, but you do not get to take it out on your friend. I think it's time you left before you say something you regret. Do you understand me?" Miranda nodded. "If I let go of your hand, are you going to leave without incident?"

"Yes, Elias," Miranda replied. Miranda dropped her hand and grabbed her things.

"Miranda, please. This is what I was trying to avoid," Addie pleaded.

"I need some time. Please don't call me for a while." With that, Miranda ran out of the room.

Elias took out his phone and dialed. "Miles? Please make sure Miranda gets home safely." He listened for a moment. "Great, thank you."

"Stellan, how could do that to her?" said Addie. "What the hell is wrong with you?"

"Don't blame this on me!"

"You knew she was going to be upset about this." Addie gaped at him. "You did it so she'd stop being mad at you and point her anger at me."

"That's a real dick move," said Elias. "Stellan, get out. Cool off, and let's try this again in a few days."

"I will end you, Elias."

"You won't succeed. Get out." Stellan stalked from the room. Elias turned to Addie. "Addie?"

"She was going to hit me!" said Addie. "I don't even know how to feel about that." She looked around the room. "And now, there's no food."

Elias wrapped his arms around her as Darian stepped into the room. "Is everything okay? Addie?"

"I'm fine. Miranda lost her shit when Stellan spilled about Elias feeding on me. And Stellan wants to oust Elias by force."

"I assume he thinks it will make him look tougher," Elias replied.

"He can't best you," said Darian. "Not in a show of strength."

"No, he can't. I am going to take Addie to get something to eat. I'll need to call a meeting with the rest of the Assembly tomorrow. They'll need to decide where they stand."

Darian nodded. "Sounds good. Feed our chanteuse, and I'll get someone to clean this all up."

"Thanks, Darian," Elias looked at his friend gratefully. Darian gave him a thumbs-up and left the room.

"Elias?"

"Yes, little bird?"

"Can we grab take out somewhere? I want to go to your place and have you fuck me until I pass out. Is that okay?"

"That," he said, kissing the top of her head, "Is more than okay. It's perfect."

This was going to get worse before it got better. He hoped he could protect Addie.

Chapter 14

"Are you feeling any better?" Elias asked Addie. They were in bed, Addie practically lying on top of Elias, their legs tangled together. His hands were in her hair.

Addie ran her fingers over the swirl of Elias's chest tattoos. "Yes, and no. I feel more relaxed, but I am still sad and angry."

"Stands to reason, little bird. Miranda spends a lot of time telling you how friends should act, but in the end, didn't act like much of one herself."

"No, she didn't. I can see now that my not telling her was also self-serving. I knew she'd act like she did, and I didn't want to deal with it."

"That doesn't mean that your more altruistic reasons aren't valid. Two things can be true."

"You're right. I guess I am used to thinking of myself as the shitty friend."

"You are not a shitty friend. You are your own person with your own personality. You not wanting to overshare what an amazing lover I am is completely valid."

Addie laughed. "Oh? You're an amazing lover, are you?"

He palmed her breast. "Little bird, you know I am."

She tweaked his nipple. "So arrogant," she teased.

"Only because it's true," he replied smugly.

Addie couldn't deny it. He really was an amazing lover. "What does this swirl tattoo represent?"

He sighed, and his eyes turned serious. "I was very unaccepting at first of being a vampire. I believed we were abominations, and I conducted myself this way for a long time—to be an abomination. Once I put that behind me, I accepted vampires were a part of the nature of life and death, the cycle of life. The tattoo represents that."

"That is beautiful," Addie said. "I hope you tell me about that one day."

"I will. But I am ashamed of it, so it's still hard for me to talk about."

"You should, though it still haunts you. Does Darian know?"

"He does. It will always haunt me, Adelaide. It always should. I was a monster then, and my life now is still about shades of grey. I am not good."

"You're good to me," she said.

"That doesn't mean I am good."

Addie sat and shook her head. "But you're doing good things. Don't give me that look—you are. You're starting to do right by Clara and the ladies. You were angry at Miranda but still made sure she got home safely ..."

"Miranda was for you so that you wouldn't worry. It was beyond time I paid more attention to how the vamps in my club were treating the ladies. But even that is down to you and your influence." Elias said. "The business of the city is dirty. I am dirty because of it."

"If Tamir ran the city, what would happen?"

"If he ran the city, there would be drugs everywhere and no rules and safeguards for the prostitution trade. That only makes me the best of the worst, Adelaide. I am the monster that keeps the other monsters at bay."

"Because it takes a monster to do that. That doesn't mean you're always monstrous. Because you've seen and been the worst, you are the one being capable of walking the line. I don't love that there are drugs in this city. I don't love that you're involved, but I understand the necessity."

"I don't love the drugs either. I see nothing wrong with sex work, though."

"Neither do I," said Addie, shifting to straddle Elias. "We can both admit we don't know each other all that well yet. But we will. Chances are I will learn things I don't like."

"You absolutely will. And that absolutely terrifies me."

"Because you think I'll leave you?" She started kneading his shoulders.

"Yes," he said simply.

"Won't happen," she said. "But we'll have to take it as it comes. I may get angry, and I may cry and yell, but I will not abandon you."

He pulled her to him. "You have to know that I would level this entire city to keep you safe. It was so hard for me to calmly handle Miranda's threat to you."

Addie's breath hitched. "I do know that. And I must admit Miranda trying to hit me was the most disappointing thing about tonight. I'd never do that. I don't think Clara would ever do that. Or Mei."

"I don't think so either. Miranda is very jealous of you; that much is obvious."

"But I don't get why. She has a great job and owns her own place. She has never had to worry about money or men."

"What do you mean she's never had to worry about men?"

"She's always had a man."

"And you? Have you always had a man?"

"No, so stop glowering. I dated when I got to college, but the only real relationship I had after Nigel was Dan, then you. Miranda always had a boyfriend. Always."

"Maybe she feels she always needs a man. But she sees you, and you sure as shit don't. And when you do finally have one, it's another vampire. A bigger, badder one than Stellan."

"Really, your arrogance," she teased.

"Compared to Stellan, it's the truth. You don't seem to need anyone to make you feel complete, certainly not another man. You were prepared to walk away if I didn't comply with your one dealbreaker. Would Miranda have done that?"

"I doubt it would have occurred to her to ask," Addie bit her lip.

"There you go."

"She's not a bad person!"

"She's not," said Elias. But if he was honest, he wasn't sure about that. "She's made some bad decisions. And you seem to be a reminder of them by making better ones."

"Well, I can't help that."

"No, you can't. Nor should you. Give her time. See what happens."

"It's what she wants, and I'll respect that. What are your next steps?"

"I will contact Stellan in a few days, but tomorrow, I will meet with the others. Let them know what's going on." He palmed her breasts. "But right now, I have a naked and willing woman in my bed."

Addie tightened her grip on Elias. "Oh no, whatever will you do with me?"

He bent her back, his mouth hovering over a breast. "Whatever I want, little bird. Whatever I want." He latched onto her nipple and sucked as his other hand found its way to her sex. She was wet for him. He pulled back. "Ready for me, I see."

"Well," she said cheekily, "You are an amazing lover."

He growled low in his throat. "Yes, and you are mine." He plunged two fingers inside of her as he sank his fangs into the flesh right above her breast. She arched under him, wrapping her legs around him and moaning his name.

He drank from her as he added another finger to the two already pumping her. He lifted his head. "Who do you belong to?" His voice was thick with passion and the heat of her blood.

"You," she said as he continued to drink from her. "I belong to you. Elias, God. That feels amazing."

"Your body is mine. I will protect it, but I will use it as I want to. Your soul is mine, you belong to me now, and I will never let you go."

He removed his fingers from her and stretched her out on her back. He hovered above her. His eyes were so dark, and she could see his fangs. She stroked one fang, then the other. "Elias, I am yours. But you are mine as well. I give you my body and my soul of my own free will. And even if you didn't ask for it, I am giving you my heart." It felt right to say it.

He looked at her, overcome with emotion. He took one hand and placed it over her heart, then placed it over his own. He could not say the words yet, but she knew what he meant. She lifted herself and dropped a kiss over his heart, where his hand had been.

He groaned her name. He put his mouth back to her breast as he entered her. He started pumping her slowly, building the tension as he continued to feed. She gripped his hair, willing him to move faster. He lifted his head and laughed softly. He licked her wound, healing it, and then licked his lips.

"Your blood is the sweetest I have ever tasted. You're part of me now." He dropped his head to her neck, inhaling her scent as he slowly made love to her.

Later, as she slept, he sat watching her. She looked so peaceful. This thing with Stellan would get worse before it got better, and he needed to be ready to protect her at all costs. The city would stay his, but if it came down to a choice, there was none. He'd choose Adelaide every time.

CHAPTER 15

Addie showed up at Clara's salon promptly at two.

"Addie! Come on back!" Clara gave her new friend a quick hug and led her to a chair towards the back.

"Hello! Thank you for taking the time to do this today," Addie said.

"My pleasure! I am dying to get my hands into that hair."

Addie sat and looked around. "This place is so nice! I didn't even realize it was here."

"Thank you! It used to be a barbershop. I got it for a song when the owner retired. He was a friend of my dad's, so I think he wanted to help me out." It had saved her life, really.

"Aw, that's wonderful! Your chair isn't in the front, though?"

"I can keep an eye on things better from back here." She ran a brush through Addie's hair. "Addie! You have virgin hair!"

"Um ... what?"

Clara laughed. "I'm sorry. I mean, you've never colored it, have you?"

Addie shook her head. "Nope. Should I?"

Clara looked horrified. "Absolutely not. Your hair is gorgeous. And Elias would kill me!"

"It's not his hair," Addie said.

"Sure, it's not!" Clara winked. "Let's get that hair washed."

Clara washed Addie's hair instead of passing her along to a salon assistant. She unthinkingly pushed her sleeves up, and as she was cutting, Addie noticed faded track marks on her friend's arms. She was not going to say anything, but it gave her a little insight into Clara's past.

Clara, though, approached it head-on. "I know you see them, Addie," she said a little too stridently.

"They are not my business," Addie replied gently.

"Sorry, I still get a bit defensive about it. I'm ashamed of them."

"You shouldn't be. They're proof you lived through something hard. Does letting vamps feed on you help?"

"It did for a long time. It eased the cravings to get high that I had. I only ever did it at the club, though. I felt safe there."

"And now?"

"I realized—thanks to Stellan, actually—I don't need to anymore. I can still do it, but only if I want to." Clara shrugged.

"At least Stellan is good for something. But honestly, Clara, I don't think less of you for having an addiction. I think more of you for beating it and thriving. We all have shit. But you made it through, and you have your own business now. Elias trusts you enough to hire you to work with the ladies."

Clara had to swallow around the lump in her throat. Her own family wasn't as understanding. "Thank you, Addie. That means a lot. So, Elias told you he hired me?"

"He did. I think it's great!"

"That's down to you, I think. Elias has changed. Keep your head still, missy."

Addie blushed a little. "I didn't do anything."

Clara leaned down. "No. You were just you, and that was enough." The two stared at each other, a moment of perfect understanding. Then, Clara straightened. "Now, tell me what happened last night, please."

Addie did, though it pained her to remember how Miranda almost hit her. She had to admit sharing it with someone who would be more objective than Elias felt good.

Clara shook her head. "Stellan does not deserve her, but you didn't deserve that, and hopefully, Miranda will come around. Are you letting her work through it?"

"Yes. Well, mostly. I texted her this morning. I let her know I love her but would be respecting her wishes. She can contact me if she wants to talk or needs me."

Clara thought it was more than Miranda deserved but did not say that. "I think that's perfect. She should make the next move." She pulled out her dryer. "Okay, let's finish you up and then maybe we can grab a coffee."

"That sounds great!" Addie did feel a little guilty about finding Clara easier to be with, but perhaps she and Miranda had outgrown each other. It was a sad thought.

Elias had set up meeting that evening with Tamir, Elizabeth and Genevieve, to discuss the whole Stellan issue. He asked Darian to sit in as well; he trusted his friend's instincts and valued his opinion.

"Stellan is out of control," Elias began. "He has decided that he wants to take the city from me by force."

Genevieve laughed. "Stellan? He really thinks he's capable of that?"

"Stellan has always had an abundance of misplaced arrogance," Elizabeth replied. "For many things." Her implication clear.

"We all did wonder at that relationship," Gen remarked.

Elizabeth shrugged. "He had his uses."

"As I was saying," Elias continued. "He has threatened to end me. I take that very seriously. I wonder if he has contacted you three yet?"

"He left me a voicemail," said Tamir. "He said it was urgent that he spoke to me. I have not called him back."

Elias nodded. "Gen? Eliza?" They shook their heads. *Interesting*. Elias. "Tamir, where do you stand."

"With you," said Tamir. Much of that was self-serving. Elias rarely interfered with his business, and never took a personal cut of Tamir's profits. Stellan was greedy and would insist on a cut of the action. He also knew there was no way Stellan could take anything by force from Elias. Elias kept the city safe, but he kept vampires like Tamir safe as well.

Elias nodded at him. "Thank you, he said. He wasn't fully convinced, but he'd keep his doubts to himself for now.

"Gen and I are with you too," said Eliza. "Even if Stellan and I didn't have history, I'd be with you. Some of the reasons serve our own interests, as I am sure it is with Tamir, but in the end, we also believe in you and your ability to lead."

Elias was surprised by this, but Eliza didn't lie. "Thank you, Eliza. That means a great deal."

"It's true," Gen put in. "The three of us have our talents, but we can't do what you do. The person who runs the city needs to wear many hats and needs to have skills we do not; you have those." Not only did Gen have spies everywhere, but she also oversaw the artistic community. It wasn't the moneymaker that the other industries were, but it was important. And it allowed her to mix in society. She saw and heard a great deal.

"And I thank you as well, Gen. Have you heard anything?"

"I've not. But I also have not been listening for that. I will remedy that situation." She hadn't considered Stellan a threat. She had been mistaken. They'd all considered him a bit of a buffoon, and she feared that mistake could cost them.

"We need to figure out where and how Stellan will strike next," said Elias.

Darian spoke up. "Elias, I think you know." His voice was quiet.

Gen nodded. "Your human, Elias. He may also be using her friend as bait."

"How the fuck do you know about Adelaide?" Elias sputtered.

Gen laughed. "Elias, please. Do not insult us both."

"Fine," Elias bit out. He was not happy about this.

"Elias, I do not plan to use this information against you or her. Please trust me on this." Elias nodded at Gen; and she smiled in return.

"Elias, neither Eliza nor I know about this human woman. Who is she?" Tamir was very curious.

Elias sighed heavily. "She is the singer in Darian's band. And she also happens to be the woman that I'm having a relationship with."

Darian looked impressed. He had not expected Elias to admit that he and Adelaide were together. "Elias, you must see that there's a very real chance that Stellan is going to try to get to you through Adelaide. He's done this kind of thing before."

Eliza nodded her head. "He is most unimaginative that way. Even if something isn't working, he hates to admit when he's wrong. So, he'll keep trying it until it either eventually works or blows up in his face."

Tamir laughed. "Hardly surprising. Tell me Eliza, what's generally the outcome for him?"

"Oh, it generally blows up in his face. But even when it does, he still will not admit that he's wrong. It's always someone else's fault."

"He's managed to drive a wedge between Miranda and Adelaide, so I am not sure he'll need to use Miranda again," mused Elias.

"Yes, but harming Adelaide is the one thing that is bound to make you lose control," Darian said. "At least in Stellan's eyes." It was not unwarranted, thought Darin. Elias' history was littered with people he had failed to save, either from his own rage or someone else's.

Elias looked at his friend. *Not the only thing*, he thought to himself. "This is true. I will have to talk to Adelaide about this. Tamir, call Stellan back, tell him you're staying out of it. That you all are."

"But that isn't true," Tamir protested.

"No, but he doesn't need to know that." Elias ran a hand through his hair. "He may be forthcoming with information if he thinks you aren't involved."

"That makes sense," Tamir replied.

Elias hesitated but decided to say what he felt. "I want to say that I appreciate your faith in me. I know much of it serves your own purposes; I am not naïve." He paused to let them acknowledge his words. "I have made a call to an old vampire friend. He has offered his assistance and his muscle."

Darian stared at his brother. "Elias? Do you mean who I think you mean?"

"Yes, I do. Dregs is coming. And God help Stellan, because that bastard is scarier than I am."

CHAPTER 16

Clara noticed the new vamp the minute she stepped inside the club that night. He was as big as Elias and twice as mean if the set of his mouth was anything to go by. Also, like Elias, he had dark hair, but it was longer and shot through with silver. He had it pulled back, showing it was shaved underneath. His eyes were covered with dark glasses, but she assumed they'd be cold.

Something in Clara reacted to him. The voice in her head whispered that he was dangerous and to stay far away, but another voice was quite firm in not caring. *Get a grip, girl.*

She sidled over to the bar and got her brother, Mickey's, attention. "Mick, who is *that*?"

"That is Dregs," her brother replied.

"Excuse me? Dregs?"

"Yup. That's his name. Dregs."

"It is not," Clara said.

"Yup, it is. He's a friend of Elias's."

"That tracks." She looked at his face. His cheeks were slightly hollow-looking. "Any of the ladies been over to him? He looks like he needs to feed."

"No, they haven't. They're a bit wary of him."

"I get that. I'll go over and see if he wants someone."

"What if he wants you?"

Clara shrugged. "Then it's me he gets." She wouldn't mind letting him feed on her.

"Clara," Mickey sounded pained. "You don't still need to do that, do you?"

She cupped his cheek. "No, honey. I don't. But I can, and I don't mind for certain people. If he's a friend of Elias's, I am willing." Plus, this is part of what Elias was paying her for.

Mickey nodded. "But no more Stellan?"

She shook her head. "Nope. Never again. What's he drinking?"

"Guinness," Mickey replied.

"Pull another for him, and I'll head over. And don't worry … I've got this handled."

Mickey pulled the beer and then watched as Clara made her way to the new vampire. He bit his lip in concern, but he needed to trust her.

"She'll be fine," Mei said quietly.

He looked at her, startled by her sudden appearance. "I know. But I'm her big brother, and I worry."

Mei smiled at him. "You're a good brother. I wish I had a brother like you. Mine is an asshole."

"I'm sorry. You can count on me as an older brother figure then."

She smiled at him. "Might be kind of hard," she replied.

"Why is that?"

She leaned over the bar towards him. "Because my feelings for you are decidedly not brotherly." She gave him a quick kiss on the lips and disappeared into the crowd, leaving him staring at her open-mouthed.

Clara straightened her shoulders as she arrived at Dregs's table in the back. He was seated where he could see everyone and everything from his vantage point.

He raised his head, took off his sunglasses, and stared at her. She couldn't help the sudden intake of breath. He had light gray eyes that made him look otherworldly. They were startling and beautiful, nowhere near as cold as she thought they would be. Though there was no mistaking the predatory gleam in them at this moment.

"Well, well," he said in a deep voice. "Who do we have here?" She couldn't place his accent, but he might be Spanish.

"Clara," she said, setting the beer down. "I work here." She waited for the inevitable smirk. But he surprised her by just nodding.

"Thank you for the beer, but what can I do for you?"

She cleared her throat. "The other women are a bit nervous about approaching you, but you look like you need to feed. May I help you with that?"

"That's presumptuous of you," he replied. His voice hard.

"Yes, it is. It's also my part of my job. I've been doing this for quite a while, and I recognize the pallor and slightly sunken cheeks." He made her nervous, but she'd hold her ground.

He smiled, and it was quite menacing. "Just a feeding then?"

She sighed. Some ladies did fuck the vampires as well. She and Mei were the exception and not the rule. "What you and one of the ladies decide is between you. I am simply trying to facilitate some sustenance for you." She sounded so prissy, even to her own ears.

"What if I want you?" he asked in a low voice that promised a world of sin.

Clara's heart raced at the image forming in her head. One she clamped down on immediately. He had to be testing her. "I am happy to let you feed on me, but I won't be fucking you. If you want that, I can send someone over may be more amenable."

Dregs looked at her a moment. She met his gaze and refused to back down. This was a pivotal moment. "You are quite formidable, *mi pequeña pelirroja*. I do not feed in public, though."

"I can arrange to have it done privately," she replied. "You would not be the first to request this." She had no idea what he had called her, and she refused to ask. She'd try and look it up later.

Dregs drummed his fingers on the table. He did need to feed, it was true. But did he want to feed and fuck, or just feed? She was staring at him patiently. He hadn't been lying to her; she was formidable.

"You," he said. "I wish to feed from you." She went to say something, and he put up his hand. "I understand we will not be fucking." *Yet.* "I do not want emotional complications, and I think you are just the person for that."

"Fine, come with me then," she replied.

He stood, towering over her. *Taller than Elias.* "Know this, though. If I feed from you, I will feed *only* from you while in town. I do not need to feed often, but I like consistency."

She narrowed her eyes at him. "Is this some kind of trick to lull me into sleeping with you?"

"No," he replied. "You do not trust in what I say?"

"I don't know you. Of course, I don't trust you. I don't trust easily."

"Neither do I. We understand each other then. Lead the way."

Elias stopped Clara on her way by with Dregs. "Use my office," he said. "Then you can go visit Addie." He handed her the key to the office. "You can return the key later."

"Thanks, Elias," Clara said. If he was offering his office, he trusted Dregs with her. That settled her nerves.

"Most welcome," Elias replied. He then gave Dregs a pointed look and was satisfied by what he saw from Dregs. His old friend would never hurt a woman, but he'd been practically a recluse for years, and he wasn't sure how Dregs may have changed.

They reached Elias's office and stepped inside. Clara locked the door.

"You sure you want to be trapped in here with me?"

"Stop trying to scare me. Elias obviously trusts you not to maul me, so I am taking this on faith. Now sit!"

He muttered something under his breath at her, it sounded like "*mocosa*," but she couldn't be sure. She rolled up her sleeve to just past her wrist and held it out to him.

He took her arm way more gently than she was expecting. He started to move her sleeve, and her hand clamped down on his. "What are you doing?"

"Something few vamps do anymore. Pulling on the wrist isn't always comfortable. I was trying to make it more pleasant for you. What's the problem?"

He was trying to make it more pleasant for her? What? "I have scars," she said quietly.

He let her wrist go and pushed up his sleeve. "So do I," he said. "It means you survived." An echo of what Addie had said.

She took a breath and slowly pushed her sleeve up. He peered at her arm, noting the faded track marks. He took her arm gently and rubbed a finger over them. He then ran his finger down her arm a few times. "I am basically trying to wake your veins. It shouldn't feel like getting blood drawn."

She nodded. "No one has ever done that for me."

"To most vamps, humans are expendable because your lives are short. It's still very rude."

With that, he bit into her wrist. She braced herself, but whatever he had done worked. It was pleasant. More than that, it felt good. He was gentle with her.

Unfortunately, she was getting a bit turned on, and she sure as shit wasn't used to that.

When he was done, he licked the wound to close it. Then pulled her sleeve back down. "How was that?" he asked.

"It was fine," she said. "You made it much more pleasant than usual."

He looked her up and down, noting how her nipples had pebbled, and he just managed to not grin smugly at her. "I'm glad. Are you amenable to being my regular person when I need to feed?"

"I am," she replied.

He nodded and stood. "Thank you for accommodating me," he said. He slid his sunglasses back on and headed for the door. "Clara," he said. "One more thing."

"Yes?"

"We are going to fuck. It's just a matter of time." With that, he was gone.

"Of all the fucking nerve!" she exclaimed. She plopped in a seat and fumed. The thing was, she wasn't mad at the idea. And that terrified her.

Chapter 17

"Come in!" Addie called to the knock at her dressing room door.

Clara bounded in, slammed the door, and leaned against it, eyes wide.

Addie looked at her in the mirror, one eyebrow raised. "You okay? You look spooked.

Clara nodded and made her way over to the chair, flopping down. "I met Dregs. I let him feed on me, and then he told me it was just a matter of time before we fucked. And he's probably right, and I have no idea what to think or do about any of it. And he called me something in Spanish, but I don't know what."

Addie pressed her lips together so she wouldn't laugh. Clara had let that all out in a rush. It both surprised and delighted her that Clara had shared this with her. "What did he say in Spanish? Do you remember?"

Clara repeated it or tried to. She mangled it a bit.

"Was it '*mi pequeña pelirroja*' by any chance?"

"Yes! That was it. What does it mean?" Clara thought a moment. "You speak Spanish? Of course you do!"

"He called you his little redhead. I do speak Spanish, though I don't have cause to often. My mother was Mexican, and my father was white." Addie pulled out a photo of her parents and passed it to Clara.

"Your mother was beautiful. You look a lot like her. You have your dad's nose, though."

Addie beamed. "She was, wasn't she? I thought she was so glamorous." Clara passed the photo back, and Addie went back to doing her makeup. "I grew up in a very white town. I think mom and I were the lone Hispanics, and me only half so."

"Were people awful?"

"Sometimes. My dad never really got it. He loved my mom, but I think he never understood her. And he really didn't understand what it was like to be a Catholic Latina in a predominantly Jewish town." Addie shrugged. "Mom was proud of who she was. I think I've lost a little of that. But I'm getting it back." Clara settled. "So, Dregs then?"

"Yyyeeaahh," said Clara. "He is super-hot, right?"

"He is. You let him feed on you?"

"Yes. He likes to do that in private, so Elias said to use his office."

"Why, though?"

"He asked me." Addie stopped what she was doing and looked at Clara. "I'm fine, honestly. I didn't need to do it. I wanted to do it."

"Truth?" Addie asked.

"Truth," Clara replied. "I know I could have said no. I didn't want to. I didn't want him to feed on anyone else, which is terrifying."

Addie squeezed Clara's hand in understanding. "What about when he does feed from others?"

"He won't. When he's here, it will only be me. He said he likes consistency. And he's like Elias; he doesn't need to often."

"And how did it feel?"

"It felt nice. He stroked my arm to help blood flow. Hey, what does *mocosa* mean?"

"Did he call you that?" Addie asked. Clara nodded. "It means 'brat,' Clara. He called you a brat." This time Addie did laugh.

"Oh," said Clara, nonplussed. "I am not sure how I feel about that."

Addie patted her hand. "Yes, you are honey."

Clara laughed. "You're right. I am."

"Are you going to have sex with him then?"

"Maybe. But I am going to enjoy the banter for now."

There was a knock, and Miles poked his head in. "Twenty minutes, Addie."

"Thank you!" Miles saluted and closed the door.

Clara stood. "Thank you. I feel better."

Addie stood and hugged her. "Of course! Keep me updated!"

Clara grinned and left. When she got back out to the front, her eyes made a beeline for Dregs—*what is his real name anyway?*—and noticed that one of the ladies had wandered over to him. Clara narrowed her eyes at the girl. But was pleased Dregs wouldn't let her sit.

Mei came to stand next to her, and Clara put her arm around her friend's waist. "Why are you looking at Naomi like that?"

"Like what?" asked Clara innocently.

"Like you want to throttle her."

"Oh, I am not! She's been gone for a while, though. When did she pop up again?"

"The other night when you weren't here. She and Elise had been partying with Tamir. But Naomi had had enough of it. She wasn't feeling well, so she took a few days off and then came back to the fold."

"Elise isn't back though, and that I don't like that. I wish there was some way I could keep the others away from Tamir. I don't trust him."

"Me neither, which is why I don't go near him."

"Same," Clara replied.

"The new guy keeps looking at you." Mei elbowed her.

"Lalala, I don't hear you."

"Yeah, you do."

Clara sighed. "Let's have lunch tomorrow, and I will fill you in."

"Sounds good." Mei looked around. "This shit is getting old."

"Yes, it is a bit. Hopefully, my brother will finally get his head out of his ass where you're concerned."

"How the fuck did you know I liked him?"

"Oh, girl." She bumped Mei's shoulder. "We'll talk about that too." Clara looked at her watch. "Fuck this, let's go pop a squat somewhere and watch the band."

"Sounds good."

But Clara spent a lot of Addie's first set watching Dregs.

CHAPTER 18

Addie had her legs wrapped around Elias's waist as he carried her upstairs to her apartment. "I can walk, Elias."

"Of course, you can, little bird. I just like carrying you." He snuggled her closer. "And you need to conserve your strength. I have plans for you tonight."

"Oh really?" she asked as they reached her landing.

"Indeed." He set her down to get her keys out. The door across the hall opened, and her neighbor stepped out. Mrs. Costello was about eighty, with a cloud of silver hair around an elfin face. She was wearing a robe and slippers.

"Oh, Mrs. Costello! I'm sorry, did we wake you?"

"Not at all, dear. Estelle can't sleep either, so we're going to watch a movie." She looked Elias up and down. "Is this your fella?" she asked.

"I am," replied Elias. "It's a pleasure to meet you, Mrs. Costello."

Mrs. Costello walked over to him and looked into his face. She was a bit under five feet, and Elias was well over six feet. He smiled down at her. "Vampire?" she asked.

"Mrs. Costello! How ...?" Addie exclaimed in surprise.

"Dear, I'm old, not stupid. I've been around the block more than a few times. I know humans from vampires. So?" She looked back at Elias.

"Yes, ma'am," he replied. "I am."

"Thought so. Dated a couple of you guys back in the day."

"Um, what?" This was from Addie.

Mrs. Costello laughed. "I've left Addie speechless; I see. I was around your age, dear, when I lost my husband, so I was still in my prime. My friends and I used to go out dancing. At the time, the club we went to had a lot of vampires." She peered at Elias again. "Never dated you, though," she said.

"No, ma'am. I'd remember that."

"Yes," she said, heading for the stairs. "You would." She shot him a wink and then started to climb the stairs to her friend's apartment. She stopped and turned back. "You going to do something about her asshole ex?"

"I'd like to, but Addie won't let me."

"Child, let him deal with the ex. That's one of the perks." A door opened upstairs. "I'm coming, Estelle!" With that, she was gone.

Addie stared at her, her mouth agape. "I am shocked, yet not at the same time." She dug her keys out and opened the door. "I feel like she has some stories to tell."

"She's a pistol," said Elias. "Almost sorry I didn't date her."

"Hey, now," Addie warned. "I don't want to be jealous of Mrs. Costello."

Elias backed Addie against the door. He gave her one slow lick up the side of her neck as he gripped her hips. "You have nothing to worry about, little bird." He ran his tongue across her clavicle, then along the seam at her lips. She opened her mouth, and his tongue swept in. It was a slow seduction. He kissed her almost languidly while his hands moved over her hips and back. She arched into him, and he almost groaned.

"You taste so sweet," he told her in a low voice. "I want to lick every inch of you."

"Elias," Addie murmured. "Please!"

"Please what, little bird? What do you need? Me?"

She nodded at him, rubbing herself against him, trying to gain friction to ease the ache at her core."

"Behave," he admonished. "Use your words, Adelaide."

"You, I need you." She tried to arch towards him again, but he wasn't having it. "Dammit, Elias!"

He raised an eyebrow at her. "What did you say?"

"You heard me." She looked at him, eyes flashing.

"I know what you're doing," he said silkily. "But not tonight." He carried her into the bedroom, setting her down carefully. "Take off your clothes and get on the bed." His tone brooked no argument. She just stood there. "Now, Adelaide. You won't deter me from my original plan. But trust me, I will remember this."

She undressed, and he opened her closet. "What are you looking for?"

"Don't talk. Get undressed, get on the bed."

"How do you want me?"

"On your back, prop your head on a couple of pillows."

She sighed but did as he asked. When Elias came out of the closet, he had three of her scarves in his hand."

"I want to bind your hands and blindfold you." She looked at him, eyes wide. But it wasn't with fear. "But once again, I need your consent. Do I have it?"

"Yes, Elias."

"Good girl." He was glad her headboard was a white vintage-looking wrought iron. "I thought of this on the way over, so you get scarves instead of rope, but I will make them secure."

"Why cover my eyes?"

"So you can concentrate on the sensations." He tightened the knot on one wrist and worked on the other. Then he covered her eyes. "Safe word?"

"Oh! I forgot about that. Do I really need one?"

"You do. Yes, you can trust me, but a safe word is a sure-fire way to get me to stop. You may not need to use it, but you need to have one. It's as important as verbal consent."

"Okay," she said, nodding. "The word 'red' is common, right?"

"Yes," came the disembodied reply. He was moving around the room.

"Let's go with that for tonight then."

"Done." He came back over to her and kissed her roughly. She arched. "I will not tie your feet, but try not to move much, or I will."

"Yes, Elias." He stood and shivered a little. The way she said his name and how she looked lying there spread out for him. He palmed himself. He wanted to tear his clothes off and fuck her, but he wouldn't. This was a slow seduction.

He found the peacock feather on her dressing table, and he brushed it gently over her breast. Her body bucked from the unexpected sensation.

She blew out a breath. "Breathe, little bird." His voice was rough. He brushed over and around her breast and then did the same on the other.

He spread her legs farther apart and settled himself between her legs. He moved up her body and gently moved the feather over her forehead, nose, cheeks, and mouth. Slowly, ever so slowly.

She sighed. She loved the feeling of the feather, but what she really loved was how his clothes felt rough against her sensitive skin. Desire pooled in her belly.

She moved against him. "Be still, little bird. Don't try to come before it's allowed." He moved the feather over her shoulders and then down her chest, between her breasts. Then he replaced the feather with his mouth, licking and sucking her skin. It was hard to stay still, but she did.

He took one nipple in his mouth while dancing the feather over the other breast. She moaned and tried not to writhe on the bed. "Elias," she breathed.

"You're doing so well, little bird." He bit her nipple, and she whimpered. Then he did the same with the other nipple. He licked down her stomach, using the feather and his tongue. He got to the juncture of her thighs and moved past it to lick her legs, still using the feather. He moved the feather slowly, torturously so, over the entrance to her sex while his free hand danced over her skin.

She hissed, and Elias laughed. "All in good time." He then reversed the direction, moving up her body this time. He stopped to lift her legs, so he could squeeze and lick her ass before running the feather along her bottom and the back of her legs. *Jesus, she's so wet.*

He stopped and then left the room. "Elias?" *Where did he go?* He returned quickly, and she yelped as an ice cube hit her nipple. "*Bastardo!*" she cursed at him.

He chuckled. "Did you just call me a bastard, Adelaide?" He had seen photos of her parents and assumed she was half Hispanic, but this is the first time she'd spoken Spanish to him. Even if it was to swear, it absolutely delighted him. But he'd keep that to himself for now.

"I did. And I am not sorry."

"We'll just add to the list of your transgressions." He rubbed the ice cube along her fevered body. He put the last of it in his mouth to melt, then kissed her again.

He could see she wanted to move, that it was almost too much for her. But he could also see how wet she was. "Are you doing all right?" he asked.

"Yes," she said.

"Swearing at me aside, you've been such a good girl. I think it's time you got your reward."

"Please," she choked out.

He got between her legs, parting her, and gave her one slow, long lick. His tongue was still cool from the ice cube, and it felt amazing. He put his hands under her ass to bring her sex closer. He whirled his tongue around her clit, then took it into his mouth, sucking none too gently. She thrashed a bit. He took two fingers and put them inside her, pumping as he worked her clit with his mouth.

He lifted his head to look at her. Her cheeks were flushed, lips parted, and chest heaving. Never had he seen anything more perfect than Adelaide right at this moment. Not in all his long life. "Do you want to come?" he asked gruffly.

"Yes," she breathed.

"Ask me nicely." She could hear the smirk in his voice

"Please, Elias. Please may I come?"

"You may," he said. He added a third finger and pumped quicker. He put his mouth back on her clit and swirled his tongue around. She was close, and as she tightened around his fingers; he bit her clit. She came on a scream.

He stood and removed the blindfold. She stared at him, breathing heavy. His hand moved to the button of his pants, then the zipper. He pulled, and his hard cock sprang free. "I took off the blindfold because I want you to watch as I slide into that pussy and fuck you. And I want to see your eyes when you come again."

He pulled her legs up and slammed into her, groaning. He started thrusting into her, hard and fast. "God, you feel so fucking good, Addie!"

She wrapped her legs around him while he gripped her hips. "Harder," she begged.

"Of course," he said. He started moving faster, thrusting harder. She crested again, tightening around him. "Adelaide, come for me. Come on my cock!" She whimpered as he pulled out and then thrust again, ramming into her, and she came again with Elias coming right after, roaring her name.

He untied her hands and rubbed them to bring the circulation back, kissing each of her wrists. He got a damp cloth to clean her while she lay there, still breathless. Then he got them water from the kitchen, watching to make sure she drank it.

He climbed into bed, pulled her to him, and pulled the covers. He just wanted to hold her now. She wrapped her arms around his waist and nestled into his chest. He kissed the top of her head, and his arms tightened around her.

"Elias," Addie said when she could finally form coherent thoughts again. "You feel free to make plans for me anytime you want."

CHAPTER 19

Addie walked back into the bedroom with a large platter and two more water bottles under her arm. Elias jumped up and grabbed the platter from her, setting it carefully on the bed. She smiled at him, handed him a water, and climbed back onto the bed.

Elias just looked at her. She was sitting naked and cross-legged, her hair piled on her head. She chose a piece of cheese and a slice of apple, popping both in her mouth. She sighed contentedly. "Is there something wrong?"

He shook his head and climbed into bed next to her. "No. I just like looking at you."

"Oh," she said. "That's sweet."

He leaned over and nipped her ear. "You called me a bastard. In Spanish."

"I did." She looked at him chagrined. "And I'm not sorry."

"Oh, is that so?" He ran his fangs down her neck, and she shivered. "Again, with that mouth of yours." He sat and grabbed the piece of cheese she had in her hand, popping it into his mouth. "I've seen photos of your mother, so I assumed you had Latin or Hispanic blood. Where was your mom from?"

"Mexico," Addie replied, popping a grape into her mouth. "She was raised by her grandmother, her *abuela*, since her parents died young. My mom decided to live with her uncle in Texas when she died. They didn't get along, so she headed out on her own. She worked and took college classes when she could."

"How old was she when she left Mexico?"

"About eighteen." Addie grabbed a photo from her dressing table mirror. "This is her back then."

Elias took the photo and peered at the young, smiling woman. "You have her smile," he said. The woman in the photo had a slim build and looked taller than Addie. "I can see how much you resemble her."

Addie shook her head. "She was beautiful. But I looked enough like her that I think it made it hard for dad to look at me after she passed."

Elias was overcome by the need to punch the dead man. "Adelaide, your mother was beautiful. So, are you."

"I don't know about that. I'm much curvier than she was."

"And?" Elias' voice had deepened with his confusion and frustration. "Do you actually buy into women only being beautiful if they're thin? That doesn't seem like you."

"No, I think it's bullshit. But..."

"You think it's bullshit for everyone except you?"

She shrugged. "My dad used to compare us, and he'd always comment on slim mom was."

He blinked at her. "So, you think you aren't beautiful, like your mother, because your dad—I'm sorry—was an asshole."

"I'm not just curvy anymore. I have a few stomach rolls, and my thigh s..."

She didn't get to finish her thought. Elias had flipped her onto her back, as he hovered over her. He leaned up on one arm while the other stroked her soft stomach. "There is not one inch of you that I don't worship. I know I spend a lot of time talking about your ass, but trust me, all of you, including your stomach rolls, as you call them, pleases me. But they should please you. Do they not?"

Addie looked at him, a little awestruck by his words. "No, I always liked my body for the most part."

"Then why are you talking about it like something is wrong with it? Why don't you give yourself the grace you would give anyone else?"

"Dan once said that I was fat, like it was the worst thing you could be I think him echoing dad had an effect on me." Addie bit her lip. She realized now how stupid it was to care about his thoughts on her body. "Jesus, I married a man just like my father."

Elias's eyes darkened. "You did. I am going to rip his dick off and choke him with it. Dan, that is." He took a calming breath. "Are you still fucking him?"

"No!"

"Then who cares what he thinks?"

"I know you're right. But it made me feel bad, and I guess I am still dealing with that. He used to say he didn't get it because both my parents were thin."

Elias dropped his forehead to Addie's, while he stroked her belly. "Addie, your body is perfect to me. There is nothing about you I would want to change Dan is an insecure asshole who needed to make you felt less than because you weren't impressed by him. You are sexy as fuck." He dropped his head to her belly, dropping kisses there. "And on stage? God, no one can look away from you. I have to control the urge to beat the fuck out of some of the younger vamps, just because of how they look at you."

Addie sniffled. "Thank you, Elias. I suppose I needed to hear that."

He looked at her. "Don't cry, little bird." He sat and pulled her onto his lap. "I wish you could see yourself on stage. Or see yourself spread out for me. If you saw yourself that way, you'd never feel bad again. No one should do that to you. Not even me. You should feel good about yourself because you're that amazing."

She wrapped her arms around him. "How is it that a very scary vampire knows how to make me feel good about myself, but my non-scary ex can't?"

"Because he's a fuckwit, and I am brilliant, with excellent taste in women. And, very scary."

"Yes, I am absolutely terrified." She fed him a piece of cheese. "Where are you from originally? If I may ask?"

"Of course, you may." He sat against the headboard, pulling the food closer to them and making sure Addie was seated comfortably across his lap. "I'm German by birth. And before you ask, I was born in the late 15th century."

"Whoa! You're so ... old!"

He tickled her side, and she squealed. "Hey now, don't make me have to punish you."

"Will it involve tying me up again?"

"It might," he growled at her.

"Oh no," she teased. "That would be terrible. I would hate that."

"Brat!" He dropped a kiss on her forehead. "Eat, please."

That reminded Addie of what she had wanted to ask him. "So, Dregs? He's okay?"

"What do you mean?"

"I mean, well ... Clara."

His sweet Addie. "Yes. Dregs would never hurt a woman. He's just private about feeding. He feels comfortable with her, I assume. Is she okay with it?" His past made him uncomfortable, and how close he'd come to ... well, it didn't bear thinking about now. Eventually, he wanted to come clean to Addie.

"She is, yes." She wouldn't mention the attraction there. She was sure he'd see it for himself soon enough. "He made it pleasant for her."

Elias nodded. "Stroked her wrist. I would do that for you if I fed from your wrist." He thought a moment. "Do I need to do it for your neck or breast? Usually, it's not necessary, but I should have checked."

"Nope. Doesn't hurt and is much more than just 'pleasant' for me."

"Good. You know I would never want to hurt you."

She twisted in his arms to face him. "Elias, of course, I know that." She gave him a gentle kiss. "What brought this on?"

"Started thinking about all of my mistakes."

"I'm here to listen when you're ready to tell me. No rush."

"Soon," he told her. "But not yet." He was worried she'd leave him once she knew about his past. For all his bluster, he'd never hold her if she didn't want to be with him anymore. But he wasn't sure he'd be able to stick around if that was the case. "Any word from Miranda?"

She let him change the subject. "Nope. Stellan?"

"Yes, actually. I invited him back to the club to talk. One more time. I said things had gotten heated last time, and maybe we could come to terms after all."

"Will he come?"

"Possibly. If he does, it won't be to talk. It will be to play tough guy. I'll need to alert the main Assembly then."

"And Dregs is here because you think it will get ugly." It wasn't a question.

"Yes, I do. Dregs can help keep an eye on things in the club as well. He's actually a really interesting guy."

"With a weird nickname."

"With a weird nickname," Elias laughed.

"He is good-looking," Addie said slyly.

"Oh, is he now?" Elias put his mouth on her neck and sucked lightly as his hand circled her breast.

"Hmm," said Addie. Her head dropped back against Elias's chest.

"There's that mouth again, Adelaide. Whatever shall I do with you?"

"I have a list," Addie breathed.

"Oh, little bird. So do I."

And for the moment, everything else was forgotten.

Chapter 20

A few nights later, Elias was sitting at his regular table, waiting for the band's first set to start, when he had an idea. He waved Clara over.

"Yes, boss?" Clara said with humor.

"Would you be willing to do me a small favor?"

"Sure!"

"Can you take some video on your phone of Addie performing tonight?"

"I'd be happy to. But why? If I may ask."

"She has no idea what she looks like on stage or how she grabs people when she's singing. I'd like her to see it. I could do it, but ..."

"You'd rather watch her. Plus, it'll be less noticeable if I do it. She looks at you a lot."

"Does she?"

Clara laughed. "Elias, you know she does."

He grinned. "I honestly don't even think about that because I'm looking at her. But I guess she does."

They've got it bad. "Anyway, it's no problem. Dregs has a great view, so I'll see if I can go sit with him." *Convenient excuse.*

"Thanks! Can you send the videos when you've got them? I promise to give you credit."

"Absolutely, and I don't care about credit. Let me go hustle over there." She threw a wave at Elias and headed over to Dregs's table.

"Well, well," he said. "*Mi pequeña pelirroja*. To what do I owe the pleasure of your company?" He smirked at her.

"Elias asked me to take video of Addie tonight. You have the second-best spot in the house." She had no doubt he knew this. He and Elias not only had the best views of the stage, but they also had the best views of the club overall. It was no accident Dregs chose that seat. "I would appreciate it if I could film from here."

Dregs looked at her a moment, then pulled a chair out next to his. He patted it. "Be my guest," he finally purred at her.

She looked at the chair. It was very close to his own. She rolled her eyes and moved it about six inches away from his chair and sat.

He quirked an eyebrow at her and wrapped a leg around a chair's leg, pulling it back to him.

She glared at him. "Dregs, what the fuck do you think you're doing?"

"I think I am moving you closer to me. Was something unclear about my actions?"

"Asshole," she said. "You know what I mean. Why are you doing it?"

"Tsk, tsk," he admonished. "Such language. I moved you closer because you smell nice." He leaned towards her and inhaled deeply.

"You are full of shit," Clara replied hotly. But she liked the compliment. She could admit it to herself. "And stop sniffing me."

"Oh, Clara, you liked it, and you know it."

She was saved from answering by the appearance of the band on stage. Clara raised her phone as Addie and Darian opened with his song. "Perfect," she said quietly.

"This song is beautiful," Dregs said in Clara's ear, causing her to shiver. "But I don't think I know it."

"Darian wrote it. I'm surprised they opened with it, but maybe Darian was feeling sentimental."

"He wrote it for someone?" Clara nodded. "Ah, that makes sense. It feels intensely personal."

Clara took a video of two other songs, including Addie singing Janis Joplin's *Piece of my Heart*. It was a favorite with the club patrons.

"Shit," said Dregs. "She really is amazing to watch."

Clara looked at him and smiled broadly. "Isn't she?"

Something shifted in him with that smile. Something he refused to entertain. He was here to help a friend, and then he was gone. He was not getting involved with anyone, least of all the redhead sitting next to him. A little fun, maybe. But that was it.

"Okay, everyone," said Darian from the stage, "We have something a little different right now. A special request for a couple celebrating an anniversary tonight."

"Oh! That's right. It's Niles's and Emma's anniversary." She laughed when Dregs looked confused. "They're regular customers. Met and fell in love in London during the Second World War."

"Our lovely Adelaide," continued Darian, "Has agreed to sing their favorite song. The first one they ever danced to. More than a few of you may know it: *A Nightingale Sang in Berkeley Square*. So, Addie, you're up."

Addie stepped to the microphone, her regular rock demeanor gone, even though she was dressed the same. "Addie used to sing this kind of music in her father's band. This is a real treat!" Clara enthused.

Dregs took the phone from her. "You watch. I'll film this."

"Oh! Thank you!" Clara said. As Addie launched into the song, Clara sighed longingly.

Dregs once again had to slam a lid on the feelings Clara was bringing out in him. He almost managed to convince himself it was because it had been so long since he'd had sex. Almost.

Elias waited by the side of the stage with Niles and Emma as Addie came off stage with the band. He had watched her sing that last song, mesmerized by how she'd looked, the feelings she'd put into the song, and how she made him feel. He was, simply put, overwhelmed by her.

"Adelaide," said Emma in her crisp English accent. "That was beautiful! Thank you so much!"

"Indeed," put in Niles. "I never thought anyone could sing it better than Vera Lynn, but I was wrong."

"Oh, that's very sweet. But I am sure that can't be true."

"No false modesty, Adelaide. It's true. And we thank you."

"You are most welcome."

"And thanks to Elias for the champagne."

"My pleasure. Please enjoy your evening, and happy anniversary."

"Champagne?" asked Addie after the couple had walked away.

Elias shrugged. "They're good customers and decent vampires. They were spies during the war for the Allied side, and they did a lot of good. They saved a lot of children during that time. Champagne and comping their evening are the least I can do."

Addie gave him a soft look. "You are very sweet."

"Please don't spread it around. I have a reputation to protect."

"Your secret is safe with me."

"Thank you. I expect Stellan tonight, but maybe I can stop by when we're done."

"I'll wait for you. I don't mind." She moved in to wrap her arms around him. "I'd rather leave together."

He gave her a quick kiss. *Did they have time for a quickie in her dressing room?* Then, raised voices drew his attention. "What the fuck?"

Stellan stood across the floor. His face was red, and his hands balled into fists. Dregs had put himself between the vampire and Clara. "Oh shit," Elias groaned. He moved toward the threesome with Addie on his heels. "Addie, go to your dressing room!"

"As if," she snorted. "Clara is my friend."

"Fuck Addie, do what I tell you."

"Oh, Elias, no. Not this time."

He growled at her, but let it go.

"Stellan," Dregs's voice was calm. Chilling but calm. "The lady has made it clear that she is occupied this evening and for all evenings that follow."

Clara was trying to come around him, but Dregs wasn't having it, and Clara looked both irritated and relieved about it.

"I don't know who the fuck you are, but Clara belongs to me when I'm here."

"Oh, is that so?" asked Elias silkily. "Do continue, Stellan."

Stellan's eyes widened. He was caught out. "I meant," he bit out, "That I have a preference for her."

"Be that as it may," continued Dregs, "The lady is spending the evening with me."

"And you are?" Stellan asked.

"Your worst nightmare if you continue to press me."

"You fucking asshole!"

"Stellan," put in Elias, "Surely we can find you someone else. You can feed and then we can talk. Calmly."

"I want Clara," Stellan fumed. He didn't care about Clara. He just didn't like being told no—about anything.

Clara slid around Dregs to face Stellan. She did not hide behind men. Ever. Addie stepped behind her to show her support, for which Clara was grateful. "You only want me because, for some reason, you enjoy causing me pain. I only let someone feed on me when I want to. I will never let you near me again. We are done."

Stellan turned to his cronies. "Do you believe this shit? Jumped up little tart."

Dregs growled and went for Stellan. Elias held him back. "Stellan, stop. Clara is my employee and my friend. I cannot allow this behavior to continue. Either settle down and behave or go." Elias seriously regretted giving the vampire another chance. And he wasn't happy he'd brought an entourage.

"Please, spare us, Elias. We all know you've fucked every woman in this place. Including your current little whore."

Addie gasped as Elias went stock still. "What did you just call Adelaide?"

"Elias, no. It's fine." Addie pleaded.

"No," said Elias. "It's not. He's insulted Clara, and now he's insulted you. So, Stellan ... care to repeat yourself?"

Stellan stepped closer to Elias while Dregs blocked the vampires trying to circle behind his friend. "You heard me. Everyone knows it. You fucked this little junkie here, and now you're fucking that little singing whore."

With that, all hell broke loose.

CHAPTER 21

Elias picked Stellan up off the ground. "I have been more than fucking patient with you. Apologize immediately!" Elias was trying to keep control of his temper.

"No, your time is over, Elias. This city will be held by moneymakers going forward, not your neanderthal antics. It's beyond time."

Elias set Stellan down. Dregs held onto the other two vamps, one hand on each shoulder. He was tensed and ready to pound them if or when Elias gave him the go-ahead. "Stellan, you'll never take or hold the city. You're weak." He needed Stellan to hit him first.

"And you're a monster. You'll always be a monster."

Elias shook his head. He was being provoked. "Stellan, I am going to report you to the Elders. And I will have you removed from the Assembly, and then I will have you banished from the city."

Stellan's face turned red, and he launched himself at Elias. Elias bared his teeth, grabbed Stellan, and threw him onto a nearby table. The vamps sitting there scattered. Dregs started fighting the other two vamps.

"Two on one isn't fair," shouted Addie at Clara. Clara could only nod.

Someone grabbed their arms and hauled them back towards the stage. "Stay here!" yelled Darian as he joined the fray, taking one of Dregs's vamps.

"No! Your hands!" yelled Addie.

"He's a vampire. They'll heal, Addie." Clara started backing her and Addie towards the doorway leading backstage.

"Clara, if you think you're going to get me in the back, you are sadly mistaken."

"Oh, I am not trying to do that. I just want us out of the way." If something happened to Addie, Elias would lose his shit. Clara wanted them out of the immediate line of fire.

Stellan stood and yelled. Several vamps stood and rushed to where Stellan stood. "I didn't come with two vampires."

"Stellan, this is *my* club. I didn't come with just two either." Several vampires, including Niles, Emma, and Clara's brother, entered the fray. Those that didn't, left quickly. By tomorrow night, every vampire on this side of the country would know about the fight.

A vampire jumped on Elias's back, causing him to grunt. He reached back and pulled the vampire over his shoulder and tossed him onto a nearby table.

"*Ay Dios mío!*" breathed Addie. "I know I should not find that hot, but I do."

Clara nodded. "No, it was pretty hot." She found Dregs unevenly matched—but in his favor—with a vampire doing more dancing around than fighting. "*Mi amigo,*" she could hear him say. "This is a fight, not a dance contest." Dregs took the opportunity to very elegantly break the other vampire's nose.

"Also hot," said Clara. "I've never seen anyone break a nose with that much class."

"Agreed," said Addie.

Stellan sucker-punched Elias while he was trying to remove another vampire from his leg. *Jesus, Stellan couldn't even hire decent fighters.*

Niles dragged the vampire off Elias and threw him at Emma, who jumped on him. "I'll make sure we keep the others away from you."

Elias nodded his thanks and squared off with Stellan. "You and me, Stellan. Just us." Elias pulled his arm back and smashed his fist in Stellan's face. Stellan tried to get his hands up, but Elias wouldn't let him. His next punch hit the vamp in the chest, then the stomach. "Have you had enough yet?"

"Hardly!" snarled Stellan.

"Give it up. You're weak. Your people are weak." He grabbed Stellan around the neck. "You can't win."

Stellan laughed. "Oh, I'll win the city. Don't worry about that."

Addie and Clara looked on with their arms around each other. None of the other ladies were around, and Clara hoped like hell they'd left. There was a crash near the bar, and her brother went flying. "Mickey!" she yelled.

Addie looked at her friend. "Go! But be careful." Clara looked uncertain. "I know he's a vampire, but he's your brother. GO! I will be fine."

"I'll be back. I have to make sure he's okay." They hugged, and Clara took off.

Addie watched Elias beat the fuck out of Stellan. Stellan was out of his league. He *had* to know that. What was his game here? She searched the floor and found Darian holding his own. They had gone through most of the vamps Stellan had brought with him.

Elias had Stellan on the floor, his knee on the other vamp's neck. "Stellan, your men are all but beaten. You're under my knee. I could snap your neck. Give it up."

"Go ahead and do it then." Stellan bared his fangs. "Do it!"

Elias looked down at Stellan, pity in his eyes. "It must be hell to never quite come in first. To always be second best." Elias stood. "Get up and get out. Take your men with you."

Stellan stood; rage vibrating off him. Elias shook his head and turned to walk away. "Elias!" yelled Dregs. Elias turned back in time as Stellan leaped for him. Elias swept his leg, kicking Stellan in the side. "I tried, Stellan. I really tried."

Stellan grunted as Elias's foot hit its mark. Elias punched Stellan in the nose and heard the crunch of it breaking. Elias punched again, ensuring two black eyes. Elias then grabbed Stellan's right arm and twisted—hard. Stellan screamed; his arm now broken.

"Do you want me to do your left one? And then your legs? Or is this enough for you?" Elias was still calm.

Stellan held up the unbroken hand. "Enough for now!"

Elias stretched his arm and made a slicing motion. All fighting ceased immediately. Even Stellan's men stopped. That, thought Dregs, was command.

Elias and Stellan stared at each other. Stalemate. Stellan could never take Elias in a fight.

A scream reverberated through the club. *Adelaide.* "Elias?" A scared, wobbly voice.

Stellan stared at Elias in triumph as he turned to where Addie stood. One vampire was holding her from behind, an arm around her waist. A second vampire had one hand on Addie's breast and the other at her neck. The vampire holding her waist lowered his head to her neck as if to bite her. His fangs bared.

Clara's knees buckled, and Mickey had to catch her. "I shouldn't have left her," she whispered.

"You wouldn't have been able to stop this, sis."

Elias's eyes turned black, and he roared. A terrible sound, full of pain and fury. And death.

"I would," he said in a voice that held no resemblance to the voice Addie knew, "Unhand her immediately if you want to see tomorrow night."

The one in front of her laughed. "No," he said. "I think she belongs to us now."

Darian looked on in horror. He moved closer to Elias. Dregs moved in next to him.

"Stellan has disappeared with most of his men. But this was assuredly his goal all along," said the Spaniard

Darian nodded his agreement. "Everyone out!" he yelled to those few who were still upright. "NOW!"

"Come on," said Mickey to Clara.

"No, Addie is in trouble, and I am not leaving her. You go."

Mickey sighed. He'd have to carry her out, and he wouldn't do that to her. "You stay. I stay."

Dregs looked over at her. "Clara, go." His voice was calm, but the command was evident.

"Fuck off." Clara glared at him. "I am not leaving my friend."

"Clara," said Darian. "Elias is not going to handle this well."

Clara shrugged. "Worry about that and not me."

Darian sighed and let it go. Dregs glared at her, and she glared back. But he had to focus on Elias now.

"I'm very sorry you're not heeding my words." Elias grabbed his shirt, ripped it down the middle and pulled it off. He stepped out of his shoes. "There is going to be nothing left of you."

The one with his fangs much too close to Addie's neck laughed. "Says you. Who the fuck do you think you are anyway?"

Elias looked at Addie. "Do you trust me, little bird?" he asked. "Do you trust me to get you out of this with no harm done to you?"

"I do, Elias," she said. She was calm suddenly. This was Elias's secret and his shame. And for her, he'd unleash it.

He nodded at her. "Well then, perhaps you two have heard of me." Darian and Dregs tensed, waiting for the words that equaled a death sentence. "Allow me to introduce myself. I'm the Butcher of Bavaria."

CHAPTER 22

"Oh shit," whispered Mickey.

"Mickey, do you know what he's talking about?"

"I've heard the name, but I thought it was a myth. Like telling your kids, the bogeyman is going to get them." Clara nodded at him. "Are you sure you won't leave?"

"I am sure. He won't hurt anyone except those vampires."

"How can you be sure?"

"Because of how he spoke to Addie. He's in control." Jesus, she hoped she was right.

Mickey put his arm around her and pulled her closer, ready to hustle her out if need be, though it would be a last resort.

The man with his hand on Addie's neck laughed and squeezed. Addie's eyes widened. "That vamp died years ago. You aren't him."

Elias clenched his fists. "Oh, he's not dead." Elias tried to remain calm, but the hand on Addie's throat challenged his control. He opened his fists and flexed. His nails lengthened to sharp points. "You are touching something that is mine. This is your last chance to let her go. If you do, your deaths will not be as painful."

The second vamp leaned down further and sniffed Addie. "She smells ... delicious."

Addie's nostrils flared, but she stayed quiet. She didn't want to distract Elias. He looked at her, then flicked his eyes to where Darian stood. She blinked at him to show she understood.

"Last chance," he snarled. "Unhand her."

The two vampires laughed and moved closer to Addie. The hand at her neck tightened again.

There was a deafening roar, and then Elias moved. He was so quick that one moment Addie was between the two vampires, and the next, she was free. The vampires lay at his feet. She ran over to Darian quickly. He put her between himself and Dregs and slid an arm around her waist. "Is there any point trying to convince you to leave?" he whispered.

"No, there isn't," she whispered back.

Elias turned and looked at her. His eyes were black with swirls of red. This wasn't normal vampire stuff. He was something different. He stalked over to them and looked at her neck. She had bruises there. He gently rubbed a finger over them. "Do they hurt?" he asked.

"No," she rasped. Elias winced. "Maybe a little."

"Your voice ..."

"Will be fine," she told him quietly. "I am not hurt otherwise."

He nodded. "They have to die," he said simply.

Addie touched his cheek. "I understand," she replied. She didn't like it, but she understood. She had to accept all of him, which meant accepting this too. Whatever this actually was.

He nodded and turned back to vamps on the floor. He picked one up. "You touched something you had no business touching." His voice deepened. "You are going to die." He raised a hand and clawed the vamp's chest. "I won't even give you the honor of having your blood nourish another." He tore one arm off, then the other. The vamp was screaming.

"SHUT UP!" Elias yelled. "You should feel lucky I don't have any of my knives handy." Elias tore his chest again. Blood and intestines spilled out. "Back in the day, I could do some real damage with those. And I could keep you alive for hours while I did it."

"Ppplleeaassseee..."

Elias ignored him and let him fall to the floor. Elias lifted his foot and crushed the man's right kneecap, then his left. "I am not going to play with you for long, though. You had your hands on her neck. You bruised her.

You hurt her voice." He punched the man in the face. "You scared her." His voice was deadly calm.

Elias stood, turned to Addie as if he was making sure she was truly fine, and she looked back at him. Steady. He sighed and turned back to the vamp. He leaned down again, took the man's head in his hands, and crushed it.

"Holy shit," whispered Clara. She looked across the floor to Addie. The woman looked a little green but was maintaining. Darian may have been helping hold her up.

"We—we—didn't know." The other vamp was staring at Elias. Pure terror was written all over his face.

"I know you didn't, but I don't care." Elias walked around him in a circle. "I am sure you did this for money. But you were going to bite my woman. *My woman.* I cannot even begin to tell you how angry this makes me."

"I have information about Stellan!"

Elias laughed. It was an awful, evil laugh. Addie's breath left her at how he sounded. It chilled her.

"Again, I do not care. You cannot tell me anything I do not know or that I cannot find out." He stood over the second vamp. "Like your friend, your blood will be wasted." He lifted his foot and slammed it on the vamp's chest. He screamed in pain.

"Does that hurt? Good!" He slammed his foot again on his stomach.

"He's going to stomp him to death, isn't he?" Dregs asked Darian.

"He is." Darian tightened his hold on Addie as she was swaying a little. "He's different now, though. He's so much calmer, almost businesslike."

Dregs nodded. "I've seen him do this once. That was enough. But I agree. Somehow, this is scarier." He looked at Addie. "*¿Estás seguro de que estás bien?*"

"*Si, estoy bien. Gracias.*" Addie spared him a small smile.

Elias was circling the vamp again like a predator playing with his prey. The man was pleading with Elias, and Elias was ignoring him. Elias broke both arms and hands and then went to work on his legs.

"YOU DO NOT COME INTO MY CLUB AND DISRESPECT ME OR MY PEOPLE!"

"Ah, there it is," Darian said quietly. "The rage."

"YOU TOUCHED MY WOMAN. YOU THREATENED HER, AND YOU THINK TO NEGOTIATE WITH THE BUTCHER?"

The vamp was weeping in pain and fear. He could no longer move. He could only lay there and moan.

"SILENCE!" Elias sighed. "I grow tired of your voice." He lifted his foot again and stomped the vamp's head. There was a sickening crunch. With that, Elias proceeded to stomp the vampire to an absolute pulp. He then moved to the other vamp and did that with what was left of him.

He lifted his eyes to the ceiling and screamed out all the rage and pain he was still feeling. He finally slumped into a chair, his head in his hands. He was covered in blood spatter and who knows what else.

Addie let out a sob and ran to him. "Elias," she said softly. "*Mi amor*, look at me."

Elias let out a shuddering breath. "How can you call me that now that you've seen what I can do?"

Her heart broke for him. This was easily the most vicious thing she had ever witnessed. She hoped never to see it again, but she might. The hero archetype was a lie. People were complicated and messy, and sometimes they were vampires. She would have to unpack how she felt loving someone who would crush a man's head because he dared touch her. Because she did love him. And she was not going to walk away from him.

"Because you are my love," she took his face in her hands. She gave him a soft kiss. He shuddered out a sob and pulled her to him. "It's okay, Elias. I'm here. It's all going to be okay." She twisted her head around. "Darian, Elias is going to need to speak to the Elder Assembly right away. Is this something you can help with?"

"Absolutely. I'll go to his office and get it set up." Darian left.

"We need to clean up this mess next."

"I'll handle it. I'll call a few people back in to help," said Mickey. "I'll also lock up." He got his phone out.

"Thank you. Dregs, can you please see Clara home? I'd consider it a personal favor."

"I can do that for you," Dregs answered. He looked at Mickey. "She will be safe with me. I promise." Mickey nodded at him, but he still didn't like it.

"Clara, please let Dregs see you home. I will worry less about you."

Clara ran over to Addie and kissed her cheek. "Of course. Are you sure you don't need me?"

Addie rested her head against Clara's while she stroked Elias's hair. "I am sure. But thank you for staying. I felt better knowing you were here."

Clara cleared her throat. "I will call you tomorrow." She and Dregs left while Mickey made some calls.

"Thank you, Mickey."

"Most welcome," Mickey replied.

"Elias," Addie said gently. "Come, let's go to your office. The sooner you talk to the Elders, the sooner we can leave and you can rest."

Elias stood but didn't let go of Addie. "I'm sorry. You're all bloody now."

"I'll live. Thanks to you."

"I would do anything for you," he whispered. "I would burn the world to keep you safe. There is nothing more important to me, than you."

"I think you've proven that tonight," she said gently. "But now, business. Then rest. Tomorrow, we talk."

He nodded. It didn't matter if he lost the city. He had Addie.

But one thing was clear; Stellan had to be stopped. Permanently.

CHAPTER 23

Addie stopped Elias outside his office. Someone had left a stack of clean paper towels on a table. Addie grabbed some and tried her best to clean Elias's face. He watched her, his eyes dark but no longer menacing and no more red swirls.

"There we go," she said. "I am not sure it helps since you're covered in icky stuff, but I did my best, and your face is a little less bloody."

"Thank you," he said. "Your voice sounds a little better."

"My voice will be fine." She smiled at him. "Now, go tell them what a fucking awful vampire Stellan is."

"Yes, ma'am." Elias opened his door, and Darian sat behind his desk.

"Yes, Elias will be here shortly," Darian looked up. "Ah, here he is now." Darian jumped, looking relieved.

Elias clapped Darian on the shoulder in thanks. He stepped behind his desk, sat, and looked at the computer screen. "Elias," one of the Elders began, "What is the meaning of this?"

"Ellicore," Elias began, "I would not have asked to speak to you if it wasn't urgent." He could not very well tell them Addie had asked Darian to make the call. "Please allow me to tell the story uninterrupted, and I promise to answer all questions you put to me afterward."

Elias told the story completely but efficiently. Facts only, his voice calm and steady as he told the Elders what Stellan had done and what he had done. He was grateful that the none of the contingent that had recently visited was present. Those vampires were ... difficult. They would have thrived off this conflict, likely spurring it on.

"Stellan is completely out of line," Ellicore said. "But we need to talk about your loss of control."

"Of course," said Elias through gritted teeth. "I am not proud that I unleashed the Butcher on them, and I admit it was an emotional reaction." He looked over at Addie standing by the door. "But I do not regret what I did. I am not sorry those two vamps are dead. I would do it again if given a chance."

"Over a human woman?" A female voice said.

"Yes, Maribella. A human woman. One I care about a great deal."

"Would you have done what you did, though, if your feelings weren't involved?"

"I cannot answer that question." Elias shook his head. "But everyone who steps into this club is under my protection. I will use whatever force I deem necessary to protect them. Those vamps were a threat, and I would have neutralized them regardless."

"Your feelings for her make you weak. You should leave her." Another male voice said.

"Never will I willingly leave her," Elias said. Addie's breath caught in her throat. As far as a commitment was concerned, that was pretty solid.

Darian stood with Elias. "I saw this happen. This was not the old Butcher. Elias was still very much in control of his actions. He was able to converse with us rationally. This was not the case centuries ago. This was not the same bloodlust of old."

"Is that so? Still, this woman ..."

Addie marched over to stand between Darian and Elias. "That's enough talking about me like I am not in the room. It wouldn't matter if Elias left me because I would not allow it. I would follow him wherever he went. I would make such a nuisance of myself that he'd have to take me back for his own sanity."

Elias put an arm around her and pulled her close. "Elder Assembly, this is Adelaide Gold. Adelaide, the Elder Assembly."

"Miss Gold, be that as it may," Maribella continued, "You are but a human and cannot help him with what he needs to do."

"I mean no offense, but that is untrue." Elias hid a smile. His Addie could be fierce when she needed to be. She was shaking a little, though, so he tightened his hold on her. "I may not have the strength of a vampire, but I am not useless. I have made him better in certain aspects of running this club. Things that, while they don't have a dollar sign right next to them, will eventually reap financial benefits when it comes to staff loyalty and attrition. Respect pays off. And quite frankly, people are stronger when they have something to fight for." She paused for breath. "He cares now where he didn't before. He will work and fight harder and smarter to keep the city. Emotion does not weaken us."

"You are quite opinionated," one of the Elders said.

"I watched someone I care about crush two vampires tonight because they dared to harm me. It wasn't easy, but I watched all of it. There was not one point during that when I feared him or for him. I saw my Elias, not this Butcher."

"My dear ..." began Maribella.

"Leave off, Maribella. The woman makes some very good points." An Elder peered at Addie. "Miss Gold, my name is Julius. I am very old, and I have witnessed much of history. And you are correct. Love does not make us weak, not on its own. But no one is infallible. Not even Elias."

Addie nodded. "Darian and I are aware of his flaws. Moreso than most, I'd say. And we are both telling you that, while a gruesome end for those vamps, it was not unwarranted. The Butcher is the exception and not the rule. I can't tell you I will never be in danger again. I am dating a vampire; that would be naïve of me. I can say I believe Elias will use appropriate force to protect me and this city."

"And to that end," Darian continued, "This will get out. The other vamps in the city will hear of this. And will think twice before going against him and the Assembly."

"And this means the Assembly, both mine and yours, will be seen as the ultimate vampire law in the land." They'd like that.

Julius smirked at them. "You three are very formidable. So be it. We shall let that go for now. Stellan has petitioned—right before Darian's call actually —to have you removed from your position on the Assembly and from the city."

"Of course, he did. He wasted no time."

"He states you attacked him, which seems to point to him being naïve or stupid, as we've had several separate reports in the last several minutes that he started the fight. Including one from Dregs, and he never involves himself in vampire politics."

"I believe Stellan is trying to cause chaos right now, in order to give him time to regroup," Elias replied.

"What do you plan to do?" Ellicore asked.

"I need to speak with the other local Assembly members, but Stellan needs to be taken out."

"I take it you mean permanently," Julius said.

"Yes. I am fine with having him drained to feed others, but I do not think he deserves it. I will abide by your decision on this."

"Please give us a moment to discuss." Julius muted their side of the conversation while they discussed it. They came back shortly. "We would prefer he be drained to feed others. He has been a good vampire for many years. That said, if you are in a position where that is impossible, you have our blessing to do what you need to do. There will be no repercussions."

"Thank you, Julius. I am honored by the Assembly's faith in me."

"You have earned it. Try and wrap this up quickly."

"I will."

"Now, all of you go home and get some rest." The screen went dark.

Darian let out a low whistle. "Addie made a friend!"

"I did? I was petrified. I couldn't tell."

"You are very fierce," said Elias, kissing the top of her head. "But yes, the head of the Assembly likes you."

"Julius? How old is he?"

"Julius Caesar was named after him. And he was already a vampire."

"Shut up! Really?" Addie was incredulous.

"Really," replied Elias pulling out his phone. "I will let Gen, Eliza and Tamir know that we need to meet tomorrow night. A virtual meeting. I am closing the club for a few days, but I am not inclined to go out tomorrow. This always took a lot out of me, and it seems that it still does."

"I am coming home with you," said Addie. "I planned for it anyway." Her tone brooked no argument.

"Of course," Elias replied.

"I will call Miles to let him know the plan for tomorrow. And I will ask him to notify everyone else," Darian said.

"Thank you. Can you also have him arrange a bonus for Mickey?"

"Absolutely," Darian replied. "How about I drive the two of you home?"

"That would be great," said Elias.

"I am going to my dressing room to get my things. I'll be back in a few minutes," said Addie as she left the office.

"Darian, I have one more very large favor to ask?"

"Of course, brother."

"I want to explain everything to Addie. I would like for you to be there. You are part of the story. And you may remember things I do not." He paused. "I'd also like you there for the Assembly meeting."

"If you need me, I'm there." He and Elias embraced. "Elias, for what it's worth, I think you did the right thing tonight. And I enjoyed the fuck out of it."

Elias cracked a smile. "Thank you. It didn't feel bad this time. I have no shame over tonight. But it brings up the shame I feel in general. I am ... I am afraid to tell her."

"She'll hold. She did tonight. When you flagged after the fight, she took over. Issuing orders like she was born to it. You won't lose her."

Elias really hoped Darian was right.

When Elias and Addie got to his place, she hustled him into the shower. He stood under the water, not moving, with his head bowed.

The door to the shower opened, and Addie stepped in. She pressed her front to his back, wrapping her arms around his waist. "It's okay, Elias. It's all okay." Her voice was quiet.

"I told myself I would never go back there. That I'd never lose control and kill like that again. I vowed to leave it behind me."

Her heart clenched. It was her fault. "I'm so sorry," she said. "This is because of me. If I hadn't come into your life, you wouldn't have gone there again."

Elias turned quickly and rested his head on hers, his arms circling her waist. "This is not your fault. It's part of me, and I should have dealt with it and not repressed it. It made me isolate myself. It made me not care about things I should have cared about. The Butcher is a part of me, and I need to accept that and learn how to use him to my advantage. I believe tonight was a step in that direction."

Addie looked at him. "How so?" She pulled away to get the body wash and a washcloth. She started to soap him up.

"You don't have to wash me," he said.

"I want to," Addie said. "Let me." He nodded at her. "Now, you were saying?"

"I will tell you the whole story tomorrow. But before, it would control me. That bloodlust. Tonight, I controlled it."

"Why do you think that is?" She moved behind him to soap his back.

"You," he said. "I didn't want to hurt you. But more than that, you've changed me for the better. I want you to be proud of me. And proud to be with me."

She circled back to face him—tears in her eyes. "Oh Elias, I am proud to be with you. To belong to you. When I call you *Mi Amor*, it's not lip service. I love you, Elias. I know it's only been a short time, but I know what I know."

He smiled at her then. It was beautiful, his smile in this moment. "You do? You love me?"

"I do."

"I love you too, little bird. My original plan was to keep this to sex only, but you wormed your way into my heart. As much as you belong to me, I also belong to you."

She brought her lips to his. "You make me better too," she said. "I feel stronger, surer of myself. Freer. So, this is a two-way street."

"No one has ever told me that before." He kissed her neck and her shoulders.

"I am glad to be the first. I am greedy where you are concerned. Now, let's finish cleaning up and get to bed. You are exhausted, and you need to rest."

"Darian has been the only other person who's ever given a shit about me," he said. "You honor and humble me."

"You deserve love, Elias. I cannot speak to the vampire you were. But the vampire you are is worthy. And you are going to win this fight with Stellan."

"It will make things harder with Miranda," he said.

"It is what it is. That will be sad, but he deserves what he gets."

"True." He kissed her. "And I will be more than happy to give it to him."

CHAPTER 24

When Elias woke the next evening, Addie wasn't next to him. He sat and rubbed his hands over his face. When they'd gotten into bed last night, he had put his head on her lap while she ran her fingers through his hair. He had fallen asleep at dawn with her singing softly to him. He smiled, thinking about it.

Pots and pans clanged in the kitchen. He sniffed. Holy shit, whatever was happening in his kitchen smelled amazing. He got up, put jeans and a long-sleeved shirt on, and headed out to the kitchen.

Addie was cooking what looked to be a huge meal. She was wearing a t-shirt that had seen better days and shorts that hugged her bottom. Her hair was piled on her head, and she was singing along to music she had playing. Elias was instantly hard, but more than that, the sight of her warmed him. He was absolutely smitten, and he was perfectly content with it.

She turned quickly and let out a yelp. "I'm sorry, did I wake you?" Her voice was still a bit hoarse, but she smiled and walked over for a kiss.

He put his arms around her and kissed her deeply. "Hello, little bird. You didn't wake me." He gestured to everything going on. "What is going on here?"

"I'm cooking!"

"I can see that. What are you cooking?" He gently rubbed the bruises on her neck.

"When I was a kid, and I was having a rough time, my mom would make a big Mexican meal. So, I am doing that for you. I am even making my own tortillas. Well, I'm trying to make them. It's been a very long time."

"You're cooking? For me?"

"I am. Is that okay?"

"It's more than okay. It's wonderful. Thank you." He hugged her to him. "But did you go out for all this today?"

"Nope. I ordered groceries and had them delivered." She looked at him. "So, I have something to put to you, but I am not sure how you'll feel."

"Just tell me." Worry was plain in his voice.

She tapped his chest. "I was thinking, maybe, while this whole thing with Stellan is going on, I should stay with you." Addie bit her lip. "I think you'll worry less if we're staying together. And you'll be able to concentrate better on what needs to be done. I know I'll worry less about you if I am here with you." Elias didn't say anything, and she frowned. Had she overstepped? "I mean, I don't have to …"

He picked her up and took her mouth in a searing kiss. She wrapped her legs around him. "Little bird, I was trying to figure out how I would ask you to do just that. You've taken a weight off my mind."

"Oh, good! I'll need to get some stuff. But that can maybe wait for tomorrow."

"Anything you want."

Addie gave him a hard look. "Elias, do you need to feed?"

He nodded. "I do. Last night took a lot out of me."

"Why didn't you say something? The food is almost ready. Darian is eating with us, but we have time. Let me feed you before I … well … feed you." She laughed a little.

He carried her to the living room and lowered them onto the couch with Addie straddling him. She tilted her head so he could get to her neck. He hesitated. "What is it?" she asked.

"We've never done this without having sex."

She smiled at him. "This is not about sex. This is about care. We need to take care of each other, and this is one way I can do that. You need this, and I want to provide it. You don't have to fuck me to get me to do it. Do you understand?"

"I do," he said.

"Good, now feed. I have to practice my tortilla making."

He leaned in slowly licking her neck. She shivered at the sensation. He gripped her hips, and she dug her nails into his shoulders. He sunk his fangs in, and she sighed, pulling him closer to her. "That's it, *Mi Amor*. Take what you need."

He groaned against her neck and drank. She rubbed his shoulders and spoke words of love to him while he drank from her. Eventually, he pulled back, licking her neck, and closing the wound.

"Better?" she asked, cuddling against him.

He kneaded her ass. "Yes, thank you. I love you."

"And I love you." She started kissing his neck, working her way to his chin.

"Are you trying to have your way with me, little bird?"

"Maybe." She wiggled on his lap.

"I thought you had to go make tortillas," he said.

"They can wait. Apparently, you feeding on me makes me a little horny." She wiggled some more.

"One would think you are trying to get me to slap this glorious ass of yours."

"Would one?" She gave his chin a quick nip and ground herself against him this time.

"Adelaide, we do not have the time for you to start this right now."

She started to reply when there was a loud knock at the door. She laughed. "It seems you are correct." She hopped off his lap.

Elias stood. "I cannot believe I have to answer the door with a hard-on. You will pay for that later."

"Promises, promises," she said as she strode back into the kitchen.

Elias looked through the peephole. He opened the door, and Darian bounded in. "What is that fucking glorious aroma?"

"Well, hello to you, too," said Elias.

"Sure, hello. No, really, that smell is amazing."

"It is. Addie is making Mexican food."

"Sweet!" Darian clapped his hands together. "Everything is taken care of, by the way. The club is closed for the next few nights. Full pay for all."

"Great, thanks. Addie suggested she stay with me until this is over," Elias gestured them towards the kitchen.

"You must be relieved."

"I am." He paused. "It's too soon to make it permanent, right? I shouldn't push?"

Darian smiled at his friend. "It's probably a bit too soon, yes. And just last night, you were worried about her sticking around."

Elias ran his hand through his hair. "I still am, honestly. Which is probably why I'm thinking about trying to keep her with me permanently." He sighed. "I should relax."

"Yes, you should." Darian glanced into the kitchen, and saw Addie cooking and dancing around. "But I get the impulse, just watching her." He grinned. "Addie! What is that heavenly smell?"

She turned around and smiled. "Oh, hey! I am making a lot of things, but we're having Tacos Al Pastor, so that's probably what you smell right now."

"Anytime you want to leave Elias, I'm here."

Addie rolled her eyes. "Firstly, you like men. Secondly, sorry. I love the big guy."

Darian's eyes widened as he looked at Elias. "And how does the big guy feel?"

"The same, my brother," said Elias. "The same."

Darian's smile was brilliant. His oldest friend, his brother, was finally in love. The night would be difficult, but it wouldn't dampen Darian's happiness over this.

Addie smiled at them. "So, what is the plan for tonight?"

"We'll meet with the Assembly. I need to tell them what I plan to do."

"And that is to kill Stellan, correct?" asked Darian.

"Yes," said Elias.

"Is there anyone on the Assembly that might disagree?" asked Addie.

"They all might. I may end up having to step down."

Addie started putting food dishes on the table, including tacos, pozole, and a large platter of enchiladas. "We're eating in the kitchen; I don't like your dining room. Why would they want that? You are taking care of a large problem for them."

"This may be too aggressive of a solution for them. In Tamir's case, I suspect they're in business together, though I am not sure if he'd ever admit to that. Elizabeth probably won't care about him dying. She has no love loss for him. Gen could go either way. She plays it close to her chest, but I don't think she'd want to see Stellan in charge of the city."

"They may not want this to reflect on them," said Darian.

"Vampire politics is exhausting," said Addie. "Okay, my tortilla skills aren't great, but they'll taste good. Have a seat."

Elias held out a chair for Addie. "You sit first. What do you want to drink?"

"Beer is fine. I had some delivered." Addie sat. "Oh, this is my childhood right here. It all smells so good! If I do say so myself."

Darian sat, and Elias brought them all beers. "And yes, the politics is exhausting."

They ate in silence for a few minutes. Elias looked at Addie. "This is absolutely amazing. I want to cancel the meeting now, so I can sit here and graze all night."

"Mmmph," said Darian shoveling rice in his mouth.

Addie laughed. "I assume that's agreement."

Darian swallowed and smiled. "Yes, it is. Sorry."

"Elias, what if they ask you to step down because of me? They may consider me a liability."

"Then I step down. The Assembly is not more important than you."

"But ..." Addie began.

"No buts, Addie. I do it because it's necessary, not because I like it. I wouldn't miss it. Stellan will still die."

"What he won't tell you," Put in Darian, "Is that Elias is the richest vampire in the city. So, he doesn't need the Assembly. They need him."

"They don't know that for a fact," said Elias. "But they suspect, as does the Elder Assembly. It's not their business. And what Darian won't tell you is that he is the second wealthiest. He's no starving artist."

Darian rolled his eyes. "Yes, it's true. Don't tell." He winked at Addie. "Though with Dregs here, I may be third now."

"Which would make me second. Dregs is ridiculously wealthy."

"I just don't want to be a problem for them," said Addie.

"They can fuck off if they think that," said Darian. "Honestly, Addie, Elias hates politics. They'd be doing him a favor."

"Okay, I will accept that." But she still looked concerned.

Elias cleared his throat. "So, after the meeting, I would like to tell you about my history as the Butcher of Bavaria. I asked Darian to stay for it in case my memory is fuzzy. He was there for some of it."

Addie took his hand. "If that's what you want," she said.

"I do. And if you decide you want to leave afterward …"

"No, stop it. I am not going anywhere."

"You don't know that," Elias replied.

"Did you harm children or rape anyone?" He shook his head. "I am sure it's bad. And I am sure there will be things you don't want to admit to tonight, but I doubt anything you have to tell me would make me not love you. Now, eat your dinner."

Addie looked at Elias and Darian eating, and despite everything going on, she felt at peace. She was worried about what he was going to tell her. She was sure it would all be fine. But what if it wasn't?

CHAPTER 25

Elias booted up the laptop in his office and started the meeting. Darian and Addie were also in the room but off-camera.

Elias was the first to arrive. Gen and Elizabeth were next. Then finally, Tamir logged in.

"Elias! What the actual fuck happened last night?" Tamir shouted.

"Tamir," Gen interjected, "This is why Elias called the meeting tonight—to explain. Please stop shouting." Gen rolled her eyes at him.

"Thank you, Gen," said Elias. "Tamir, please do not interrupt until I'm done. I promise to answer all your questions. But it's best if I can tell the story with no interruptions."

"Fine, get on with it then," Tamir groused.

Elias told them what happened but had to mute Tamir, who kept trying to interrupt, despite being warned not to. "Tamir," he said when he was done, "I meant it when I said no interruptions."

Elizabeth laughed. "Tamir, you deserved that." Tamir glowered at her. "Elias, you say Stellan was the aggressor here. He has contacted each of us, insisting it was you."

"No doubt," replied Elias. "He has counted on the fact that I have a reputation. That said, there were witnesses."

"Darian and your human can be considered biased," put in Tamir.

Elias didn't like how he sneered the word 'human,' as if Addie was any less than him. "Tamir, you will keep a civil tone when you speak about

Adelaide. That is her name. Please use it." He ran his hand through his hair. "There were a number of people at the club, and they have provided eyewitness testimonies to the Elder Assembly."

"If it wasn't for her …"

"Tamir, I would not continue with this," said Gen. "It's not productive" Gen, ever the pragmatist. "Stellan would have done this regardless. He is most determined to unseat Elias."

"Agreed," put in Elizabeth. "The one out of the ordinary thing here is Elias going back to his roots."

"Ah yes, the Butcher." Tamir's tone was derisive. "You wouldn't have gone there if it wasn't for your little plaything."

Before Elias could reply, Addie marched over to the computer. "I'm in the room, Tamir. And I do not appreciate your tone."

"How dare you speak to me that way!"

"No, Tamir. How dare you," thundered Elias. "I realize you use humans and toss them away, but not all of us are like that."

"No, they are not." Gen had had a human lover for years. He was well into his seventies now, but she adored him no less than she did when he was younger. "And it is nice to meet you, Adelaide."

"It's nice to meet you all, as well. Well, most of you."

Gen laughed. "Is Darian there too?"

Darian sidled up on Elias's other side. "I am, hello."

"So," said Elizabeth. "What do you plan to do?"

"He should be removed from the Assembly, effective immediately." He paused. "Additionally, I am going to kill him," Elias replied calmly.

"Removing him from the Assembly is bad enough, but killing him? Absurd!" Tamir was shocked. "The Elder Assembly won't allow it."

"I've spoken to them. And they have agreed to it. He attacked another vampire without cause. He put human staff and guests in harm's way. He is dangerous." Addie stiffened, as Miranda sprang to mind. He put his arm around her waist and pulled her closer, as if sensing her thoughts.

"So, this isn't personal?" asked Elizabeth. Her tone was more curious than accusatory.

"It is partly personal. He put Addie, specifically, in danger, and I will not let that slide. He's not going to stop, so he must be stopped."

"We appreciate your honesty. You must care for Adelaide deeply." This was from Gen.

"I love Adelaide. I will do what I can to protect her, even if it annoys her," he said, as Addie's mouth popped open to say something. She narrowed her eyes but stayed quiet.

Gen laughed. "Fair. I think you may get an earful later, though."

"No doubt. I do not wish to involve the three of you. I will step down from the Assembly if you all wish it."

"Not necessary," said Elizabeth.

"Not so fast," Tamir said. "Maybe you should."

"Why on Earth should he?" asked Gen. "He's not asking us to assist him. And we all know what Stellan has been like."

"Yes, why the change of heart, Tamir? The last time we spoke, you took Elias's side." This was from Elizabeth.

"It feels like a large jump from kicking him off the Assembly to killing him."

"Tamir, he escalated. Significantly."

"I am aware of that, Eliza. But to kill him still seems excessive."

"Or perhaps," said Gen. "You don't want him dead because he's been funneling funds to you." The vampire casually examined her nails while she said this. "It would appear you two are indeed in business together."

"Lies!" Tamir pounded his hand on his desk.

"Oh? So, he's giving you money for no reason? He gets nothing for it?"

"Genevieve, I do not appreciate this!"

"I am sure you don't, but it's true. I thought, at first, he was lending you the money so you could get yourself out of the hole you seem to be in. But it appears you've given him a piece of the action."

"You're in a financial hole, Tamir? Is this true?" Elias narrowed his eyes at him. Tamir had been providing them with falsified financial documents if this was the case. But Gen's words confirmed what Elias suspicions about Tamir and Stellan.

"I am outraged at these lies!"

"Tamir, it would explain why you care about Stellan's continued existence," Elizabeth said. "For myself, I do not care if he dies." She shrugged.

"As for being aggressive," said Gen. "We are vampires. Aggression is how many of us have survived so long." She sighed. "Really, Tamir, do not insult me. My information is good, and you know it."

"I do not support murder. And I will go to the Elder Assembly."

"Feel free," said Elias. "I don't mind that. I will mind greatly if this conversation gets back to your business partner." Elias smirked at him.

"I won't tell Stellan," Tamir said.

"None of us believe you," said Gen. "Why wouldn't you?"

"She's right," put in Elias. "Tamir, if you do. I will add you to the list. Do not make an enemy of me. You do not have to support me, but you must stay out of it."

"I know it's forbidden to break the confidence of these meetings." Tamir's look was cunning. "But if you step down…"

"He's not stepping down!" Eliza's voice was sharp. "You are outvoted. Stellan is now off the Assembly, and his life is forfeit. You will remain neutral and quiet." It was times like these that Elias remembered Elizabeth had once been nobility. She expected people to obey her, and they did with that tone of voice.

"Fine! I am done with this tonight!" Tamir logged off.

"Not quite as satisfying as watching him storm from the room," laughed Gen. "He will be a problem. I shall keep an eye on him."

"Thank you, Gen."

"You threatened him. He may act on that once he thinks about it," mused Elizabeth.

"He's a pampered coward," said Elias. "He knows he can't beat me. But it's still likely he'll tell Stellan."

"Oh, he most definitely will," Eliza put him. "Tamir will always be loyal to those who provide the money."

"We always knew his loyalty came with a price." Gen shrugged. "Who knows what Stellan has told him."

"All very true," replied Elias.

They spoke for a few more minutes, then Elias closed his laptop.

"Well, that was fun," said Addie. "Tamir is really ridiculous. I like Gen and Eliza though."

Darian laughed. "Tamir is an idiot. It remains to be seen whether he's just an average idiot or a dangerous one."

"True. And now onto the next part of the evening." Addie raised an eyebrow at him. "It's time you knew my history and how the Butcher of Bavaria came to be."

CHAPTER 26

"Elias, we don't need to do that tonight." Addie put her hands on his chest, looking into his face.

"Yes," he said firmly. "We do. It's time."

"It won't change my mind about you." Addie crossed her arms in front of her chest.

"It might," Elias replied.

"It won't," said Darian, putting his arm around Addie's shoulders. "If you were still the Butcher today, maybe. But you aren't that vampire anymore."

Elias sighed. "Let's go into the living room." Elias stalked away, and Darian squeezed Addie's shoulder before he ushered her along.

Darian poured them whiskey and then sat in an oversized chair. His long legs stretched out before him. Addie sat on the couch, and Elias sat on the opposite end. Addie didn't like that, but she let it slide for now. She sensed he needed a little distance to tell his story.

"I was born around 1477 or so. I don't remember the exact date, but I believe I was around forty when I became a vampire, best as I can recall. I can tell you I became a vampire not too long after Martin Luther published his *Ninety-five Theses.*"

"That kicked off the Reformation, correct?" Elias nodded at her. "Are you that old?" she asked Darian.

"No, I came along later," he replied.

She nodded. "I'm sorry. I interrupted." She gave Elias a chagrined look.

"You," he said, leaning over to drop a kiss on her nose, "May always interrupt me." He sat back. "Printing had become popular, so there were religious pamphlets all over. I was born into a Catholic home, but I was not religious. I was a soldier, well, more of a mercenary. I fought for money."

"There is nothing wrong with that, Elias." Addie's voice was gentle.

"No, I never thought so either. I fell into a conflict somehow between nobles. A noble by the name of Schrader was who I fought for. Baron Schrader. We only saw him at night, but I thought he was just eccentric." Elias paused to take a sip of his whiskey. "But in truth, he was an ancient vampire. He was also insane, as it happens."

"Truth," said Darian. "He was a religious zealot. But he was psychotic. And very powerful." Darian took a sip of whiskey. "Mercenaries who fight for money do not ask questions about the nature of the fight." He looked at Elias. "That is not a judgment, brother."

"I didn't take it as one. I was a good soldier. No, I was great. I reveled in the killing. It made me feel powerful. Well, it made me *feel*. I had gotten to a point where I didn't feel much besides aggression. So, I craved the violence." He looked at Addie. Her gaze was steady, but she betrayed nothing of her thoughts.

"He saw me fighting one night and decided he wanted to make me a vampire. An *uber* vampire, if you will. One bred for a kind of psychotic violence. He'd been sired by a vampire who had the same idea, and Schrader was the perfect creation. Until me." Elias rubbed a hand over his face. "All I can think is that it must have been something in the bloodline. In all my years, I've never known another vampire's eyes to swirl with red when the Butcher takes over."

"He'd tried to make such soldiers before, but it hadn't worked. He had turned them into vampires, and when they didn't become what he wanted, he left them to die in the sun." Darian looked grim.

Elias was grateful he didn't have to tell this story alone. "Exactly. But he saw me and my capacity for violence and my lack of anything resembling a conscience and thought I'd be perfect."

"And you were," Addie guessed.

"I was. I became a monster. He would capture vampires and humans, and I would torture them. Generally, with a whip. I was excellent with a whip."

"Did you kill them?"

"Yes. That's when the knives came into play. I would toy with them before I actually killed them."

"And this was about religion?" Addie asked.

"At some point maybe, but then I think he liked watching me do it. He got off on it. I didn't know until much later about the girls he raped. He kept that away from me."

"Why?"

"Because even I had boundaries. I would not harm a female. Any female. I did not care what they were accused of. And I did not harm children."

"Schrader had a cadre of vampire killers who would do that. Unbeknownst to Elias."

"What would you have done if you had found out?"

"Killed him sooner," Elias replied.

"Why do you think you had that rule about women and children?"

Elias shrugged. "I no longer remember. I have vague memories of my mother and siblings, so I assume it stems from there."

"Reasonable. Go on."

"So, this went on for years. So many years, I honestly lost track of time. And I became colder and emptier inside. But the thing about the Butcher was that he was out of control." He paused. He was the Butcher, and he needed to own that. "I was out of control. I would let the violence consume me, and I would become the monster that was the Butcher. That Butcher would never be able to have a conversation with you. That Butcher would never have cared about your well-being. When I was in the throes, I didn't just commit violence, I was violence." He shuddered.

Addie moved close to him and took his head in her hands. She kissed his cheek. He put his head on her shoulder as she put her arms around him. "It's okay, Elias."

"I know I am glossing over a lot of the details..."

"I don't need them right now. I am a reader and an only child; I have a very active imagination." She paused. "What about women?"

He shook his head. "There were none. Not human, not vampire. When I wasn't torturing anyone, I kept to myself. I only took blood from males." He took her hand and kissed it. He stretched out, putting his head on her lap. "Just for a moment," he said, closing his eyes briefly. He didn't deserve the comfort, but he needed it.

"Tell her about the rest from where you are," said Darian. "I think it will help." He hated the shame and pain on his friend's face.

"He's right," said Addie, stroking his hair. "Tell me when it changed." She didn't need more details right now; she got the picture well enough. There'd be time for her to learn more.

"One day, two humans were brought in—brothers. I don't even remember what their transgressions were." He looked over at Darian. "Do you?"

"Yes, they were caught stealing bread because they were starving. And, as it happens, they were protestant. They had no home. They only had each other. So, they traveled around and worked when they could."

"Such a small thing, really. But to me, it didn't matter. It meant I could inflict pain. I told you I was a monster."

"Stop," said Darian softly, pain lacing his voice. "Please just stop. What you did for them was not monstrous."

Addie suspected Darian was one of the brothers, but she wanted to let them tell it their way.

"They were tied up tight. I had done it myself, and when I raised the whip to deliver the first blow, I looked down and stopped dead. One of the brothers was not a brother. She was a sister."

"A woman?" Addie asked incredulously.

"Yes," said Darian. "My sister. I am sure you've guessed that one of those travelers was me." Addie nodded. "My sister posed as a man because it was safer that way."

Elias nodded. "Her name was Ilse. Darian's real name is Heinrich."

"Hated it then, hate it now." Darian grinned and took a sip of whiskey.

"Is Elias your given name?"

"As far as I know, yes," he answered. "Anyway, I saw it was a woman and put my arm down. Ilse begged me not to kill her brother. I could do whatever I liked with her but leave her brother be."

"She was older than me, and she thought to protect me. I should have protected her."

"You did. Do you not remember? When I put my arm down, you crawled in front of her. They both had been beaten badly by the vamps who had captured them. I asked why he should be kept alive, and she answered that he had the voice of an angel."

"Elias laughed and mocked us. But I saw how he looked at Ilse, and I knew he wouldn't kill her. Though, I was afraid he'd rape her."

"He didn't know I would kill anyone who raped a woman. I dragged them inside the castle and into my rooms, making Darian sing for me." He looked at his friend again. "It was the most beautiful sound I had ever heard."

"You do have a beautiful voice, Darian." Addie smiled at him. "Why don't you sing lead in the band?"

"I don't like being a front man. I prefer being just one of the musicians."

"Fair. I'm sorry, continue."

"Elias tried to hide us in the castle. He threatened to kill the few on-lookers from earlier if they told Schrader what happened. But someone did eventually."

"I carried on as if nothing happened. But I wasn't putting my back into anymore, as it were."

"You were still a scary bastard."

"I had to perform. But when Schrader found out, he had Darian brought to him. He made him sing. Then, he turned him into a vampire, so he could always sing for him. Then he told him he would make Ilse his whore, and there was nothing Darian could do about it."

"He brought me into his room and told me exactly what he would do to me. And then he told me—" Darian paused and took a few deep breaths. "He told me exactly what he was going to do to Ilse. Said I could watch if I wanted to. Vamps were holding me. There was no escape."

Addie tensed. "What happened then?"

"I was held, drained, and made a vampire. I passed out, and when I woke, Ilse was alive, but Schrader was not."

"When I heard, I was frantic. I ran to Schrader's chambers. It was too late to save Darian. He had fallen into a new vampire slumber. But Schrader had Ilse bent over a chair and was trying to enter her. She was fighting him, but she was losing energy. He was old but still a vampire. I didn't even think about it. I tore him away from her. It was a bloody fight. But I had more strength than he did. I crushed his head between my hands. His perfect killing machine had killed him, in the end."

"You saved Ilse, though."

"Yes," he said. "And then I broke. I destroyed everything I could get my hands on. I gave the females a choice; loyalty to me or leave by the next evening. And then I killed every male vampire loyal to Schrader. That was most of them."

"I can't say as I blame you," Addie said, still stroking his hair. "What happened next?"

"We found a cleric who assisted us in getting the castle deeded over to Ilse, citing she was a long lost relative of the Baron's. Those things were not easy back then. We were able to scare up several people to corroborate the story," Darian said. "Luckily, the cleric was also a vampire and helped me through my first days."

"Yes, because after I completely lost my shit, I went catatonic. I did not move or eat or do anything for a week."

"What knocked you out of it?"

"Ilse. She braved coming to see me. The cleric was fine, but Darian needed me. We were brothers, and he was flailing and needed to be taken in hand. His sire was gone, and I was the closest thing he had to one now."

Addie dropped a kiss on his forehead. "Some monster," she said.

"Addie," he looked at her, pain in his eyes. "I killed—I tormented—I tortured hundreds of people during my time as the Butcher."

"But when it came down to it, someone managed to find the kernel of humanity you had left. I am not romanticizing, condoning, or excusing what you did. But you did change. You were capable of change."

"And you still had rules," put in Darian. "You saw Ilse was a woman, and you stopped. She affected you."

"Did you love her?" asked Addie.

"Yes, but I never told her or touched her."

"She knew." Darian's voice was quiet. "She loved you as well. But she knew you were not meant for each other, just as you knew. But you gave her something better. Independence. And the means to live her life on her own terms. That was heady stuff back then for a woman."

"It still is," said Addie. "Elias, it is well beyond time to forgive yourself."

"I will never be rid of the shame. And guilt." His voice was full of grief.

Darian came over and sat on the floor next to him. "Elias, she's right. You have done such good in the intervening years. It doesn't erase it, but your books aren't full of red. The violence didn't consume you last night. You controlled it. He was like a berserker back in the day."

Elias was crying. "All those people—all those lives."

"All the people you've saved since then, including Addie the other night."

Addie hugged Elias to her the best she could. "I love you. I see the good in you. You must learn to let this go. That doesn't mean you forget them, just give yourself some grace. We can have as many conversations as it takes to help you do that. You can unburden yourself to me, and I will hold you. No judgment. And I will not leave you."

Darian clasped his friend's hand. "I told you that you wouldn't lose her. I mean, you almost killed me, and I stuck."

Elias smiled at his friend. His brother. "Couldn't get rid of you if I tried."

Darian stood. "I think that's enough for tonight. Be easy, my friend." He dropped a kiss on both his and Addie's head and let himself out.

Addie let Elias cry quietly in her lap. He eventually stopped and looked at her. "What now?"

"Now," she said, kissing him softly, "You rest."

"You will stay with me?"

"For the rest of my life," Addie promised.

CHAPTER 27

Addie opened her eyes to find Elias watching her. "What time is it?" she asked.

"A little after five in the morning," he replied, winding a lock of her hair around his finger.

"You should be resting, sleeping," she said.

"It's hard for me to sleep when it's still dark. I will drop off soon. I do need to sleep."

"Can I get you something?"

"No, little bird. I know I shouldn't have been staring at you, but you soothe me."

Addie smiled. "It was a little disconcerting to find you doing it, but I can't be angry with that reason. You do the same for me." She moved closer to him until her nose pressed into his neck and her hands on his chest.

"This is even better," he said. His arms wrapped around her, and his head rested lightly on hers. "Thank you," he said quietly.

Addie didn't need to ask why he had thanked her. "You are very welcome," she responded. "Anytime you need to talk about it, I am here to listen, and I won't judge."

"You may judge at some point, and that's expected."

"I will try not to. No one can judge you harsher than you already judge yourself."

"I was not good. I did monstrous things."

"Yes, you did. But you stopped, and you've spent the ensuing centuries trying to not do harm, even though you turned your emotions off completely. You cannot right those wrongs. The damage is done. All you can do is better. And you are."

"Old vampires can learn new tricks."

"That they can." She leaned back to look at him. "You kept his last name."

"I did. By that point, I wasn't even sure what my original last name was. And it is a reminder of who I used to be, and who I will never be again."

"That makes perfect sense." His hand moved slowly to her backside. "Later, Elias. You need to get some sleep. Tomorrow, you need to figure out how to kill Stellan. And I need to figure out how to get Miranda away from him."

Elias squeezed her bottom, then moved his hand higher. "Do you think you can?"

Addie sighed. "No, I don't. But I am going to try." Addie bit her lip. "Elias?"

"Yes?"

"Did you ever feed on Ilse? I'm not jealous, but I am curious."

"I did," Elias replied hesitantly.

"I'm sorry, I shouldn't have asked. That was rude."

Elias pulled her tighter to him. "I am not mad you asked. It was the night she came to get me out of my stupor. I'd not fed much at all. I was not well. She offered me hers so that I could help Darian. I took it. But that was the only time."

"That seems reasonable," said Addie. "You've lived a long life. It would be very naïve of me to think you didn't love someone before me."

"Addie, Ilse was so long ago that her memory is hazy for the most part. Like a dream. But I can tell you there has never been anyone like you."

"What a sweet thing to say."

"It's true."

"Then I can tell you that I was indeed a little jealous."

"Naturally," he said. She pinched his nipple and he laughed. "Darian doesn't know about me feeding from her."

"I won't say anything." Addie yawned. "Okay, time to sleep. For both of us. Sweet dreams," she said.

"I think," Elias said, "Tonight, they just might be."

When Elias stepped into the living room the next evening, Addie was on a video call with Miranda. He stayed far out of frame, but Addie sensed him coming into the room.

"Miranda, he's lying to you. He started this, and he put those people in danger. He put me, your friend, in danger."

"You were never in real danger," Miranda laughed. It was an odd, hollow sound. Miranda was acting very strangely.

Addie peered closely at her friend. Miranda's eyes didn't seem right. "I was in danger, Randi. And I was scared." She paused. "Are you okay? Your pupils seem a little large." Addie took a quick screengrab on her phone to show Elias.

"I am fine. Addie, why are you doing this? Are you jealous? Maybe Elias is jealous of Stellan."

Addie wasn't even going to dignify that with a response. "Randi, do you honestly not give a shit that I could have been hurt or killed?"

"I care! Or I would. But I don't think it happened the way you said."

"So, now I'm a liar? You've known me for years!"

"You lied about Elias feeding on you," Miranda said.

"You're right. I didn't tell you, so it was a lie of omission. But I honestly didn't want to upset you. It was wrong of me, but my intentions were good ones."

"Sure, they were." Miranda sounded petulant.

Addie was now good and pissed off. "Miranda, you know what? I am sick of your shit. Stellan is dangerous, and I am worried about you. But I will not let you make me feel shitty anymore. I was the best friend I knew how to be to you. I did my best. Perhaps not telling you was somewhat self-serving, but it is true I didn't want to hurt you."

"Maybe he's awful at it, and you didn't want to admit that!"

"Oh, Miranda, you fucking wish," Addie snapped. "Let me tell you something, it is amazing! Absolutely fucking amazing! I am sorry Stellan doesn't want to feed on you, but don't give me shit because Elias does and does it very well!"

Elias nearly choked on his coffee at Addie's comments. Her temper had been well and truly engaged.

"If you were any kind of friend to me—" Miranda began.

"Oh? I'm sorry. Is trying to warn you about your psychotic boyfriend not being a friend to you then?" She paused a moment, debating this next statement. "You never accepted the person I am. You want to change me, which makes you as bad as my ex." Addie let out a frustrated growl. "You know what, Miranda? If you need me, if you need help, I will help you. Otherwise, I think we're done here." Addie hung up and then let out a rapid-fire stream of Spanish. He assumed she was swearing.

When she wound down, he brought her some coffee. "I am both turned on and a little afraid of you right now," he said.

"I want to say I shouldn't have said all of that," she took a sip of coffee, "But it felt good."

"Standing up for yourself can feel good."

"Yes! I have been on mute for so long, just letting things happen, and now I know I have my mom's temper." She smiled. "I am delighted!"

He hugged her to him. "You were great, little bird. Show me the picture you took."

"Oh, that's right!" Addie showed it to him.

"Yeah, her pupils are huge. She's high. But I am betting she doesn't know it."

"Has Stellan done this kind of thing before?"

"Years ago, but we thought he had stopped or I would have mentioned it to you. He got into a lot of trouble for it."

"What do you think he's given her?"

"No idea. But it probably came from Tamir. I will see if Dregs can see him with me later tonight. Maybe you and Clara can hang out while we're doing that."

"That would be nice."

"Good. I figured I would take you to get some stuff, and if she's free, we can grab her on the way back."

"Works for me. I'll text her." Addie shot Clara a quick text and got an immediate reply. "She's in.'

"Great. Let me shower and get dressed."

"How about I shower with you?"

Elias grinned wolfishly and picked Addie up. "Perfect! Will there be shower sex?"

"I was thinking of a shower blowjob," laughed Addie as he stalked towards the bathroom.

"God, I may never let you leave!"

Chapter 28

Addie and Elias climbed the stairs to her floor when Mrs. Costello stepped out of her apartment. As soon as Addie reached the landing, the old woman pulled her into a tight hug.

"Thank goodness you're okay," she said shakily. "I have been so worried."

Addie's arms came around her neighbor, and she hugged back gently. "I am so sorry I worried you. I should have let you know where I was."

"It's just—" She pulled back and scanned Addie's face to make sure she was truly fine, "—when the men broke into your apartment, I thought for sure something was wrong."

"Men?" asked Elias.

"Is this your doing, young man?" asked Mrs. Costello.

Elias wanted to smile at being referred to as a young man. The old lady knew what he was, after all. "I'm afraid it is."

"If this lovely woman gets hurt because of you ..."

"Mrs. Costello, I'm fine. Honestly."

"Call me Marina, dear."

"Marina, I love him."

That brought Marina up short. She peered at Elias. "And you?" she asked with a snap.

Elias smiled. "And I love her. But I may also be a little in love with you right now."

"Naturally, but please stop flirting with me." She smiled at him.

"Apologies, ma'am." He smiled back. "But can you tell me about the men?"

"Yes, they came rolling in late last night. They picked the lock quietly—I think they were hoping you were there—and then trashed the place. I stayed in my apartment. But once they left, I rescued some items in case they came back—photos, your guitar, a few books."

Addie was upset. This was *her* personal space. She nodded at Mrs. Costello and opened her apartment door, gasping at the mess. "Oh no! Oh, look what they've done to my place!"

She turned and pressed her face to Elias's chest. His arms came around her. "I'm so sorry, little bird. We'll get it cleaned up; I promise."

"I know," her voice was muffled, "But they invaded my personal space! They touched my things!" Addie was upset, but also furious at the invasion."

"But," put in Marina, "They didn't get you. And it was you they were looking for. They destroyed the place out of anger at not finding you."

Addie pulled her head back. "Apparently, trying to kill me once wasn't good enough for Stellan."

"What? They tried before, and what did you do about it?" Marina demanded of Elias.

"I destroyed the ones who touched her."

"Good! Adelaide, sweetheart. They are just things. And you can get this all cleaned up, and Elias will kill the others. It will be fine." Marina was rubbing Addie's back, trying to comfort her.

Hearing her elderly neighbor discuss killing in such a casual way gave Addie the giggles. "Thank you, you're right." She looked at Marina. "I am going to be staying with Elias for some time. Until this is cleared up."

"Smart. Give me your phone number. I can call if something happens or someone else shows up."

While they were doing that, Elias sent a couple of texts. "Mrs. Costello, I will have a clean-up crew here tomorrow, humans. I am letting you know, so you don't worry."

"Did you want to ask me first, before discussing it with my neighbor?" Addie huffed at him. "It is *my* apartment after all."

"This is my fault. I am going to fix it."

"But it's not your apartment, Elias!"

Marina looked at the two squaring off. "I am going back inside now. I am glad you're fine. Don't fight too hard, and come get your stuff before you leave." With that, she disappeared into her apartment.

Addie stomped into her apartment. Elias followed, shutting the door behind him. "But you are my woman, and I take care of what's mine."

"Oh, for fuck's sake! Are you going to caveman style carry me home next? Your woman! Like I'm a piece of furniture or something."

"No, Adelaide, you're the most important fucking person, besides Darian, in the world to me."

"That does not give you the right to decide what is best for me and my apartment. I worked too hard to get here to let another man make my decisions."

"What the fuck was I supposed to do?" he growled at her.

"Ask me! *Hey Addie, I have some people that can do the clean-up. Would you like me to do that? Or do you want to take care of it?'* It's simple."

"I'm not ... I'm not used to asking."

"Then get used to it. I've let you get away with a lot, and I know that. But not anymore."

"Why not?"

"We love each other. We need to be partners for this to work. I've already had a father and a shitty husband. Do not be my third bad decision."

"I am nothing like either of those men. I was doing this ...." he stopped suddenly as her words hit him. He was taking over, making decisions for her. Like her father and Dan had done. It didn't matter if it was for a different reason. It didn't matter if it was because he loved her or felt guilty or wanted to help. It amounted to the same thing—not taking her feelings into account. He should have asked her first, not just taken over.

She was staring at him, waiting for him to finish what he was saying. He ran his hands through his hair. "Fuck," he said. "I'm sorry, Addie. You're right. I'm no better than they are if I try to take your autonomy away. I apologize. Would you like me to cancel them?"

She looked at him and smiled. "No, thank you. I am happy to have your help. But you need to ask me when it concerns my own life and space. It's important to me." She put her arms around him. "Can I pay them?"

"I have them on retainer. But you and I can work something out in that regard if you insist."

"Sounds good," she said. She knew though, he'd never take her money, so she'd need to find another way to even things out.

She walked around the living room and kitchen and tried not to cry. They destroyed all her plants and ripped open cushions. They destroyed all the cheap art on her walls, and the keyboard was in pieces all over the living room. "I don't know how or why my guitar is intact, but I'm grateful."

She walked into the bedroom and wailed. Elias hurried to her. "Oh, my God," he said. The bed was on its side, the frame smashed, along with the headboard. All the bedding and pillows were destroyed, along with her dressing table. She was holding a ripped photo of her parents in one hand. In her other, she was clutching something, but he couldn't see what it was.

"Addie?"

She held it out to him. It was a very old rosary, now in pieces. "It belonged to my grandmother, then my mother. Now it's mine. I am not religious, but it's not the point!" She sobbed. He scooped her up and sat on the floor with her.

"Please don't cry, little bird. Please don't."

"Haven't people taken enough of my mother away from me? She died. Dan sold her piano and now her rosary and ripped photos. When will it be enough?"

"It's enough now. No one is going to take anything more from you." He rocked her while she cried. "I promise. I will make all of them pay."

A little later, there was a light tread on the stairs and a soft knock. "Addie? Elias?" It was Clara.

"Come in, Clara," he called. "We're in the bedroom."

The door opened, and there was an intake of breath. "What the actual fuck? I'll kill that fucker myself." Clara appeared in the doorway to the bedroom. "Killing is too good for him," she said, scanning the room.

Addie looked up, her eyes red, and Clara's heart lurched at the sight. "Hey, Clara. Like what I've done with the place?"

Clara squatted and ran a hand over her friend's hair. "Looks great," she said softly. "I know you were going to pick me up, but I thought I'd come by and see if I could help you pack."

"We're having it taken care of tomorrow. But I am glad you're here to help."

"If I have stuff left to pack," she said sadly.

"If you don't, we'll online shop and you will drink wine while Elias and Dregs go scare Tamir. It will be fun." Clara took Addie's hand and pulled gently. "Come on. Up! Let's go."

Addie stood and went into her closet. "Well, I still have some clothes, and my suitcase is fine."

"See? Bright side!" Clara clapped her hands.

"Do you know someone who can fix jewelry?" Addie asked. "My mom's rosary was broken."

"Let me see." Addie handed her the broken rosary. "Okay, this should be easy to fix. I can do it. I have the tools. We need to stop at my place so I can grab them."

"You can fix it?" Addie sounded so hopeful that Elias was nearly undone by it.

"Yup. I took up simple jewelry repair during rehab. Helped me focus. I've made some simple pieces, but I honestly prefer fixing to making."

Elias looked at the two women. "I will be in the other room. I will leave you to it."

Addie looked after him. "Okay, let's see what I have left."

Clara hugged Addie. "I know it's hard to see your stuff like this. But it will be okay. And Elias will kill Stellan, and we'll even try and help Miranda."

"Jesus, what did I do to deserve you?"

"You are very lucky. So am I, for that matter. Let's do this!"

CHAPTER 29

Dregs peeled the girl's hand off his bicep and gently pushed her off in another direction. It didn't matter where, just away from him. She gave him a sour look and staggered away. "This place is insane. And I do not like it."

"It wasn't like this when the Elders visited. I have to wonder if that was staged. Or if it's degenerated in such a short time?"

"Tamir is very good at smoke and mirrors. As you well know. Though maybe you've forgotten. Or just didn't care."

"True. And I've been letting a lot slide. He's been providing us with strong financials, he hasn't had any citations or run-ins with the police, and I didn't think there was any need to be in his business." For all the good he had tried to do over the years, the shame had gotten to him and he'd shut down. He'd missed a lot, and this was the price to be paid.

"You were wrong, my friend." Dregs, like Darian, was always honest with Elias. It was one of the reasons he liked the vampire. He always called Elias on his shit.

"I was," said Elias. "Tamir is not the main problem right now, but he is a problem. Gen has known something was wrong for a while. She mentioned it the other night."

"That was the first you'd heard of it?" Dregs seemed surprised by this.

Elias shrugged. "Yes. She may have been waiting to use the information when it would serve her best."

"That sounds like her."

"It does. But he could put all of us at risk."

"You need to examine his books. The real ones, not the fake ones he's been showing you all," Dregs said. Elias looked at him, a question in his eyes. Dregs sighed. "Fine, I'll do it."

"It's not my fault you have an exceptionally good head for numbers." Elias looked across the floor. "Ah, here comes Tamir now."

"Elias! Dregs! Welcome to my little piece of sin!"

"Jesus," muttered Dregs under his breath. "He's a lot, as the kids say."

Elias let out a low chuckle. "Tamir, good evening. Thank you for seeing us on such short notice."

"Of course! Let's go back to my office. Once we handle our business, you should sample the delights." Tamir's tone from the other night seemed to be a thing of the past. It put Elias on alert. Something was very wrong here.

Dregs shuddered as Elias answered for them. "Unfortunately, we have other business this evening." Even if Elias wanted to stay—which he didn't—Addie would have his balls if he stayed to party.

"Ah, such a shame. Though, I expect your little human is the sweetest berry there is." Tamir pushed his office door open and ushered the other vamps inside.

"Tamir, if you ever talk about Adelaide like that again, I will use your head for target practice." Elias's voice was deceptively mild.

"My apologies, Elias. I fear I may be a little giddy this evening."

High as a kite, thought Dregs. He must have been drinking from a fair number of drugged-out humans to have said something so stupid.

"Don't do it again." Tamir and Elias sat while Dregs made his way over to the window and leaned on the sill. He was positioned behind Tamir.

"What can I do for you two this evening?" Tamir asked as there was a knock on the door. "So busy this evening. Come in!" he called.

A human woman opened the door and came in as if nothing was going on in there. She was wearing a very small dress and stiletto heels she wobbled on. Dregs made a small gesture to Elias, who looked at the woman's eyes. Her pupils looked like Miranda's had. "Tamir! You left. Why did you leave me?"

"My dear, I have business. I'll be out soon."

The woman finally seemed to realize there were other people in the room. "Oh? Do they want to join our party?"

Elias sighed. "No, we do not." He gently guided the woman back to the door. "Go play somewhere else, dear."

"You're cute. You sure?"

Elias closed the door on her and locked it. "What is she on?" Elias asked.

Tamir shrugged. "Who can say?"

"You, Tamir. You can say. The way her pupils are enlarged is one thing. The mental synapses seem to be something else."

"Mental synapses?"

"Tamir," put in Dregs, "We've had a look around. The humans on this drug do not seem to be working on the plane that we like to call reality."

"And they don't seem to realize they aren't putting two and two together. Miranda is a prime example."

"Stellan's Miranda?"

"Yes. Now answer me!"

"Why is it that anything with drugs is blamed on me?" The two men said nothing. "Fine. It is me. It's a concoction of my own."

"What's in it?"

"It's part Miasma, cut with heroin and a few other things." Miasma was a vamp drug humans took to help vamps get high when they fed.

"Heroin is bad enough," said Dregs. "What other things are in it?"

"Nothing!"

"Tamir, you're lying and I am losing patience. Now, tell me!" Elias raised his voice just enough to raise the hairs on the back of Dregs' neck.

"Hell Fire," Tamir admitted. "Not a lot of it, just a little."

"What the fuck, Tamir! Hell Fire is outlawed in vamp society. It was all destroyed. Where did you get it?"

"He made it," said Dregs, holding up some papers. "And you're using more than just a little of it."

"Those are mine!"

"Tamir," Dregs said, trying to hold onto his temper. "You have made a drug that has been outlawed for years. It's not only highly addictive, but it also kills humans!"

"Not always!"

"More often not." Clara's face flashed through Dregs' mind. A drug like this could undo all the work she'd done to get clean. Worse, it could kill her. The thought made his blood run cold.

"Whose idea was this?" Elias bit out. "Because I don't think it was yours. You're not quite that stupid."

"Stellan's. It was his idea. He came to me with it and the recipe. He knew I needed the influx of cash."

"You're selling it?" Elias was horrified.

"No, I am selling the new drug. Not Hell Fire. I swear it!"

"Stellan could be, though," Dregs replied. "I bet you didn't think of that."

"I ... no ... he wouldn't!"

"He's giving Miranda your new drug without her knowledge, I suspect. Who's in charge of the supply chain for this?"

"He is," Tamir rubbed his hands over his face, sober now. "Elias, it's such an amazing high. If you would try it, you'd know."

"You're lucky I don't kill you for that comment alone."

"What are you going to do?" Tamir looked frightened.

"I'm closing you down as of right now. No more parties, no more drugs. You will hand over your books—your real books —to me by tomorrow night. Your personal little shipping business stops as of now as well. No contact with Stellan. You go dark."

"If I don't do what you say?"

"I will contact the Elder Assembly and report you for the creation and distribution of Hell Fire and this new drug."

"We call it Hell Raiser," said Tamir.

"Of course, you do." Dregs sounded disgusted.

"Tamir, the Assembly won't just call for your removal—they will call for your death."

Tamir's eyes widened. Maybe the vamp was indeed that stupid.

"You are shut down. My people will arrive shortly to make sure nothing goes wrong." He'd leave Dregs here, but he had other business to deal with, and he wanted the other vamp with him. "For now, you will remain on the Assembly, but do not test me further."

Tamir nodded. "It will be done." Tamir paused. "Stellan is using your human's ex-husband. I don't know what he's doing exactly, but Daniel has been here with him several times."

Elias nodded. "Thank you," he said. Daniel was on his list for this evening, and it was good his instincts were correct. "We're going to clean this up, Tamir. It's at an end."

Tamir nodded. "I don't want to die. I will do what you say." But the words rang hollow, and Elias couldn't bring himself to believe the other vampire. Time would tell.

It was another hour before Elias and Dregs were able to get away. Elias was satisfied Tamir would behave in the short term. It wouldn't last, so time was of the essence.

"Where to next?" Dregs asked.

"Addie's ex, Daniel. We're going to pay him a visit." Elias bared his fangs.

"Are we going to kill him?"

"No, probably not. We're going to frighten him, though."

"How much?"

"Oh, quite a lot. I am going to enjoy this."

Chapter 30

Elias pounded on Daniel's front door. The asshole was home. His car was in the driveway, and his lights were on. There was a second car in the driveway, so it looked like he had company.

"Do you think you can pound on that door any harder?" asked Dregs, amusement in his voice.

"I do, yes." To prove his point, he did just that, coming short of splintering the whole thing. "Daniel! Open the fucking door! I know you're in there."

There was shuffling, a crash, and then the door opened. "What do you want?" hissed Daniel.

Elias poked a finger into Daniel's chest and pushed. Daniel stumbled backward, allowing Elias and Dregs to enter the house.

"Danny, is that the food?" A young blonde woman poked her head out of the living room. "Oh! Are you delivering the food?" She was wearing a tight, short red dress, barefoot.

Elias sighed and walked into the living room. He picked up her shoes and her jacket and handed them to her. "Time for you to go, miss." He gently guided her towards the front door. "Put your shoes on now."

"Danny?" she asked, entirely confused. Dan, for his part, stood there, staring at Elias with horror and confusion written all over his face.

"*Danny* has business to do. Shoes on, miss." Elias's tone brooked no argument. The woman put her shoes on and held her jacket out to Elias. He let out a sigh and held it for her as she slipped into it.

"I don't understand, though. Danny and I had a date tonight. Danny, what is going on?" Her tone had turned a little whiny. Dregs couldn't blame her.

Still, Dan said nothing. Elias handed the woman over to Dregs. Dregs led her to the door and opened it. There was a man on the other side of it with a food bag. "Well," said Dregs. "What timing. I'll take that." He grabbed the food bag. "Now, miss, be sure to get home safely." He ushered her out and shut the door on both her protests and the delivery person's stammered thank you. Dregs set the food bag on the floor.

Daniel had finally found his voice. "What the fuck do you two think you're doing? Barging in here and interrupting my date! Did Addie put you up to this?"

Elias bared his fangs and hissed at Dan. The man cowered. "Dregs, can you please bring him? I do not trust myself to touch him right now."

"Don't you fucking touch ..." Dan bit off the rest of his sentence as Dregs grabbed him by the neck and pushed him into the living room.

"Sit!" Elias ordered the man.

"I will not!" Dan exclaimed as Dregs pushed the man into a chair.

"Daniel," Elias began. "I don't like you, solely based on your treatment of Adelaide. It would not take much provocation for me to kill you. I will assume Stellan has apprised you of my reputation and what happened the other night?"

Daniel said nothing. "Answer him," said Dregs, holding one long fingernail to the man's neck and pressing none too gently.

"Yes," it came out a squeak, and Daniel tried again. "Yes, he did." His voice came out still wobbly but a bit steadier.

"Did he tell you he had two vampires threaten your ex-wife? How does that make you feel? I know she left you." The dig was petty, but Elias couldn't help himself. No, he could have. He just didn't want to. "But you did care about each other once."

"She said *she* left *me*?" Dan sounded affronted.

"She did. You aren't going to try and convince me differently, are you? Do not insult her or me."

Dan's face turned red, but he left it alone. "Can you tell him to back off?" He gestured to Dregs.

"No, I can't. The thing is, Adelaide could have been badly hurt. If she had been, you'd be dead by now." Elias stalked over to stand in front of Dan. "I would have assumed you had something to do with this whole thing. It would not have mattered if I was right or wrong. I would just need to vent my rage, and it's not like you'd be the first human I've killed."

"You can't threaten me!"

"Yes, I can." Elias smiled, but it was a cruel smile. "You'd never see me coming. I wouldn't even bother to feed from you." Dregs stepped back, and Elias grabbed Dan by the neck and lifted him from the chair. "I'd just rip your head off."

Dan grabbed onto Elias's hands. "Put me down!" he gasped.

Elias squeezed harder. "Daniel, do you want to die?" Dan shook his head or tried to.

"Then I suggest you tell Elias what he wants to know about Stellan," put in Dregs.

"If I put you down, will you?" Elias asked in a growl.

Dan nodded, and Elias dropped him into the chair. "I should call the cops!" Dan's voice was a little hoarse.

Elias shrugged. "Go ahead. It won't help you. I have cops on my payroll. No charge will ever stick to me. Now, are you ready to answer my questions? Or do you need me to make my point again? Dregs wouldn't mind drawing your blood."

Dan didn't say anything but glowered at Elias.

"Good. Now, what do you know about the new drug Stellan and Tamir are making?"

"Hell Raiser, you mean?" Elias nodded. "Did Addie tell you what I do for a living?"

"She said you're a money guy," Elias replied.

Dan nodded. "I am. But I also do ... well, other things."

"What other things?" This was from Dregs.

"I find things for people."

"I take it that it's not entirely legal?"

"No, Elias, it's not legal in any sense of the word. I always thought Addie knew, and that's why she left."

"She didn't know, and she left you because she was unhappy with you." Elias experienced a certain glee telling Dan this. "Now, continue."

"I didn't realize Stellan was a vampire when he came to me. I didn't even know about them. He opened my eyes to the fact there was more going on than I could ever imagine." Dan rubbed his face. "He told me he was looking for a recipe for a drug, called Hell Fire. He had heard I was good at finding things."

"And he offered you a lot of money to help him find it?" Dregs crossed his arms.

"Not just money."

"Ah, he told you he'd make you a vampire." Elias was not surprised by this.

Dan nodded. "Yes. He said as soon as he got rid of you, he'd make me a vampire. He'd put me on your Assembly, and he told me ..."

"What else did he tell you?" asked Elias in a deceptively mild voice.

"He told me he'd make sure I got Addie back. That he'd make sure she became much more, well, biddable, I guess."

"Oh shit," murmured Dregs.

Elias blinked a few times; his eyes blackened, and his hands fisted at his sides. He was standing stock-still, trying to get himself under control. "You do realize he was planning on keeping her drugged and under his control, not yours. For you, yes. But in the end, she'd belong to him." His voice was a low growl.

"I ... didn't think ..."

"No, you didn't. Hell Raiser does something to the mental synapses. Things don't connect. But now it seems like it makes them suggestible as well." Such a powerful drug also had to be made with vampire blood. There was no other way it could be this strong.

"This has Stellan written all over it," Dregs said. "Do you think Tamir knew?"

"It's possible," replied Elias. "Where can I find the vampire that had the Hell Fire recipe?"

"Dead. Stellan had him killed."

"And that was okay with you?" Dregs asked. "Don't humans usually denounce murder?"

"He said if I were going to be one of you, I would have to play by a different set of rules."

Elias managed to calm down. "Daniel, it's possible Stellan would have made you a vampire, but it's more likely he would have killed you." Elias gave him a hard look. "He still might."

"What? Why?" Dan started to rise, but Dregs pushed him back down.

"You, my friend, know where the bodies are buried."

"Oh, my God!"

"Not even close, Danny, my boy. I am going to handle Stellan. And if I find out you are more involved than you've let on, I will kill you."

"I'm not. I swear I am not."

"We'll see, but I will have people watching you. So, I suggest you behave." Dan nodded. "You may want to think about leaving town for a bit. That's up to you."

"I have a cabin on a lake. Maybe I'll go there." Dan, for his part, looked absolutely terrified right now. Elias wished he could take a picture to enjoy it at his leisure.

"One more thing," Elias walked over to Dan's chair and put his hands on the arms, leaning into the man's face. "Since you're the find it guy, you're going to find something for me. For free. Your life, you waste of humanity, depends on it."

Back in the car, Elias called Gen and made sure there were eyes on Dan constantly. A cabin at the lake was no match for Gen's spies. "Thanks, Gen. Let me know if he steps out of line." He listened for a moment. "Great, thank you." He ended the call.

"You enjoyed that quite a bit, didn't you?" asked Dregs.

"I did." Elias texted Addie quickly, telling her he was on his way home. "The thought of Addie being fed that drug makes my blood run cold."

"I know," said Dregs quietly. "Stellan would likely do the same thing to Clara." Knowing her history, she might not survive that.

"Christ, you're right. The drug must contain vampire blood. Powerful vampire blood."

"Agreed. Psychotropic drugs aren't new, but to be this potent? There has to be vamp blood involved."

"We need to wrap this up quickly. But I am afraid getting the drug off the street completely will be difficult and time-consuming." But do it, he would.

"I'll stay until that's done." Dregs's voice was calm but firm. "I'll not only examine Tamir's finances, but I will also take charge of overseeing shipping operations. No more parties. No more nonsense. And I will see if I can figure out who's blood they've been using."

"I can't ask that of you," said Elias.

"I am offering my services to you as a friend. But Elias, if you're going to run this city, run it correctly from now on. You need to do more than pay it lip service."

Elias nodded. "You're right. I see where my neglect has gotten us." He looked at Dregs. "Does any of this have to do with Clara?"

"You know her past?"

"I do."

"I want this drug gone. I want it gone for her and Addie, for everyone who could be hurt by it."

"So, it's not personal then? You aren't interested in her?"

"No! And fuck off!"

Elias laughed. "Fine, have it your way." Dregs was very interested in Clara, even if he didn't want to admit it. It's been a very interesting night, thought Elias. Very interesting, indeed

CHAPTER 31

Elias heard laughter floating out the apartment door and smiled at the sound. Addie and Clara were curled on the couch, a bowl of popcorn between them. Addie had wine, but Clara was drinking water.

"Elias!" Addie jumped up to kiss him. "I am glad you're back!"

Clara gave him a look. "You haven't shown her the videos yet. I asked."

"With everything going on, I forgot. I promise I will, though."

Addie rolled her eyes. "How did it go? Was it a shit show?"

"It was." Elias rested his head on top of Addie's as he wrapped his arms around her. "You're feeling better then?"

"I am. I'm still mad and upset about it. But it's done. Clara has been good company."

"I'm glad," he said into her hair. "I don't like seeing you so upset."

Addie smiled at him. "Do you and Dregs want a drink? You can tell us what happened." Addie smiled at Elias. "Hey, Dregs, have a seat."

"Thank you, I will." He moved the popcorn to a nearby table and sat next to Clara. She rolled her eyes at him. "What have I told you about that attitude, *mi pequeña pelirroja?*" he whispered to her as Addie and Elias got drinks.

Clara snorted. "Don't poke the little redhead," came the retort, "She bites."

"Oh, I hope so." Dregs's voice was a low growl, and Clara reddened, despite herself.

She was saved from responding as Elias and Addie came back over. Addie set a whiskey in front of Dregs. "*Gracias*, Adelaide."

"*De nada,*" she responded. She sat next to Elias on the loveseat.

Clara watched as Elias draped an arm around Addie's shoulders and pulled her closer to him. Addie dropped a hand on Elias's leg and squeezed. Clara sighed quietly.

Dregs looked over at her and saw the look in her eyes. *Longing.* That's what longing looked like. Clara, for all her talk, was lonely.

Something in Dregs shifted. He had kissed her the other night when he'd driven her home. It had been a whim. He walked her to her door, and when he'd looked at her to say goodnight, she reached out and put her hand on his chest as she looked at him. Before re-thinking what was probably a bad decision, he lowered his head and grazed her lips lightly. She'd sighed. It was the same sigh she had just made, he realized with a start. Was she thinking about their kiss?

He needed to finish here and get the fuck out of town. This was not good. He mentally shook himself and tuned into Elias telling the ladies what had happened that night.

"Did Dan pee himself?" asked Addie when Elias got to that part.

"Did he ... what?" asked Elias, totally taken off guard by the question.

"Pee himself. This one time, we went out to dinner, and we got mugged on the way back to the car—this big scary dude. At first, Dan tried to act tough, but the guy was pretty big compared to him. He got so scared, he peed himself." Addie laughed, remembering it. "I know getting mugged is awful, but it was so hard not to laugh."

"Did the mugger hurt you?" asked Elias.

"No, *Mi amor*, he did not. He took our wallets, wedding rings and Dan's watch, then left quickly. I suspect he too wanted to laugh."

"What happened after that?" asked Clara.

"We called the police. They did laugh. It was very obvious."

"Your ex-husband is an idiot," said Dregs.

"Yes, he is. So, did he?"

"No, he didn't. At least not while we were there."

"Damn! What next?"

"I arranged to have Dan watched. But Gen called a few moments ago, and Stellan has disappeared."

"But he didn't take Miranda with him?"

"Well, he may have. She's not been to work."

"But if she disappeared with him, why would he be okay with her answering my call?"

"My guess is that this happened after you spoke to her. He was likely still resting when you two spoke. He's a late riser compared to Dregs or myself."

"Gen has people looking for him, as does Elias. We'll find him sooner or later," said Dregs. "We're also watching Tamir."

"He may lead you right to Stellan," Clara put in. "That would be handy."

"It would be, but I am not counting on it being that easy." Dregs stood. "It never is. I think it's time to head home. Clara, I can drive you home."

"I can get an Uber. Or a cab."

"I am sure you could, but that isn't necessary. I'll drive you."

"Dregs, you don't get to make decisions for me."

He raised an eyebrow at her. "No, but there is a vampire out there who knows you and didn't get what he wanted from you last time you saw him. I know you can take care of yourself. But you are no match for a vampire. Even if it is Stellan."

Elias and Addie watched in silence, fascinated by the exchange. Clara looked over at them and blew out a breath. Dregs was right, though she hated to admit it to herself. She was being difficult. But that kiss the other night had been unexpected, and she didn't know if she wanted a repeat or not. No, she did know, and that was the problem.

"Fine," she said through gritted teeth. "You make good points."

Addie stood and hugged Clara. "And I'll worry less."

Clara hugged her friend back. "Then I definitely can't say no."

Elias also stood and turned to Dregs. "Let's talk tomorrow evening. We need to find Stellan soon."

"What about the club?" asked Addie.

"Closed until this is settled. I don't want a repeat of the other night. I don't want anyone else getting hurt. Everyone still gets paid, though."

Addie nodded. "That makes sense. But I'll miss it."

"It won't be too long, I don't think," said Dregs. "Stellan is too arrogant to stay hidden for long." With that, he and Clara took their leave.

Elias wrapped his arms around Addie. "Now, woman, give your man a proper kiss."

"Oh, 'my man,' is it?" Addie nuzzled his neck, inhaling his scent. "I missed you this evening."

"But you had a nice time with Clara?"

"I did. I feel guilty for saying this, but she's much easier to be with than Miranda." Addie looked at him. "Am I an awful person?"

Elias smiled at her. "No, you're not. Miranda is a difficult person, and she's maybe not the friend she should be."

"Maybe," Addie replied. She would put it aside for now. "Show me those videos!"

Elias laughed and took out his phone. "I had Clara do this to show you what we see when you're performing."

Addie watched the videos quietly. Then watched them again, assessing her performance. "I always thought my mom commanded a stage when she performed and that I'd never be like that. And I think when I was with my dad's band, I wasn't. But even I can see it here." She laughed. "I'm good!"

"It's because you're doing what you love. And you want the audience to love it too. And we do."

"Thank you for showing me these. It makes a difference." She smiled at him. "Didn't you say something about a kiss?"

"I did." He lowered his mouth to hers, teasing her lips with his tongue. His hands made their way to her waist as he lifted her. She wrapped her legs around his waist and her arms around his neck. "Open for me, little bird." He nipped her bottom lip lightly.

She opened her mouth, and his tongue swept in, meeting her own in a dance. "You taste good," she said. "Like whiskey, and I don't even know what else. I can't get enough of you."

"I'll never get enough of you," he said gruffly as he carried her to the bedroom."

He set her on the floor in front of the bed. He backed up slightly until he was sitting on the bed. "Take off your clothes, Adelaide."

His tone made her weak-kneed but also powerful. "Yes, Elias," she said, pulling her top off slowly. She undid her jeans and shimmied out of them; grateful she had taken her shoes off earlier in the evening. She then pulled her bra and underwear off, standing naked before him.

He stared at her with glittering eyes. "Your nipples are already hard. Touch them for me."

She licked her lips and did what he asked. "Like this?"

He nodded. "*Schönn,*" he replied, using the German word for 'beautiful.' He didn't use German often. But it fit.

Addie started to rub her breasts, while he watched her. He stood and removed her hands. He took her mouth in a hard kiss while rubbing her breasts and pinching her nipples. She moaned against his mouth. "Does that feel good? Does it feel good when I pinch them?"

"Yes, Elias," Addie moaned.

"Good. I like doing it." He pinched them a little harder, and she cried out. "Do you want me to stop, little bird?"

She shook her head. "No. No, I don't want you to stop. More."

He raked his nails across them, and she grabbed onto him to steady herself. He laughed softly. "How do you want me to fuck you tonight?"

"From behind," came the prompt reply. "I've been thinking about that all day." She bit her lip. "Also ..." she stopped.

"Also, what?" he asked.

"I want to try something if it's okay."

He looked surprised. "What did you want to try?"

"I'd like you to tie my hands behind my back."

Elias's hard cock twitched. He cleared his throat. "Really? You want that?"

"Yes. And I have a new safe word: *watermelon.*"

He blinked rapidly several times. "You are a constant source of surprise and delight."

CHAPTER 32

Addie smiled. "I admit I spent some time doing research today." Her search history would never be the same.

"Is that so? And this piqued your interest?"

"Yes! The internet was very forthcoming with both information and photos. The photos, I admit, were how I decided what I wanted tonight."

"Then you've read about aftercare?" She nodded. "I've been doing what I thought you might want, but I think you should now tell me what you want and need." He should have done this before now, but he was going to fix his mistake.

"I do like what you've been doing, to be honest. I'll want to continue to cuddle. Tonight, I may be quieter because this is new, and I am thinking more intense, but I will need to see, honestly. I also do like it when we shower together afterward." She gave him a shy look. "What will you need?"

"No one has ever asked me that before." But why would they have? He wasn't always concerned with what his partners wanted or needed. He had a lot to get right this time. "I will want to hold you, and I will need reassurance you're okay and enjoyed it."

"Easy enough."

He walked over to a dresser, opened it, and pulled out a long black scarf. "On the bed, Adelaide. Face down, ass up."

"Yes, Elias." She got on the bed exactly as he instructed. When he turned back to her, he groaned. "Christ, woman, you may kill me yet."

He quickly took his clothes off and went over to her. "You remember your safe word?" He made sure she had a pillow under her head and shifted her lower half to try and make her as comfortable as possible.

"Watermelon."

"Use it if you need to," he said. "I'm serious."

"I promise."

"Good. Put your hands behind your back." She moved her hands to sit on her lower back. He took her hands gently and wrapped the scarf around her wrists before securing the knots. "I don't have any rope as I haven't done this in years, and I never brought anyone here regardless. The scarf will have to do. How does that feel?"

"It feels fine. Not too tight, but just tight enough." Her research had helped her determine her comfort level should be. And this felt good. This was a position she'd always liked. And there was something about being at Elias's mercy that she found exciting. It's how she had felt that night at her apartment when he'd blindfolded her and tied her to the bed.

"Excellent." He stroked a hand over her hair and down her back. She shivered. "Do you know how unbelievably sexy I find you right now? I'm so hard looking at you this way. That gorgeous ass in the air—your hands tied. I can't wait to fuck you—to make you scream my name as you come."

She wiggled, and he laughed, slapping her ass. "No wiggling, Adelaide." His hand slid to her ass and squeezed. His fingers teased the rosebud there, and she moaned.

"Please, Elias. Please."

"Please what, little bird?" Her head was turned to the side, and he leaned down, kissing her quickly.

"I want you inside me," she said tightly.

"I will be soon." He stood and climbed onto the bed behind her. He pressed against her, his cock against her ass. He leaned over her and dropped kisses on her back. His hands kneaded her breasts. "You're mine, Adelaide. Mine. And now I get to do what I want with you. You are at my mercy." His fingers sought her sex. She was wet, ready for him. He played with her clit, and she ground against him.

He pinched a nipple hard. "Be still," he said.

"I can't help it," she replied. "It all feels so good." It was a lot of sensation, but she was fine with it. More than fine. She closed her eyes to concentrate more on how it all felt.

"I know, little bird. But be still while I touch you. Your pussy is so wet. I did that to you, never forget that." He ground himself into her as his fingers entered her, pumping, and his thumb pressed against her clit. He ground his cock against her, and soon, she was panting. "That's it, Adelaide, that's it." He continued to pump her and pressed harder on her clit as she came apart on his hand. He gave her a few moments to settle herself after her orgasm.

"You're such a good girl, aren't you?" he crooned. "Are you ready for me? Are you ready for my cock?"

"Yes, Elias. Now, please."

He smiled to himself at her bossy tone. He grasped her tied wrists with one hand, the other on her hip, as he slammed himself into her. She screamed his name as he started thrusting hard into her. "Is this what you wanted, little bird?"

Addie couldn't answer. It was so much. How he felt inside her—how he was pulling on her wrists—his hand on her hip. The sensations made her practically dizzy, but she loved every minute.

"Are you going to come on my cock like a good girl, Adelaide?" He thrust into her harder and faster while she moaned and cried out. "Come on, baby, show me what a good girl you are, and come for me."

Addie lifted her ass higher, eliciting a groan from Elias as he thrust into her. She was getting so close again. "Elias ... Elias ..." she choked out. "God, please." He took her higher, faster, and she soon came again.

But it didn't stop. He scooped an arm around her waist and pulled her up. He kept one hand around her middle and grabbed her hair with the other as he continued the vigorous pounding. She started grinding against him again, wanting to help bring him to his orgasm. "Addie, God!" He slammed into her once, then twice, and on the third, he roared and found his release.

He let go of her waist and untied her hands. He rubbed her wrists gently before she lowered her arms. He massaged her shoulders and arms. "Adelaide?" he croaked. "How are you doing? Was that okay?"

Adelaide turned to face him, taking his face in her hand and kissing him gently. "I am fine," she said. "That was amazing."

His eyes searched hers. "Truly? You didn't mind being tied up?"

"Not at all. I rather liked it." She stroked his shoulders. "I did a lot of reading today, and I think I have an idea of other things I'd like to try."

"Oh? What were you reading about exactly?"

"A lot of things, but mostly about Shibari."

"Rope bondage?" She nodded and gave him that shy look again. "Huh. Well, I'm out of practice, but we can ease into that."

"Great!" She gave him a quick kiss. "So, I say we shower, then cuddle. I do need a little quiet time."

"Sounds perfect," he said. He got off the bed, picked her and carried her into the bathroom.

"I can walk," she laughed.

"You always say that. I *know* you can walk. I like carrying you."

"Hey," she said. "I love you."

"And I love you, little bird."

CHAPTER 33

Clara and Dregs didn't say much on the ride to Clara's apartment. He parked the car and shut off the engine. "We should talk about the other night," he said to her.

"No, we don't need to," Clara asserted. "I am sure it was a weak moment on your part."

He raised an eyebrow. "On my part? You reached out to touch me first if I recall."

Fuck, she had. "A weak moment on both of our parts then. It had been a long, stressful night."

"So, you're suggesting we move on and forget about it?"

"I am." She opened the car door. "You'll be moving on once this is over. Let's not start something we can't finish." She got out of the car.

"Fuck!" he snarled, getting out of the car. "Clara!"

"You don't need to walk me to my door."

"Yes, I do." He caught up with her. "What if I don't want to forget it?" he asked her. Why was he doing this? She was giving him the perfect out. All he had to do was take it. So, why wasn't he?

She didn't say anything, opening the door to her building and making her way to her apartment. She stayed quiet as he held out his hand for her key and walked through her place to make sure it was safe for her.

She was standing inside her front door when he returned. "Dregs, what would be the point of moving forward? You'll leave, and I'll be where I always am—alone."

Any argument he could have made died on his lip with those words. He stared at her as he handed her keys back. As he started to walk out, he heard the small, choked sob. "Of course," she said to herself. "Never really worth fighting for, am I?"

He pivoted so fast she had no time to react. He yanked her to him, his arms around her like steel bands. "Clara, you may be the *only* thing worth fighting for." With that, he kissed her, willing her lips to part, and groaning softly when they did. Her hands kneaded his shoulders as she kissed him back. She took everything he gave her and returned it. Kissing Clara was like having light poured on his soul. It filled the empty spaces inside of him. It was a dangerous and heady feeling for a man like him, who was used to the shadows—used to being solitary as he moved through the world.

He ended the kiss sooner than he would have liked to, but he had to get some space. He stepped back from her. "I am going to leave now, but it's not because I don't want you. It's because neither of us is ready for what will come next. But know this, since I've met you, I think about you constantly. It really pisses me off, but there you have it." His accent had gotten thicker, evidence of his current state of arousal.

"Same," she replied. "I don't want to want you."

"Then we understand each other. But Clara, it will happen. You'll beg me to make you come."

She shook her head. "Not if you beg me first."

"*Mocosa*," he replied. And with that, he was gone.

Clara shut the door, locked it, and then sagged against it. She had not been kissed like that since ... Well, ever. No one had ever kissed her like she might be the one thing that could save them.

She didn't like it.

No, she couldn't lie to herself. She liked it too much. He purposely pushed all her buttons, teased her, and frustrated her. And she gave it right back to him. She looked forward to it. She imagined him feeding from someplace more intimate.

She let out a frustrated yell and took her phone out. She wanted to talk to someone about this. Addie. She wanted to talk to Addie about it. She sent a text.

Do not answer this tonight but call me tomorrow. I have something I want to chat with you about. NOT AN EMERGENCY.

With that done, she made herself a cup of tea and crawled into bed. Maybe she'd watch a movie, something to take her mind off that kiss. But deep down, she didn't think that was likely.

Dregs stared at Clara's window until the light in the living room went out. He tried not to imagine her getting ready for bed and failed miserably.

What the fuck was wrong with him? He had a chance to walk away, free, and clear. But her words and that sob had broken something in him. His tough little redhead had a soft heart that had been wounded too often. *His? His redhead?* When had he started thinking of her that way?

He shouldn't have kissed her. He should have explained he'd be leaving soon, and ... it wouldn't have mattered. That fucking sob! Maybe they could have an affair and then go their separate ways.

Dregs laughed. *Imposible!* There was already too much between them to be a casual affair. They understood too much about the other person and had since the beginning.

"Well," he said to himself, "You are well and truly fucked."

Addie saw the text the next morning when she got up to make coffee.

You awake? She texted her friend.

It was seconds before a *Yup* was texted back

Is this a phone call, or should I come by?

I'd love for you to come by. Will Elias be okay with that?

Let me check in with him. I am not going to be a prisoner here.

Addie went back into the bedroom, and Elias was still awake. "*Mi amor?*"

He grinned at her. "I know that tone. You're going to ask me something I won't like."

"Clara has a thing she wants to talk about, and I would love to talk do it in person at her place."

"Is it about Dregs?"

"I can neither confirm nor deny that. Even I know you don't break girl code that way."

Elias sat up. "Hmmm. I do have human bodyguards I keep on retainer. There are daytime tasks they run for me. You could be today's task."

Addie clapped her hands together. "That would be great! I expected a fight."

"I know better. I'd rather send you out with protection than have you sneak out with none."

Addie looked affronted. "I would never do that!"

"Yes," Elias said, picking up his phone, "You absolutely would."

By lunchtime, Clara and Addie were happily ensconced in Clara's apartment, snacking, and chatting.

"So," said Addie, eating a piece of cheese, "You two kissed. How was it on a scale of one to ten?"

"It can't be measured with human technology." Addie hooted. "No, this is bad!"

"Why is it bad?"

"Because he's not going to stay. He's going to help deal with Stellan and Tamir, and then he's gone."

"Isn't he taking over Tamir's job and cleaning up all the shipping issues?"

"Only temporarily. I don't want to start something neither of us can finish."

"Have you ever thought maybe starting it will change things?"

"Huh?" Clara looked a little confused.

"So, he plans to move on. What if being with you is what he needs to stay?"

"I don't want to ruin his plans."

"What plans?"

"I don't know, Addie! I assume he has some."

"Perhaps you two are being giant wusses." Clara made a face at her. "Look, I get it. You both have been through shit and been hurt. But maybe you need each other to heal."

"Christ. You fucking fall in love, and now it's all flowers and hearts with you! I needed pragmatic advice. I can get the lovey-dovey shit from Mei."

Addie laughed. "Okay, that's fair. Look, you're both overthinking it. Enjoy it. Enjoy that tension, enjoy the kisses, enjoy his company. Don't force it. If it happens, enjoy it. When he leaves, Mei and I will be here with junk food and some really great mocktails."

"Now, that's what I was looking for!" There was a loud noise outside Clara's door. "What is that?"

"I'm not sure." There was a yell from the bodyguard who brought Addie. "I am going to text Elias."

But there wasn't time. The door burst open, and four huge humans came in and went right for Addie and Clara. Addie tried to fight back. "Jesus, the chubby one is a fighter," said the one with a bald head and a scar down his face.

"The redhead is no slouch either," said a large burly Black man with dreadlocks.

"You fucker! Let me go!" shouted Addie. Then blackness descended as the man holding her knocked her out.

CHAPTER 34

Elias hadn't expected to sleep, but he did drift off during the afternoon. When he woke, the apartment was quiet, and a feeling of cold dread snaked down his spine. There was no singing or cooking. He couldn't even smell Addie.

He grabbed his phone. No texts or phone calls had come in. He called her, but there was no answer. He put on a pair of sweats, and headed to the living room when someone pounded at his door.

"Elias!" Dregs was yelling. "Open up! We have a very large problem!"

Elias opened the door. "Dregs, are the ladies okay?"

Dregs came in and started ranting in Spanish. "Dregs, I don't speak Spanish. English, please!"

"*Lo siento,*" Dregs replied. "I pivot to Spanish when I'm upset. They're gone, Elias. I went over to see Clara, and the door was off its hinges. Your man was just coming around. There was a fight, but they stuck him with something. He went down."

"Fuck! I did a Stellan and overslept. Maybe ..."

Dregs shook his head. "It happened while it was still light."

"Any sign of my other men?"

"Nope. And of course, none of the neighbors heard anything."

"Naturally." Elias was trying desperately to remain calm. He punched in a number and put it on speakerphone.

"Elias," Gen said. "What can I do for you?

"If Stellan was going to kidnap someone, where would he take them?"

"Adelaide?" the female vamp asked.

"Yes," replied Dregs. "And her friend, Clara."

"Ah, Clara. I know her." There was muffled discussion on the other end. "I've got Eliza here."

"Eliza, any ideas?" Elias ran a hand through his hair, frustrated and panicked.

"Yes. There are a few places he likes to take people. I will text you a list."

"And I'll send you a couple places Tamir uses that he thinks no one knows about. Did humans take them?" Gen asked.

"Yes," Dregs said. "It was during daylight hours."

"Then Tamir is involved. Stellan uses humans for many things. Muscle is not one of them."

"I was hoping I would not have to kill Tamir," Elias said. "But that's changed now."

"I expect he's disappeared as well. The snake," Gen replied.

"I'll contact the Elder Assembly for you," said Eliza.

"I will also send some of my people over to you. They're good at stealth and will come in handy."

Dregs's phone rang, and he moved away to answer it.

"Thank you. Time is of the essence. Stellan and Tamir have created a new drug, Hell Raiser."

"Holy fucking shit! Tell me they didn't use Hell Fire as a base." Gen sounded pained.

"I cannot tell you that, unfortunately. It's not only Hell Fire, but Miasma and heroin cut into it. We also think they added vamp blood to amplify the psychotropic properties by quite a bit."

"That's a death sentence." Eliza's voice was frigid. "The Elders will sanction Tamir's kill, no problem. Those two will have a dishonorable death sentence imposed within the hour." A text came in with a ding. "That's the list. I doubt he's bothered to get any new ones. Lazy bastard."

"Thank you, Eliza."

"You're right, though," put in Gen, "Time is running out. We will let you go. Let us know if you need something."

"Thanks again, and I will." Elias hung up. The text from Gen came in.

Dregs came back over. "Darian is on his way. That was him on the phone."

"Fine. I am going to get dressed. Make yourself a drink." Elias stalked back into the bedroom. He shut the door and leaned against it, closing his eyes. He had never known this kind of fear. He couldn't have found his Adelaide just to lose her now. If anything happened to her, he wouldn't be able to survive it. He wouldn't even want to.

Hold on, little bird, I'm coming to get you.

Addie opened her eyes and groaned. Her head was killing her. She was on a cold, hard floor, and the light was dim. It took a moment to come back to her. "Clara?" she whispered, the fright in her voice evident.

Someone touched her leg. "Here," Clara whispered. "I'm so glad you're awake. I was worried. And it sucks to be this angry and frightened by oneself."

Addie snorted, then groaned. "My fucking head," she said. "I don't suppose you know where we are."

"No clue." Clara put her arm gently around Addie. "You have a bump but no blood. I checked earlier."

Addie snaked her own around Clara's waist. "Thank you for that. Are you okay?"

"I am. My guy didn't pop me quite as hard. But I woke in this room with you passed out next to me."

"Stellan, I am sure."

"No doubt. I'd also surmise Tamir is involved." Clara sighed. "Elias and Dregs are going destroy them."

"Yup. Hope I get to watch."

Clara barked out a small laugh. "Me too."

There was noise at the door, and the two women huddled closer together. The door opened suddenly. Bright light shone in, shadowing the person in the door. The door closed, and the lights went up.

Addie gasped. Miranda was standing by the door, staring at them.

CHAPTER 35

"Miranda?" Addie looked at her friend in surprised horror. Miranda's pupils were enlarged, and her skin was sallow.

"She's high off her ass," whispered Clara.

"Addie! And what was it? Clara?" Miranda said with a sneer.

"That's right," said Clara. "You feel okay, Miranda?" Clara's voice was gentle.

"Oh, I feel great! Stellan's been feeding on me. That makes all the difference." Miranda started pacing around the room. "You'd know all about that. Right, Addie?"

"Sure, honey. But I don't think it's that."

"Not worth it." Clara shook her head. "She'll never believe you."

"Believe what?" Miranda demanded. She looked at them huddled together. "Well, aren't you two buddy-buddy?" Her tone was petulant.

"Miranda, you know we're prisoners here, right? Stellan had us kidnapped."

"Only to get Elias's attention. He's not going to hurt you, silly." She looked at Clara. "You, he'll probably hurt."

"I'm sure," Clara answered dryly. "He's dangerous, Miranda."

"Hah! You're just jealous! Because he wants me and not you." Miranda got in front of Clara. "I bet he's never even fed from you."

Clara pushed up the sleeve of her left arm. "You see that scar? Your fucking vampire-in-rusty-armor did that to me. He likes to cause the women he feeds from pain." Miranda paled, and Clara grabbed her arm, pushing her sleeve up. "See, Miranda?" She pointed to a fresh wound on Miranda's arm. "He's done the same to you."

Miranda pulled her arm away. "No!"

"Yes, but you convinced yourself that you liked it."

"I thought you said not to bother?" Addie put in.

"I know," said Clara. "But I'm pissed off, and my mouth ran away from me. I'm pissed at Stellan, not her. She can't help it." Clara looked at Miranda. "Okay, maybe I'm a little pissed at her, too."

"Randi, Clara is trying to help. He's keeping you high on a new drug and feeding on you so he can feel the high. He doesn't care about you."

Miranda glared at Addie, raised her hand, and slapped her. "You jealous bitch!"

She raised her hand again, but Addie grabbed her arm. "No. You get one free pass, Miranda. Hit me again, and you'll be sorry." Addie's father had done a lot wrong, but he had taught his daughter how to defend herself if necessary. She knew it was the drugs Miranda's system, but she would not allow the other woman to hit her again.

Miranda's face fell. "Addie, do what he wants. He wants you, and I am okay with sharing him with you. We're friends. It will be fun."

"He's convinced of you this with help from the drug. It's dangerous."

"I feel so good. You'll feel good, too. You'll see. He'll make it good." She looked over at Clara and then back at Addie. She had a sly look on her face. "I can even put in a good word for Clara."

"I'd rather die," Clara responded.

"That," said a voice from the door, "Can be arranged."

"So, we've separated the city into four quadrants, based on the information from Eliza and Gen," said Elias to the assembled vampires in his apartment. "I want to keep the operation small so we don't draw unwanted attention. Dregs, Darian, Mickey, and I will each take the lead for each quadrant." Elias had called Clara's brother because the vampire should know. He'd made it over in record time with ten other young vampires in tow. He might be wasted as a bar manager with that kind of hustle.

"We only have a finite amount of time tonight to search, as we've already lost a good bit of the night." Darian ran a hand through his hair. "What happens in daylight?" Darian had called the other band members, and they had shown up, ready to help in any way they could.

"Human team takes over."

"Fat lot of fucking good they did today!" This was from Mickey. Elias gave him a look, and the younger vamp blew out a breath. "Sorry. That was uncalled for. I'm upset.

"I understand, Mickey. Clara is your sister, but we need to try and remain calm. My man is excellent, but you cannot do much when you get jumped by more than one guy, and they've already taken your team out." Elias said this with considerable calm. But on the inside, he felt like Mickey did. That was fear talking.

Mickey nodded. "Again, I apologize." Mickey didn't want to explain that Clara had gotten kidnapped to their parents. They had just stopped looking at her like she would fall off the wagon any minute. They'd somehow think she had brought this on herself.

"Getting back to this," said Dregs. "Each team will take two of Gen's men with them. But don't be stupid about it. Dawn comes, text us, and then go the fuck home. Don't be goddamned heroes."

"If you see anything, contact either Dregs or me immediately. Questions?" Everyone shook their head. "Okay, let's move!"

Darian sidled over to Elias. "We'll find them, Elias. It'll be fine."

Elias gave Darian a bleak look. "I hope you're right."

"I'm always right." Darian moved towards the door. He hoped this time was no exception. He wasn't sure what would become of Elias if something happened to Addie.

Stellan stood in the doorway. Miranda jumped up and ran over to him. "I was trying to convince them, baby. Just like you told me to do."

"Good girl," Stellan said, absently stroking a hand across Miranda's hair.

Addie rolled her eyes. "Jesus Christ," she whispered to Clara under her breath.

"Well, well, ladies. Here we are, together at last. Now, what were you saying, Clara?"

"I was saying I'd rather die than belong to you."

Stellan tsked. "Clara, junkie whores like you should be grateful for whatever you get."

"Hey, Stellan, how about you go fuck yourself!" This was from Addie.

"Adelaide! Don't talk to Stellan like that. Clara ..."

"Miranda, I wouldn't go there." Addie's voice had turned to ice. Miranda closed her mouth and hung her head. Addie hated what Stellan had done to her. But Addie couldn't help her right now.

"Adelaide, you will submit." Stellan smiled menacingly at her.

Oh, I am going to enjoy watching you die. "Stellan, Elias will kill you."

"He'll never find you. Not in time anyway."

Clara laughed. "You took the woman he loves. You are a marked man, Stellan."

Stellan looked from one woman to the other. "You two will learn. And you will submit. And you'll be glad of it. I promise I can make it fun for you. You'll never have to worry about anything as long as you live."

The two women said nothing, staring at him.

"Breaking you will be fun." With that, he swept out of the room, taking Miranda with him. She waved at them on the way out, a sure sign she wasn't connecting all the dots.

"You know," said Addie, "I always thought he was arrogant, that he was callous about Miranda and you. But I didn't think he was actually a psychopath."

"He's obviously very good at hiding it. He liked to cause pain, but that didn't mean he was crazy. Lots of vampires are that way with humans."

"Not Elias. And not Dregs."

"No, not them." Clara sighed. "I should have been more careful about Stellan."

"You couldn't have known."

"You're right, but I still hate that I missed it."

"Let's try and get some rest. I think we're going to need our energy."

Time quickly began to have no meaning for the two women. Food was practically thrown at them, and if no one took them to the bathroom, they had to use a bucket in the corner. They slept on the floor with two awful blankets and were not allowed to do much more than throw water on their faces when they finally got to an actual bathroom.

And they weren't left alone. There was a steady stream of humans during the day and vampires at night. And Stellan always stopped by. They were never physically harmed, but many threats were made.

"I really hate that I smell," Clara remarked.

"Same," Addie said as she and Clara tried to do some stretches. "I keep fantasizing about a nice, hot shower."

"Oh, God," said Clara. "Stop it. I am going to start crying in a minute." Clara looked at Addie. "Okay, I'm jealous. I can't do tree pose."

"Because your balance is for shit, whereas mine is excellent."

"Nice. Real nice." The two joked with each other mostly to keep the fear at bay. But the only upside to all of this was they had ample time to get to know each other. And the more they talked, the more they liked the other. They were suited to being friends in a way they often weren't with others

They would have reached this anyway, but forced proximity sped up the process. They had nothing else to do—talking and yoga.

"The guys are going to come for us. Right?" Clara would invariably ask.

"They are," Addie firmly replied. But she really wished they would hurry.

Chapter 36

They didn't find them that night, the next, or even the next two nights. Tempers were short, and nerves frayed. Darian was usually able to escape in music, but it wasn't working. Addie had become like a sister to him, and Clara reminded him of his biological sister with her intractable will.

The thought that Stellan—and Tamir, for he had disappeared—could be harming the two women was almost too much for him to bear. It was one of the few times in his life that music hadn't made him feel better. In this case, it made it worse when he thought about how Addie shared his love of it.

Elias had destroyed his office at the club after the second night of searching. The only two people who were brave enough to speak to him were Dregs and Darian. Dregs was mostly silent, preferring to take his anger and frustration out on inanimate objects.

After Elias had unleashed on his office, they came outside to find Dregs standing near his car. He stared at it like it was the architect of all his problems. Dregs did not say one word. He just walked over to his car, put his hands on it, and flipped. He stalked away after that—all in total silence. Elias stood next to Darian, watching impassively.

"That's the closest I've ever seen him come to losing his temper," said Elias. "He has amazing control. Then again, he's had to."

"Oh?" asked Darian. He'd known Dregs for years but didn't know his history.

"His time as a human and a young vampire was … not good. A sure-fire way to infuriate those hurting you is to remain silent. He learned that early."

"I had no idea." Darian looked at Elias. "He didn't give himself his name, did he?"

"Not to start. But he made it his own." Elias sighed. "Go home, Darian. It's almost dawn, and I don't wish to lose you as well."

"You haven't lost Addie either. Will you sleep today?"

"I will not rest or feed until we find Addie and Clara." Elias walked away.

Darian watched with sadness. But like his friend, he wasn't going to rest or feed until the women were found.

It was dusk on the fifth evening when Darian got a call from a human assigned to his team. "Darian! I think we've got them!"

"How long do you think we've been here?" asked Addie.

"I think this is the fifth night, based on Stellan's appearances and change of clothes. He comes at the top and bottom of the evening."

"Good observation skills. And he's usually high as a kite when he visits the second time."

"As much as I want to punch your friend Miranda, she's doing a pretty good job of ensuring he doesn't stay too long." Even if she managed it with a fair amount of whining and simpering. Stellan had made the poor thing completely dependent upon him and his whims.

"She doesn't want him paying any attention to us. Well, you. Her reasons are completely self-serving. But they work in our favor."

"I still don't get it. Why does Stellan fixate on me?"

Addie looked at her friend in confusion. "You really don't get it?" Clara shook her head. "It's because you don't care about him at all. His ego cannot stand that. Coupled with the fact that you prefer Dregs's company. In Stellan's mind, he can't even fathom that you'd prefer Dregs to him. Even if there were no Dregs, you still wouldn't want anything to do with Stellan."

"No, I wouldn't."

"Deep down, he knows that. He's cruel to you to make you pay. But also to try and convince himself he doesn't want you. He'd kill both Miranda and me if he thought you'd have him."

"I'd kill him in his sleep!"

"And he knows that too. And it makes him both hate you and want you more. He wants to break you." Addie didn't matter to Stellan. But she mattered to Elias, and that's the only reason she was important.

"How do you know all this?"

"I'm a big reader—gothic romances. Stellan is the villain. Now, we just need to be saved by the hero. Or heroes, in our case."

Clara was about to reply when the door banged open, and Tamir strode in.

"Look what the cat dragged in," said Clara.

"Ladies! I apologize for not visiting you sooner, most rude of me." He wrinkled his nose. "Forgive me, but you two smell."

"Well, it may have something to do with the fact that we were kidnapped, and have been prisoners here, thanks to Stellan." This was from Addie.

"Thanks to you as well, it seems," said Clara.

Tamir shrugged. "I'm a businessman. And Stellan was the best choice for me, at present."

"Because he has no problem with the fact that, at heart, you're a drug dealer who doesn't care if humans die."

"I am not a drug dealer, Miss Gold." Tamir sounded offended. "I am merely a purveyor of fine entertainment for the vampire community." He ignored the look of disgust on their faces. "And when you've lived as long as I have, you need to develop new ways of staving off boredom. And it can all be so very boring."

"You created a dangerous psychotropic drug because you were bored? You don't care what the long-term effects could be for humans, including Miranda!" Clara sounded outraged and scared. If forced to take the drug, Clara may not survive it. And she knew that.

"Your lives are so brief, but there are more of you than us now. Why should you not be used to make our lives better?" Tamir paced the small room. "You run to us. You find us exciting and maybe you hope for long life. And once we have you, we know you'll do anything for us. Your friend Miranda, that little whore Elise. They beg for it."

Addie was going to vomit. She didn't like Elise, but she didn't deserve that. And Miranda sure as shit didn't deserve this. "You're a monster," she said.

Tamir laughed. "My dear, if you think Elias is any different, then you are a fool." Addie said nothing in reply. "Ladies, time is running out for you. Stellan hoped keeping you here, making you wonder what would happen next could convince you. But all you two do is snipe at him, and he's increasingly annoyed by it."

"Did you think keeping us in a small, damp room would sway us?" Clara was incredulous. "You've been feeding us as little as possible, chaining us when we need to use the bathroom, and insulting us at every turn. Is this how you meant to convince us to submit?"

"I know this is inelegant. I may have handled it differently. Perhaps we should have kept you comfortable. But would it have mattered?"

"A gilded cage is still a cage," Addie replied.

"Exactly." Tamir yawned. "You're both very irritating. And boring."

"I am so sorry we could not entertain you more." Addie's tone was sarcastic. "Why don't you fuck off?"

"Very rude, my dear." Tamir turned away. "For two people that are prisoners, you are very arrogant."

"Why be conciliatory? You're just as likely to kill us either way," Addie replied.

"If you kill us," said Clara, "Your lives will be forfeit. Elias and Dregs will rip the two of you apart."

"I highly doubt it." But Tamir looked worried. "We'll be taking those two down next."

Addie and Clara looked at each other and burst out laughing. "Highly doubtful," Addie said in between laughs.

"You two are impossible! I tried to help you see reason."

"Oh, Tamir, you do not give a shit if we live or die. Just go!"

Tamir stared at them for a moment, then calmly walked out. The force he used to slam the door closed was the only indication at how angry he was.

"You know," said Clara. "We have too much bravado for two people who are probably going to die."

Addie snorted. "We do, but what else can we do? It's the only power we have right now." She took Clara's hand. "Shit, I hope we don't die."

"I hope we don't either."

"Should we have a plan in case they try?"

"Fight like hell," said Clara. "Then fight some more."

Sometime later, the door banged open again, and a vampire came in bearing two trays with food on it. Another vamp stood at the door, watching them.

He casually dropped the trays on the floor, scattering most of the food onto the floor. "Dinner!" He looked down and sneered at them. "Eat up, now!"

"A little hard when most of it has landed on the floor," Addie replied.

The vampire shrugged. "You can miss a meal or two anyway."

The one at the door leered. "Bigger girls are better in bed, you know. They have to try harder."

"Fine, you can have her, and I'll take the redhead."

"You really think Stellan will let either of us fuck these two?" The door vamp scoffed.

"He might." The vamp pushed the dinner trays closer to them. "Come on, eat for me." He was looking directly at Addie. "Do what you're told."

"I'm not hungry," Addie said.

"First time in your life, I bet." He laughed like what he'd said was terribly funny instead of cruel.

"Why don't you both leave and let us eat in peace." Clara's voice was shaking with fear and rage.

The vamp leaned down. "I like the fear I can smell on you. It turns me on. I can't wait to get my hands on you." He reached out, touching her hair, and Clara tried very hard not to throw up on him.

"Come on, Deke! We need to go. Stellan doesn't want us in here long."

Deke stood. "Fine, you're no fun." He looked at the ladies. "Eat the food. You'll need your energy." Both vamps left.

Addie picked up a tray, throwing it at the door, and immediately regretted it. "I'm sorry. We'll call that my tray. I'm not hungry anyway."

"Don't be silly," replied Clara. "We'll share what's left. We may not have appetites, but we need to keep our strength up."

They ate the meal in silence. It was plain and not very good, but it did the job. "I don't mind telling you," Addie said. "I'm absolutely petrified. Something about those two got to me."

Clara nodded. "Me too. I am not sure I can pretend to be brave anymore." She rubbed Addie's shoulder. "I'm sorry they said those things to you."

"It doesn't bother me. I'm fine with my body. And it's not the first time I've heard that shit."

"I'm still sorry. We should rest before we get the end of the night visit from Stellan." Clara grabbed the dirty, coarse blankets and put them over them.

Addie held out her arm. "Come here, cuddle up. It's cold as fuck in here."

Clara moved in to cuddle under her arm and put her arms around Addie's waist.

Neither slept, worried about what might be coming next.

CHAPTER 37

The door banged open not too long after dinner, and two vampire goons came in, followed by Stellan and Tamir. One goon grabbed Addie, and the other got Clara.

"Get your fucking hands off me!" shouted Clara as Addie tried to struggle.

"Ladies, fighting is useless. You aren't strong enough to take on a vampire. No human is."

"They're going to separate us," Addie said frantically to Clara while trying not to panic.

"Yes, Adelaide. Very good. We are indeed going to separate you since there is no reasoning with you together."

"Stand firm," Clara said. "Don't back down. Elias and Dregs will come for us."

"Oh, my dears, no. I am afraid time has run out for both of you. Bring them!"

Dregs, Elias, and Darian stood fifty yards from the warehouse. Cameras were mounted all around the building, but they were in a blind spot.

Mickey and another vampire attempted to interrupt the camera feed so they could patch in their own footage on a loop.

Darian looked at his phone. "Okay, it's done. You need to get in there quickly, though. They'll need to revert the cameras to the live feed after ten minutes."

"Got it," said Elias. "Per the plans Gen managed to find, there's a hidden side door on the northeast corner of the building."

"How do we find it?" asked Dregs.

"Eliza says there is a slightly different colored brick. You'd need vamp eyes to see it."

"How did Gen even get these plans?"

"She won't tell me. I assume she killed another vamp for them."

"Huh," said Darian. "Okay, you all have eight minutes. Go!"

Elias and Dregs sped off and disappeared around the other side of the building. Darian stayed put, keeping watch. Once the two were in, he and the rest of the team would move into position to swarm the place.

Gen and Eliza had sent them more vamps to help, and Elias had rounded up everyone he could find. No one involved in this kidnapping would leave alive. Should anyone escape, they'd run into a contingent of vamps on the outside, ready to give chase.

Elias was not only rescuing Clara and Addie, but he was also sending a very real message to anyone who thought it was a wise idea to cross him in the future.

Darian was tapping his foot and checking his phone every ten seconds until he finally received a text saying they were in and it would be obvious where the hidden door was.

When Darian and the others got there, he could see why. The heads of three vampires propped the door open. Darian snorted.

"Okay, let's go. Addie and Clara should not be harmed. If you run across Stellan's girlfriend, do not harm her either. Subdue and get her out. Questions?" There were none. "Be quick, be quiet, be lethal."

Stellan took Addie, while Clara ended up with Tamir. Miranda was standing in the corner of the room. Her eyes were even glassier than before, and Addie wasn't sure her friend could even focus them at this point.

"Randi, are you okay?" It didn't matter what Miranda had done; Addie was still concerned.

"Don't you worry about me. Worry about yourself now," Miranda replied.

"Quiet," replied Stellan. "She's right, you should be more concerned with your own well-being." The goon standing behind Addie's chair tightened his hold on her shoulders. It hurt, but Addie was damned if she would show it.

"I tried to be patient with you. I tried to be nice about it. But you and your friend tested my patience at every turn. Why could you not do as I wanted you to? You'd be safe and comfortable now."

"And high. Don't forget high," Addie said. "And if you lose your patience after, what—five days—then your patience isn't worth shit."

Stellan walked up to Addie and slapped her hard across the face. "Speak to me like that again, and it will be worse for you."

Miranda looked shocked by the slap. It was the first real emotion Addie had seen from her. "Please, Addie, do as he asks."

"No," said Addie. "Go ahead and beat the shit out of me. That will make Elias even angrier when he finds me. And that will make your death a whole lot worse. I'll enjoy that." Addie was playing with fire, but she couldn't help herself. She was both angry and scared, and that always made her mouthy.

"Miranda, don't interrupt me again," Stellan snapped.

"Sorry, Stellan. I will be quiet."

Addie's eyes narrowed. She wanted to make him pay for what he did to her friend. Stellan had likely done permanent harm to Miranda.

"Big man," she said. "You need to make women feel small and worthless to make yourself important. You're a pissant. You aren't good enough to wipe Elias's shoes."

Stellan's face turned red. Addie had gone too far. But Stellan stepped away from her. He looked at the vamp standing behind her and nodded. The goon grabbed her by her hair, yanking her out of the chair.

He threw her against the wall, and it was sheer will that she didn't fall to her knees. "You can't even do your own dirty work."

"Oh, I can. It's just more fun to watch." He turned to Miranda. "Pay attention to your friend. This is what happens when you misbehave."

The goon pulled his fist back and punched Addie in the face. She did fall then. *Shit, that hurt.* The goon lifted her again, but there was a crash outside the door.

"Put her down and go check that," Stellan snapped.

The goon dropped her onto the floor as he exited, and Addie rolled onto her back.

The noise outside ratcheted up.

"Looks like you have a reprieve. You're going to have a black eye, I'm afraid. Probably two."

"Fuck off!" Addie spat.

Stellan walked over and kicked her hard in the ribs. "Bitch, it's time you learned some fucking respect." He pressed her ribs, and Addie screamed in pain.

There was a giant roar outside, and then the door was gone. Standing in the doorway was Elias.

"Oh, thank fuck," Addie whispered to herself.

"Elias! This isn't what it looks like."

"Really? Because it looks like my woman is on the floor with your foot on her ribs." He looked at her face. "Are you the one who punched her?"

"No," rasped Addie. "It was the bald vampire with the scar."

"Good thing he's dead then. I wish I could kill him again. Did Stellan hurt you at all?"

"He slapped me earlier. And he kicked me in the ribs."

"Are they broken?" Elias was trying very hard to remain calm.

Addie shook her head. "I don't think so. I've had broken ribs before. I think these will just be badly bruised."

"Okay," he said, the violence in his eyes dimmed slightly.

"Fucker couldn't even manage to break my ribs properly."

Elias wanted to grin at her words. His tough little songbird. He looked at Stellan. "You're not leaving this room alive."

"I have other men here!" Stellan looked petrified.

"Not as many as you did ten minutes ago." Elias walked into the room, and two huge vampires took positions in front of the door. One faced in, one faced out. "No one leaves. Not even the other woman. Understood?" They nodded.

He walked across the room and stood in front of Stellan. "I believe you're touching something that belongs to me." He pushed Stellan, and the vampire sailed into the far wall, crumpling to the floor.

Elias squatted next to Addie. "Little bird?" His voice was full of anguish at seeing her hurt and relief at seeing her alive.

Addie got herself into a sitting position, though it hurt, and put her hand on his cheek. "I knew you'd come, *Mi amor*. I never doubted it."

He removed her hand from his face and kissed her fingers. "Are you sure you aren't too badly hurt?"

"I'm sure. Your timing was really good."

"Do you want to leave while I handle this?"

"No, I want to watch you kill him."

He grinned at her. "That's my good girl." He helped her to the other side of the room to stand with Miranda.

"I want to leave!" Miranda whined.

"You are staying!" Elias shouted. He pivoted to her. "The only fucking reason I am not going to kill you is because of Addie. But don't push it."

"Elias, Stellan is keeping her high. She does not have a firm grip on reality right now. Ease back some, huh?"

Elias looked back at Addie, and his face softened. "For you, anything."

He went over to Stellan, still slumped on the floor. "I didn't hurt you. Get the fuck up."

Stellan slowly got to his feet. "Elias ..."

"Do not test me, Stellan."

"You can't kill me!"

"I can. Not only has it been approved by the Elder Assembly, but I have also been given carte blanche to kill you as I see fit."

"Which means?"

"I am going to tear you apart with my bare hands and then pound you to dust. And I am going to enjoy every fucking second of it."

CHAPTER 38

"No!" Miranda started to move towards Elias, but Addie stopped her.

"Stop, Miranda. Don't get involved."

"He'll kill Stellan!"

Addie sighed. "That's rather the point, honey. I'm sorry, but it has to be this way."

Miranda wailed and dropped to the floor. Elias turned to look at her, and whatever Miranda saw there convinced her to be quiet.

He turned back to Stellan. "Now, where was I? Oh yes, your imminent death. Let's get this over with, shall we?"

Stellan snarled and leaped at Elias, who caught him squarely in the nose with his fist. Stellan dropped again. Elias threw him against the wall again, harder this time. "Come on, Stellan. At least try and land a punch."

Stellan stood again and put up his fists. "You think you're so tough! You're nothing! That's what you've always been, and you'll never be anything but a butcher."

"You know what? I can live with that. Because now the Butcher is on the right side of history. Now stop being boring and fight."

Stellan threw out a fist, but Elias blocked. They moved in a circle, Stellan trying to land a punch but never managing it. Elias was playing with the other vampire. Elias kept taunting Stellan about his lack of fighting prowess while easily missing getting hit. He actually slapped Stellan at some point, then tripped him.

Elias also laughed at him. And that was the worst thing you could do to Stellan. The more Elias laughed; the quicker Stellan unraveled. Elias was emasculating him.

Finally, Stellan roared at Elias. "Just fucking kill me then and get it over with, you monster!"

"I thought you'd never ask." Elias reached out and grabbed Stellan by the neck, squeezing. "You kidnapped the woman I love. You scared her, hurt her. All because you couldn't accept that I am better than you. You grasping, sad little man. It's time to end this."

"Miranda, cover your eyes. You don't want to see this," said Addie.

Miranda looked at her. "Is it going to be really bad?" she whispered in a broken, confused voice.

"Yes, it will be. Turn to the wall, close your eyes, and don't look until I tell you it's okay." Addie couldn't let her watch this.

"I don't ... I can't ...."

"Please, do what I tell you to," Addie snapped. That did the trick. Miranda turned to the wall and closed her eyes. Addie kept her eyes on Elias.

Elias let go of Stellan's throat, grabbing his arm instead. "Fair warning, this is going to hurt a lot."

"Are you going to break it?" Stellan asked.

"Oh, Stellan, no. I'm going to destroy it. And you." Elias pulled, and the bones in Stellan's arm shattered. He then twisted and pulled his arm out of the socket.

Stellan screamed, and Miranda whimpered. *Fuck*. Addie should have told her to cover her ears as well. But that wouldn't really have helped. She put her hand on Miranda's head and stroked her hair. It was all she could do.

"I was born for this, Stellan. Literally. I was created to inflict pain and misery on people. And if I am telling the truth—" He gripped Stellan's other arm and yanked that off as well. "—a part of me absolutely relishes it. Especially today."

Stellan was screaming and weeping. "Monster!" He managed to yell.

"Yes, I am. I could play with you longer, but I want to take my lady home. Your blood will nourish no other vampire. You bring shame and dishonor on your kind."

Elias put a hand on either side of Stellan's head and squeezed. Stellan's eyes registered what was happening before they were crushed between Elias's hands. He stomped on Stellan twice when the body dropped, shattering the torso and then the legs.

He couldn't lie to himself; it had felt good because it also had been right. Stellan was no innocent, and justice had been served.

"It's over," Addie whispered to Miranda. "Don't look over there, but it's done."

Miranda turned but made the mistake of looking at what was left of Stellan, which wasn't much. "NO!" Miranda tried to get over there, but Addie held her.

"Elias? Help?"

Elias rushed over and grabbed Miranda, but she started thrashing. "Miranda, hold still. I'm not going to hurt you!"

"You're going to kill me! His blood is on your hands!" Miranda was hysterical.

"I'm not going to kill you, I promise." He grabbed her arms, but she kicked.

Addie knocked her friend unconscious with a punch to the jaw.

"Who taught you how to throw a sideswipe?"

"My dad," she answered.

"He taught you how to fight?" That was one thing the man had done right then, Elias thought to himself.

"He did. He was a boxer in his twenties. My uppercut is better."

"You're fucking amazing!" He hoisted Miranda over his shoulder. He leaned down, kissing her quickly. "Let's get out of here."

"Wait! Clara!" Addie grabbed his arm. "She's with Tamir."

"Dregs is getting her. He'll kill Tamir. I am almost sorry to miss it. He's a very elegant murderer."

"Okay, can we wait outside until I see her?"

"Of course, little bird. Anything you want."

When they got outside, Elias gestured to two vampires standing off to the side. "Addie, this is Hank and Amanda. They're doctors."

"But Miranda?"

"We'll look after her, too," Amanda said. She was tall, with braids piled on top of her head. She and Hank had a brief conversation in another language.

"That's beautiful. What language is that?" Addie asked.

"Fula," Amanda said. "Hank and I are originally from Senegal. That's the language spoken in the part of the country where we're from." Addie nodded. "Now, let us take care of you and your friend."

Addie looked at Elias. "You won't leave, will you?"

"Not for anything, Adelaide. I'll be right here with you." It would be a while before Elias was okay with her being out of his sight. He was surprised and pleased that she seemed to feel the same. Finally, Elias let out the breath he'd been holding.

CHAPTER 39

Dregs had to torture a handful of vampires before finding out where Clara was being kept. He killed all of them, even the one who finally gave up the needed information. He would have liked to linger over it, but time was ticking away.

He made his way to a basement level. It was dark and dank, and Dregs knew he'd found where Hell Raiser and Hell Fire were made. They were likely cutting the heroin here as well. Two vampires stood outside a door, so he walked that way.

They saw him coming and turned towards him, hissing menacingly. He laughed. "You two are adorable. But it will do you no good. I will kill you both."

They ran at him, and Dregs stood there, waiting for them to get close. Dregs rolled his shoulders and shook out his arms as they got closer. As they were about to strike, he snapped out his arms, grabbed each vamp by the neck, and squeezed.

"You're really no match for me, gentlemen. I have been doing this a long time." He sighed. "I'd like to play with you, but I do not have the time." His grip tightened on their necks as he cut off their air. Then, he relieved them of their heads, stomping them under his feet.

A large skeleton key peeked out of a pocket. "Well," he said, "This must be my lucky day."

Inside the room, Tamir had Clara on the floor as he straddled her. He had a syringe in his hand. "Clara," he said silkily, "Don't you miss it? The sweetness of that high? Not worrying about anything or anyone except how good you feel?"

"Leave it to you to romanticize addiction," Clara said between gritted teeth. "You have no idea what it's like. I don't miss it at all. This will kill me, Tamir. I won't survive it!"

"Ah, well, that is the chance we will have to take." He raised the syringe, and Clara thrashed. "Stop it!"

"No!" Clara was frightened. She was worried about dying but also worried about being addicted again. She didn't miss that awful feeling of being sick all the time, but the initial high? She dreamt about it sometimes, how it felt in the beginning. She'd wake with an awful yearning until she reminded herself of how it had ruined her life. She had to rebuild it piece by piece, earning her family's trust and getting healthy again. The euphoria of a high was temporary. She would never trust it again.

Neither heard the key in the lock and the door slowly opening. Clara was too busy trying to keep the syringe away from her, and Tamir was too busy trying to get control back.

Tamir was winning. Clara was near tears when suddenly, he was gone. She looked to her left, and Tamir was rolling across the floor with Dregs.

He came. He came for her. And for the first time since she was a child, Clara believed in miracles.

Seeing Clara on the floor with Tamir over her had loosened a cold fury in Dregs. He had seen the terrible fear on her face as the syringe got closer. Tamir would die for that alone. He took a calming breath and launched himself at the other vampire.

He rolled them across the floor, and this time, he was straddling Tamir. He pulled back and punched, breaking the other vampire's nose. He looked over at Clara. "Are you hurt?"

She sat and shook her head. "No, Dregs. He didn't hurt me."

"No drugs in your system?"

"None. I promise."

He nodded and looked at Tamir. "Ah, Tamir, what shall I do with you?"

"Let me go! This is Stellan's fault. He threatened me if I didn't help him! This is his doing!"

Dregs sighed and stood, pulling Tamir with him. "Now, we all know you are lying. Please don't insult my intelligence."

Tamir's eyes widened. "I will do whatever you ask!"

Dregs looked over at Clara, then back at Tamir. He was eerily calm as he looked at his nails. They were longer than most modern vampires kept them. "You will do whatever I ask you to do?"

"Yes, Dregs! Anything!"

Dregs smiled, but it was cruel. "Then," he said, "I ask you to die." Dregs lifted his hand and raked his nails across Tamir's neck, hitting his carotid artery. "Your life is a waste, and your blood will not be used to feed any vampire. You are dishonored." His words echoed the ones Elias said to Stellan. He snapped Tamir's head from his body and set it on the floor. He looked around the room and found a wastebasket in the corner. He grabbed it and set the head inside. He pulled out a lighter and set the head alight. He wiped his hand on Tamir's clothing before turning the torso to dust.

Clara sighed in relief and stood next to Dregs. She grasped his arm with her hands and leaned against him while the head burned. "Thank you for coming to get me," she said quietly.

Dregs dropped a kiss on top of her head. "Clara, I will always come for you when you need me. It does not matter what happens between us going forward."

"I know." The knowledge settled her like nothing else. "I cannot believe I am calmly watching a head burn like it's nothing."

Dregs laughed softly. "Shock, maybe? You are made of strong stuff, Clara."

Once the head was nothing but ash, he nodded. "Let's go."

"Addie?" she asked.

"Elias was getting her. And from what I heard, he succeeded."

"Oh, thank God!" She looked at him. "What will happen here?"

"We'll destroy everything in here. I really want to blow the place up, but Elias thinks it will draw too much attention from the human police. He can only pay so many of them off."

"He's likely right. You'll destroy all of the drugs?" She gripped the front of his shirt. "All of them! Do you promise me you'll do that?"

"I promise you, *princesa*. I will burn all of it, and then I will stay until I get it off the streets."

"Thank you," She shook, and his arms came around her. "I'm sorry. Can we stand here for a couple of minutes?"

"You have nothing to be sorry for."

"I was so scared of dying. But I was also scared I wouldn't, and I'd get addicted again."

"I don't believe in a lot," Dregs told her in a low voice, "But if there is one thing I do believe in, it's you."

"Thank you," she whispered. Clara didn't know how much she had needed to hear that from someone. She couldn't count on him being around in the future, but for now, she would do what she never did—lean on someone else for a moment.

Addie was watching the door and biting her lip. "What is taking so long?"

"She'll be out soon, little bird." Elias was confident Dregs would get to her in time because the alternative was unthinkable.

"Adelaide," said Amanda, "You've had a great shock. Please try not to get too agitated. All will be well."

Addie nodded and tried to stop fidgeting.

It was another few minutes before Addie caught sight of her friend's red hair. She started to run towards her and then grimaced in pain.

"Adelaide," said Elias, "Please be careful of those ribs."

"You're right," she said, stopping.

Clara pulled away from Dregs, and ran to her friend.

She grabbed Addie and pulled her into a big hug. Addie grunted. "Oh, my God!" Clara pulled back. "I'm sorry! Are you hurt?"

"Bruised ribs. It's nothing! I am so happy to see you! You're okay?"

"Yup. Dregs found me before Tamir managed to stick me."

The two women stood just holding each other as Dregs and Elias approached.

"Is that little fucker dead?" asked Elias.

"Indeed, he is. I am sorry I couldn't take my time with him."

"You're scary, my friend."

"Says the Butcher of Bavaria," Dregs responded.

"You're both scary," said Addie. "Shut up, now." She leaned back and wiped away from tears. "I'm going to make you Chicken Molé. The sauce takes forever, but you deserve it," she told Clara.

"I'm sorry, what about us? We killed the bad guys!" Elias exclaimed.

"Fine. Molé for all!"

"How is Miranda?" asked Clara.

Elias shook his head. "Not good. She's being taken upstate to a vampire friendly hospital. Even though she's human, it's the best place for her. They'll call her parents. Hank is taking her personally."

Addie shook her head. "I feel like I failed her."

"She is an adult," said Elias. "She made her own choices. They were bad ones, unfortunately. But you didn't fail her." He looked around. "We still have more to do. I decided you were right, Dregs. We're going to blow the building."

"What about the cops?"

"Gen and Eliza are going to help smooth things there if I can't. But I want the ladies well away from here."

"I am not leaving without you!"

"You won't be. It'll take a while to set up, so humans will need to carry it out. I will leave them to it."

"Clara!" Mickey came running over. "Are you okay? Are you hurt? I am so happy to see you!"

Clara hugged her brother. "I am so happy to see you too, Mickey! You have no idea. I'm fine. Oh, God, Mom and Dad!"

"I covered for you. Like always. They know nothing."

"Thanks, bro!"

"Look, I need to help them grab the computers before they blow the fucker. But I am coming to see you tomorrow night." He looked at Dregs. "You'll get her home safely?"

"Of course," Dregs replied.

Mickey nodded, hugged Clara again, and shot off into the night.

"Do you feel safe going home?" asked Elias. "You can come to my place with Addie and me."

"Thank you, no. I want to go … Oh wait, do I have a door?" Elias nodded. "Then yes, I just want to go home, shower for a year, and crawl into bed."

"Oh man, that sounds great," Addie said. "Me too."

"Off we go then."

CHAPTER 40

Clara sighed when she stepped inside her apartment. "I was a little worried I'd never see my apartment again" She looked at Dregs. "Thank you for taking me home.".

"Of course." She stood unmoving in the middle of the living room. "What's wrong?"

"I am a little nervous about being here, even though it's my home. The peace I found here has been tarnished."

It made sense. She and Addie had been nabbed from here after all. "Don't let them win by robbing you of your sense of home."

"You're right," she responded quietly. "I do know that."

"Would you like me to stay for a while? Until you fall asleep?"

"That would be nice. You don't mind?"

"Not at all." He shouldn't do it. He needed to be distancing himself from Clara. But he couldn't walk out on her right now. He walked her into her bedroom and turned on a small lamp by her bed. "Go take your shower. I will be right here when you get out."

She kissed him softly on the cheek, then gathered what she needed. She went into the bathroom and turned the water on.

He sat on the bed, took off his shoes, and sat against the headboard. He looked around the room. It was small but very neat, blues and greens being the predominant colors. He picked up a paperback and leafed through it,

221

raising an eyebrow as he read some. Clara liked to read smut, and this was raw stuff. He smiled to himself, imagining her in some of these positions.

He slammed the book down. *No.* He could not think like that. She had just been through a terrible experience. It was awful to be thinking of her like that now. And she wasn't meant for him, it would be unfair to start something he couldn't finish.

The shower stopped, and a few minutes later, Clara emerged in a pair of sleep shorts and a t-shirt. Her wet hair was brushed, and her skin flushed from the hot water.

"You're still here." She sounded surprised.

"I said I would be." He looked at the windows. "You have black-out curtains, I see."

She nodded. "You don't work nights and not have them."

"Makes sense." He had wondered if it was for a vampire lover, but her answer made more sense, knowing what he did about her. He wasn't sure why he cared, but he did.

She climbed on the bed and wiggled under the covers. "Are you sure you don't mind staying a bit longer?" She bit her lip, and he almost groaned.

"I'm sure." She looked like she was going to say something else, but he interrupted her. "Clara, lay down and close your eyes. I'll stay until you fall asleep."

She nodded slowly. But instead of laying down, she scooted close to him and put her head against his arm. Without thinking, he lifted it and put it around her shoulders. She snuggled into him.

Dregs looked down, and she closed her eyes, letting out a contented sigh. Within minutes she was asleep. *Shit.* She trusted him. So much so that she had fallen asleep laying against his arm after being held captive for the last week.

He should leave, but his body stayed put. He stayed long after she had fallen asleep. But, by the time Clara woke the next day, he was gone.

Addie stood under the hot spray of water; her eyes closed. She groaned at how wonderful the water felt.

"You okay?" Elias asked as he stepped into the shower.

"Oh yes. The hot water feels amazing!"

"How are the ribs?"

"They hurt like a bitch." She looked at the bruising. "And they look as bad as they feel."

Elias frowned. "Are you sure they aren't broken?"

"Yes, baby. I am. And so was Amanda. Just badly bruised." She gave him a rueful look. "She also said no sex for a few days."

He encircled her in his arms. "Little bird, I am so happy you are safe and with me that waiting for sex is no problem."

"I was terrified. I knew you were looking for us, but I was starting to worry that you wouldn't find us in time."

"I was worried too."

Elias gently washed her, taking extra care by her ribs. "The black eye is also coming along nicely," he said as he washed her back.

"Isn't it, though?" She laughed. "Elias, I am not sure my ass is that dirty."

"Can't be too careful." He came around to give her a quick kiss.

She narrowed her eyes at him, taking in the planes of his face. "Elias, have you fed?"

"Not since you got taken," he admitted.

"Elias! You didn't rest either, did you?"

"How could I?" He grabbed the shampoo and gently worked it into her hair. "I was trying to keep my panic at bay. I was so frightened I wouldn't find you in time." He rinsed the shampoo and then repeated the process with the conditioner. "Addie, if I hadn't gotten to you in time ..." his voice broke.

She put a hand on his cheek. "But you did, *Mi amor*. You did. And I am here and whole. And now, you need to feed."

"You're hurt and bruised, no. I can wait."

"You could, but why should you?" She sat on the shower bench, and he followed her over, dropping to his knees and resting his head in her lap. She guided his head to her breast, and he groaned. "Feed, Elias."

"I don't want to hurt you."

"You won't. I need this as much as you do."

Elias gave in, piercing her breast gently, and she let out a moan. "That feels wonderful. Now, touch me."

His head popped up. "I thought Amanda said no sex."

"She did. I didn't. I know my limits, and I need you to touch me."

"I can deny you nothing." His head dipped to her breast again as his fingers found her sex. He rubbed her clit in languid circles as he drank from her.

"More, Elias, more. Please!"

Elias put two fingers inside her while his thumb stayed on her clit. He pumped her slowly, matching the rhythm of his sips. She fisted his hair, and her head fell back against the shower wall.

He took his time drinking from her and fucking her with his fingers. He licked the wound closed and then took one nipple in his mouth, sucking and biting. Then the other.

"Elias, faster! Please."

"You want to come, Adelaide? You want me to make you come?"

"Yes!" Her ribs were bothering her, but it was worth it.

"Then ask me nicely, little bird." He gave her a wicked grin.

"Please, Elias, please make me come."

"My pleasure." He opened her legs more and dove in between her legs. His tongue touched her nub while his fingers still pumped inside of her. He sped up, pumping her hard and fast. When she reached the edge, he took her clit in his mouth and bit gently. Addie came with a scream.

"Holy—ow—shit. That was amazing!"

"Did I hurt you?" What had he been thinking?

"No, baby. Breathing with these ribs is not fun. But that was worth it." She let out a jaw-breaking yawn.

"Time for bed," Elias said, turning off the water. He got out of the shower and put a towel around his hips before taking two more towels to Addie. He gently toweled her body, then used the second towel for her hair.

"I should dry it, but I think I'll braid it and hope for the best."

"I'll braid it," Elias said.

"You can braid hair?"

"Yes." She glowered at him. Whose hair had he braided? "Centuries ago, my hair was long, and I sometimes wore a braid."

"Mmmm," she said. She supposed it could be true. "I have no business being jealous, but I am."

He gently led her into the bedroom and braided her hair before peeling back the covers and ushering her under them. He got in on the other side, and she immediately cuddled up to him. "I think I'd like to stay here with you a little longer, if I may."

"Addie, you can stay as long as you like." He wanted her with him all the time, but he was trying to do what Darian suggested and relax for now.

"Okay, great." She yawned again and closed her eyes. "Thank you for rescuing me."

Elias looked down at the person who'd come to mean the world to him. The person who had helped him begin the process of forgiving himself, who had convinced him that he could be worthy of love. "I didn't rescue you, Adelaide. I just came and got you. You rescued me."

EPILOGUE

One month later

Addie had visited Miranda a couple of days ago and had been sad ever since. Her friend detoxed from the drugs in her system, but her mind was shattered.

The hospital was in a beautiful location and was as nice as a place like that could be, but it was still a hospital. An expensive one. And it was likely Miranda would be there for the rest of her life.

"I don't know how her parents are affording it," she had said to Elias. "She's a schoolteacher, and he's a mechanic."

"They aren't. I am."

She looked at him. "You are?" He nodded. "Elias, that's so lovely of you."

"I feel responsible. I know she made her own choices, but my unwillingness to see what was going on caused this. And she was your friend ... is your friend. I wanted to do it for you, too."

"What did you tell her parents?"

"That an ex-business associate of mine had gotten her addicted to drugs without her knowledge. I stayed as close to the truth as possible. They did try and fight me on it, but I told them it would be my honor to do it."

"I should call them and see if there is anything I can do." She stroked his thigh. "You're a good man, you know."

"No, I'm not. And that is why we're here." He tapped the steering wheel. "I'm trying to be better, though. You help make me better."

"Any sign of Elise?" Elise had disappeared, along with a handful of other men and women who had been regulars at Tamir's. They'd all turned up in one way or another: dead, strung out, hurt. But not Elise.

"No. And I don't like it." He eased the car into a parking space in front of her apartment. "But I know your last visit to Miranda made you sad, so I have something I hope will cheer you up."

"At my apartment?" she laughed.

"Yup!" He came around, opened her car door, and helped her out.

"You know, my ribs are better now."

"I do. I'm just polite."

"Sure." She looked at the bag he was carrying. "What's in the bag?"

"Rope," he said, a wicked grin on his face.

"Oh, really? For me?"

"Oh yes, little bird. I have such plans for later tonight."

"I cannot wait," she said breathlessly. She fished for her keys as Elias sent a quick text message. When they stepped inside the building, neither noticed a pair of eyes watching them from the shadows.

They were heading upstairs when they heard piano music. She turned to look at him. "That is a piano," she said.

"Man, you really know about music. I am impressed."

She hit him on the shoulder. "You got me a piano?"

"Nah, it must be someone else." But he laughed as she jogged upstairs. He hurried after her and caught up to her as they reached her landing.

Mrs. Costello was standing by Addie's open apartment door. "Addie, dear! You're looking well."

"Thank you, Mrs. Costello."

"Marina, dear."

"Of course. Marina."

"Well, come on now," said the old woman. "Come see what your vampire has done for you."

Addie looked back at him. "What did you do?" she whispered.

"Go and see," he replied.

Addie walked into her apartment, and Darian sat at a piano. He stood. "Hey, you two."

Addie was staring at the piano, unbelieving. "Elias," her voice breaking. "This is my mother's piano!" She walked over to it and lovingly stroked the keys. She peered at the underside of the lid to where her and her mother's initials were etched.

When she straightened, there were tears in her eyes. "How did you do this?"

"I had a little talk with Daniel. I convinced him to take a really good look for the bill of sale. He found it very quickly. So, I talked to the new owner."

"And they sold it back to you?"

"They did." It had cost him a lot, but it was worth it.

Addie launched herself at him. "Thank you!" She rained kisses all over his face. "Thank you, thank you!"

"I knew how much it meant to you, and I want you to be happy."

"Isn't it lovely, Marina?"

The old woman answered past the lump in her throat. "It truly is." She looked at Darian. "Young man, why don't you and I go have some whiskey and give these two a moment?"

"Sounds good."

"Come on by when you're done," Marina said as she and Darian left.

Elias looked at Addie. "Happy?"

"Very. Thank you again. I love you a lot." She couldn't believe it. He had gotten her the one thing she really wanted back. Books were replaceable, but this piano was not.

"And I love you, little bird." He kissed her deeply.

"Did you kill Dan or the other person, though?"

"No. But I did scare Dan. Quite a bit."

"That I would have enjoyed seeing." Addie laughed.

"I can describe it in detail."

"Sounds good. Okay, enough, let's go drink with my elderly neighbor."

The eyes watched the apartment for a long time after the lights went out. Eventually, they faded back into the alley. Elias, Addie, and even Clara were safe ... for now.

ACKNOWLEDGEMENTS

Vampire's Kiss was brought to life on Kindle Vella and I enjoyed writing it so much, that I wanted more people to read it. Hence, you now have this book in front of you.

Thanks to my breasties (you know, besties but with...breasts. You get it), for their unwavering love and support. Get you a group of friends where you can take turns being the one who has their shit together, and the one who is a spicy disaster.

Thanks to my beta readers; Erin, Caitlin, and Suzanne. The feedback as always, makes the book better. Suzanne read the story while it was on Kindle Vella and sent along feedback as she was reading it, which was invaluable for fleshing out the rest of the story and when it came to finalizing the manuscript for publication.

Lane, you are STILL the best worst sister, love you.

Thank you to my editor Kyleigh who once again put me on the right path. Any errors you see are mine. And GetCovers did a brilliant cover. I love it so much!

Do you Discord? I didn't until this year and was lucky enough to land in The Romance Riot Discord. Those ladies (and a couple of gents) have been a source of information, advice, laughter, and bawdy discussions. They have brightened my life in a myriad of ways, and I love the hell out of them.

Finally, thank you, the reader. For reading and hopefully enjoying this book. And thank you for supporting indie authors. Without you all, we writers would just be sitting in dark rooms, banging away on a keyboard with no one to read our work. I mean, we do that, but at least we have people who read our books.

Stay tuned for the further adventures of Elias, Addie, Clara and Dregs (I bet you want to know what his real name is, huh?)

About the Author

Lori-Anne Cohen is an urban fantasy and paranormal romance author, living and working in Massachusetts. She is a cat mom, sometimes actress, and she never uses a level when hanging things on the wall as she likes to live dangerously.

Want to know where to find me, or about my other titles? See the QR code below.

TITLES BY LORI-ANNE COHEN

Demons of Paris Series
Demon's Consort
Demon's Guardian
Demon's Holiday
Demon's Heart – Coming 2025

Vampire's Kiss Series
Vampire's Kiss
Vampire's Trouble – Coming 2025/2026

Marked by the Vampire

Riding the Dragon

Gwendolyn, please stop doing that." Anya looked over at Gwen, exasperation plain on her face, her voice sharper than she'd normally be with her friend.

"Doing what?" Gwen feigned innocence.

"Drumming your fingers on the taxi door."

Gwen looked chagrined and stopped the drumming. "Aren't you nervous? This is weird."

Anya was working an old coin, flipping it between each of her fingers, something she'd been doing since she was a child. It was a trick her father had taught her, and it was something she did when she was feeling out of sorts. This was the only sign that she might be a little agitated. "I am a bit nervous," Anya admitted. "But your tapping is not helping. Can you not do something quieter?"

Gwen pointed a finger at Anya's hand and made a flicking motion. The coin sailed neatly over to Gwen, who held it suspended midair. A flick of her wrist and the coin started flipping over, and then back again.

Anya smiled at her friend, even though she really wanted her coin back. "Gwen....my coin, please." She paused, wanting to soften her tone. "Though, you're really getting quite good at that."

"I've been working on it. It makes a nice change from spell work, though that is what I should be concentrating on. If nothing else, Methuselah is entertained by it."

"I'm sorry, who?"

"Methuselah. The cat."

"I thought the cat's name was Morrigan?"

"It felt too Irish."

"You *are* Irish." Anya looked at her friend, exasperation warring with affection.

"I know. But it felt too on the nose honestly. I am enough of a stereotype, being an Irish witch with a black cat."

"So, you changed it to Methuselah? Before this, he was Morrigan. And before that, Maximus. Why do you keep changing the cat's name?"

"Because it's not right. Neither is Methuselah, but it will do for now." Anya rolled her eyes. "Names are important."

"Whatever you say, you tiny weirdo."

Gwen knitted her brows at her friend. "Just wait, he'll tell me his name eventually."

"Uh-huh. Sure"

Gwen made a face at her friend and sat back in her seat, looking out the window as they slowly made their way towards the Marais.

"My coin, please? It was a gift from Natalia. She insists it belonged to the last Tsar of Russia." She grinned. "I don't believe that. But it is as old as she is."

Gwen flipped the coin back to Anya, who caught it, without looking and began working it through her fingers again. "If Natalia is Russian and not really your grandmother, why does she insist you call her that? In French?"

Anya smiled. "Natalia is very affected and likes the sound of it. She likes being called '*grand-mere*' because it makes her feel matriarchal and frankly, it's just easier when talking about her to people who don't know what she is. I called her *babushka* when I was very small, and she was not pleased. She lectured me very soundly in both French and Russian for about an hour. I owe my early French language skills to her. She thought shouting in French sounded classier. I prefer shouting in Russian."

Anya's own accent was mostly Russian, though she occasionally sounded French from having lived there for so long. Most people she met found the accent, coupled with the deeper timbre of her voice, exotic. Anya found this annoying and would get prickly anytime it was brought up. She didn't put stock in many people and as such, didn't give a damn what anyone thought of her accent. She was not an exotic creature and it irritated her that anyone would think this. She didn't let people get close as a rule. Well, until Gwen. When she'd realized the blonde could drink most men twice her size under the table, she'd known they would be friends. Anya had opened up to her in a way she'd never done with anyone else. Anya had not realized that she had been lonely, until Gwen came into her life and had filled it with friendship.

When Anya had decided to come clean to Gwen about their task tonight, she'd been hoping that with her being a witch, she'd be more open to the fantastical. Gwen had been shocked, but in the end, she'd come around. It had taken two bottles of wine and a lot of questions to get there. Witches were one thing, but demons were apparently a bigger stretch. Gwen still had so many questions whirling around in her head, she didn't know where to start sometimes.

But what stymied her the most, was how parts of Anya's life had been mapped out for her since she'd been born. Natalia had seen to that. It was both fascinating and a little horrifying.

Gwen smiled. "Does Natalia do that imperious thing with her voice that you do?"

"What imperious thing? I do no such thing!"

"Anya, I've heard you lecture." Anya was a literature professor.

Anya looked affronted. "That is just not true!" She thought for a moment and shrugged. "Well, ok. That's fair. I suppose I do get imperious sometimes. Maybe." Anya huffed out. In Anya's case, it was a defense mechanism designed to keep people away. Gwen knew that Anya was, at heart, warm and loving, but she rarely let anyone see that side of her.

Gwen sighed. "Why tonight?" she asked, bringing it back to the task at hand. "What's the rush now?"

Anya rolled her eyes. "Apparently the Council has been badgering this demon about it being time for him to take a consort. They met with him recently to hammer it home some more. Natalia is absolutely sure that it is destined to be me, so she wants me in there before someone else gets there." Anya paused. "I am still not really fully convinced to be honest. She has said that it was an ancient demon who told her this, that it was part of some prophecy or something. It's just...well...it's just that it's always felt so far away. Something I didn't have to worry or think about. And as I've been looking back at my life, I see how Natalia has been pushing me in the direction she's wanted me to go. This has been informing my decisions as an adult, even if I haven't realized it, hasn't it?"

"Annie, come on." She thought about it, but she owed it to her friend to be honest with her. "To a certain extent, possibly. Yes. But you're a strong person. I don't think in the end that you do anything because you're expected to. Did Natalia really want you to be an academic?"

"Not really, no."

"But you are one. Because you love to learn and study."

"True. Though teaching is another story entirely. In the circus, she wanted me to do high wire. I didn't want that. I wanted the knives."

"Exactly!" She paused. "You know, we don't have to do this."

"I am forty-two years old and my whole life has been wrapped up in preparing myself for this. Or at least it feels that way to me. So, I am going to do this and see what happens next."

"So, you don't believe you were meant for this?"

"I am not sure what I believe. The closer I've gotten to it, the more my doubts have ramped up. And beyond telling me his name and where to find him, Natalia, that old bat, has refused to answer any more questions. Something that is really pissing me off, by the way."

"What if he's awful?"

"Then I walk. Period. I am not tying myself to some kind of tyrant. And Natalia can just fucking deal. I am fairly sure she's worried about newer demons wanting to take over Eastern Europe, so she's trying to protect Vlad and herself. The one thing she did tell me is that he can't come into his full power until he takes a consort." Anya shrugged.

Gwen didn't really get the whole Council thing, and she was more interested in the demon himself. "What does it mean? His full power?"

"Well, he's destined, so Natalia tells me, to be a much more powerful demon one day. He will likely sit on the Council, sometime in the future."

"Oooookkk. But doesn't he need to rule a larger area than just Paris."

"He rules all of France. And Belgium currently.""My question still stands though." Anya gave Gwen a pointed look and light dawned. "Western Europe?"

"Western Europe. But I also really don't get how. There is already a Demon of Western Europe, but our guy rules both France and Belgium. It's got to be weird demon politics."

Gwen smiled. "This is a puzzle. And you want to figure it out."

Anya started to deny it, then sighed. "Yes. It's a puzzle and I cannot just walk away from a puzzle."

"No, I know you can't. You'd be powerful then?"

"Well, he would be. I assume I would also share in that some."

"Would you be more powerful than Natalia?"

"Possibly." She thought for a moment. "Oooh, she'd hate that."

"Hmmm, this whole thing is a bit shady."

"You think? She and Vlad must have some kind of plan here."

"You're being awfully casual about this whole thing."

"It's not me being casual, Gwen. It's just something I need to figure out. And I need to figure out why I've been guided here. Natalia tried to make me into a little mini her. Which failed spectacularly."

"Did she think the highwire was a more feminine pursuit?"

"One can only assume. I think she thought high wire would be a more romantic story. More...dramatic maybe. Knives are messy and she doesn't like messy. She has been very good to me in a lot of ways, but I suspect in the end it was to her own gain to do so." Anya and Gwen never really discussed a lot of her childhood, and she had never told Gwen about what happened in Russia and why she'd left when she was still a child. She needed to tell her soon.

"Does he know you exist?"

"Not that I am aware of. I am not sure how he's going to feel about it. About me. It could be a non-starter. He could see me and run the other way."

"Why would he do that?"

Anya smiled indulgently at her friend. "Because he doesn't want this whole thing, he doesn't like tall women, or redheads, or Russians. Maybe he already has someone. Any number of reasons."

"He'd be a fool. And then I may have to curse him."

"Pretty sure you cannot curse a demon."

"Pretty sure I'd try anyway."

"How have we gone from you doubting I should do this to cursing a man who may not want me?"

"Loyalty knows no logic."

"You may also be a wee bit biased."

"Naturally. But honestly, I don't think the issue is going to be him not liking how you look."

"What do you mean?"

"Oh my God! Are you fucking serious? Do you not see any of the attention you get?"

Anya was 5'9' and curvy, with large breasts and generous hips. Her pale skin and dark auburn hair made her naturally violet eyes stand out. Her nose had been broken and that kept her face more on the interesting side. She looked soft but looks could be deceiving. Anya had a lot of strength, and she was quick. She was also lethal with a knife or dagger.

"Ridiculous!" scoffed Anya. "You are much prettier than I am."

"Yes, I am pretty." Anya looked at Gwen. "What? It's true, and I am not going to deny it. I am also smart and funny and have magic coming out of my pores. I don't deny what I am. You do. All the time."

"I own my brains."

"But you've never owned your looks. You may not be traditionally pretty, but you are someone people look at. And who has violet eyes? Not deep blue, violet!"

"Are we having this conversation to get my mind off what we're doing tonight?"

"Maybe? Is it working?"

"A little, actually." Anya thought she was weird looking, same as when she was a kid.

"But he's old timey, right? He may like how old timey you look." Gwen grinned at her friend.

The taxi screeched to a halt, causing Anya to smack into Gwen. "Was that really necessary?" Anya asked the driver in French.

He shrugged. "Not the easiest address to find," he replied in English, causing Anya to roll her eyes. That was not a reason, to her mind. But she let it go.

"*Bien, merci.*"

"We should get out," Gwen said.

"We should." Neither moved. The driver started tapping his fingers on the steering wheel and staring at the two in the rearview mirror. Anya sighed, pulled out some bills and paid the man. She had added in a healthy tip and he smiled at her. Always a bit of a soft touch, thought Gwen.

"*Merci, madame!*" She nodded at him and got out of the car, followed by Gwen.

"Where exactly are we?" asked Gwen.

"His club."

"Nightclub type club?"

"Yup. He owns and operates this one, and a handful more so I'm told." She paused and looked at the awning and unobtrusive entrance. A large man, demon most likely, in a dark suit stood out front. Security, by the look of him.

Gwen leaned into Anya. "Is that a demon?" The man was over six feet and was built like a square block. He had a large scar running down one side of his face and when he saw Gwen looking at him, he winked at her.

"Yes."

"They look like people."

"Gwen, they are people. Well, they were."

"Point taken. Well, at least we can get a drink."

"We can." Anya didn't move.

"So, how do you know...how will he know..."

"If we're meant to bond, he should be able to feel a bit of a tug."

"A tug?"

"Apparently. Look, I don't know. I know what I was told, but I have no clue how any of this really works. I am just as much in the dark as you, at this point." Anya was very agitated. She had put the coin away and she wished she hadn't.

"Annie, it's ok. You're nervous now."

"I am. Natalia told me we'd recognize each other, if indeed we are destined to be mated, but that's about it. I am not even sure how we've managed to avoid each other."

"Run in a lot of demon circles, do you?"

"Fair point well made. It's just…"

"What?"

"Something is niggling at me about this whole thing. Something odd. Not bad, just off. "

"Do you want to go?"

"No."

"Ok, then let's go in."

"I don't even know what he looks like!"

"He's the owner, it won't be that hard to find him. What's his name?"

"Declan O'Shea."

"Oh, An Irishman! That's nice then! Ok, let's go in and get this Declan O'Shea." Anya breathed and pulled out a card. "What's that?"

"We need this to get in. It's a really exclusive demon club. Humans need to have this card. Natalia sent it to me."

"Fine." She began to propel Anya towards the large demon standing at the front door of the club. "We're going in. You're buying."

Declan sat brooding in his office. His meeting a few days ago with the Council hadn't gone as planned and he was still pissed off about it. They had insisted that he find his consort and begin the bonding process. It was ridiculous and archaic, but so was the Council of Demons.

The Council was run by eight Demons, who each ruled over a part of the world. The de facto head of the Council was Anaranth. He was the ninth, non-voting member, and was sometimes called upon to break ties. He could also overrule a vote he didn't agree with. That was something he rarely did though. All Council took a human consort who ruled with them. The consort became immortal, so they lived as long as their demon. Even Anaranth had one from when he had been a voting member. Only demons destined for the Council were *allowed* consorts. The whole thing sat badly with Declan. It felt elitist and he hated that. Why should he be allowed to mate because he was meant for bigger things like the Council? It was appalling that class distinctions were still a thing with the demons.

"Declan," Anaranth had said, "You are eight hundred years old. It is well past time that you found your consort. You will never come into your full power until you do. And now is the time. She is out there and it's time you found her." The threat was clear. Western Europe would never belong to him otherwise, he'd never hold it. Declan didn't really care about that. He never had, and this ironically, was why he had done so well. He didn't rule his territory like a monarch on a throne. He ran it like a business. He valued loyalty, but that and respect were earned. And he paid his employees, both human and demon, very well. He would not rule from fear, ever. He was not one to cross, but as long as you did your job and followed the rules, there was never a problem. Betray him or steal from him and you would pay. Dearly. It was how he had amassed so much wealth over the last several hundred years. Matthew, Declan's number two man, called him the demonic answer to Bill Gates.

"What if I don't wish to mate. What if I don't care about power."

Anaranth had laughed. "My boy, there is no such thing as not caring about power!"

Declan sighed. Another of his inner circle Dougal, had referred to the Council more than once as a "bunch of old farts." That wasn't entirely unwarranted.

There was a knock at the door. "Come in!" he barked.

Christian, his general manager entered. "Someone is in foul humor this evening, I see."

"Christian, my patience is thin right now, please just tell me what you want."

"I just have some papers that you need to read and sign. Updated supplier contracts."

"Leave them." Christian stared at him. "I will sign them, but not at the moment. I am just as likely to incinerate them right now."

"I will nag you tomorrow about them, then. And cheer up...the club is packed, and we have some very lovely new blood in the building."

"The last thing I need right now is a woman."

"There is nothing so wrong that a night in the arms of a soft female, or a hard male for that matter, cannot cure. But have it your way, be a misery." And he swanned out of the room.

Declan rolled his eyes at his manager's words. He liked women; he liked the idea of having someone. But he didn't like the idea that he was going to consign someone to immortality as the consort of a demon. It seemed selfish just to have some company. And who knew what he may end up with? She may be a lunatic, like Liliana. Or, have no backbone like Mikhail. There had not been a new consort in hundreds of years. The elders on the Council were bored and wanted some new blood. And some good gossip fodder. Declan was in no mood to give it to them.

He sighed, got up and left his office, making his way downstairs to the heart of the club. The closer he got, the louder the music and noise got. He had learned to let it wash over him and not concentrate on it, otherwise the buzz of human energy would get to him. And with that, came their thoughts sometimes. He really disliked that it was one of his special Demon gifts. He kept it under tight control, but the initial blast when he hit the club was always a bit of a problem.

He stopped at the top of the last set of stairs leading down. He could immediately tell something was different. He frowned. The energy was off. Not bad, different. But it was jarring to him.

Something...someone was down there, throwing it off. There was a witch down there, but they weren't the problem. They had some power, but it wasn't threatening. It felt almost gentle. He stood stock still and opened himself up to find the cause. It took no time at all. His eyes flicked to the bar where a redhead in a deep eggplant dress sat with a petite blonde, who was the witch he had felt. But the redhead was the issue here. The back of his neck started to tingle, as did the tips of his fingers. Slowly, the redhead turned towards him, knowing exactly where to look. Their eyes locked and she smiled, smirked really. *Well fuck*, he thought. There she was—his fucking mate.

www.ingramcontent.com/pod-product-compliance
Lightning Source LLC
Chambersburg PA
CBHW060542190726
48283CB00003B/836